Also by Phyllis Wachob

Teachers Abroad Mysteries

#1 Revolution Revenge
#2 Oasis Assassin
#3 Turkish Delight Gone Sour
#4 Singapore Fling

Kern Kapers Mysteries

#1 Body in the Orchard
#2 Killer Kern
#3 Hot Tub Homicide
#4 Cuyama Cold Case

Hot Tub Homicide

Phyllis Wachob

Dedication

This novel is dedicated to my late mother, Betty Hylton Wachob, who loved the idea that her daughter was an author of murder mysteries and read them all.

Acknowledgements

This series of mysteries would have been impossible to write and bring to fruition without the help of many friends and family members. The critique and change of cover design, contents, flow, and characters would not have been enjoyable, in fact, agonizing and slow, without their help. So, thanks to my many friends who listened to the tellings and retellings, my cover designer Doug Thompson, my photographer Francisco Montesinos, and my proofreader Tere Swagler. A special thanks goes to all my fellow members of the Writers of Kern, who keep the encouragement coming.

Preface

Some of the places in this novel are real, for example Dewar's, Beale Park and the resident parakeets. These places of Bakersfield and Kern County are easily found in histories, maps, guides and on the web. However, Darrell Pitt's office and the community where Very lives are fictional. In its essence, this is a work of fiction. Names, characters, places and incidents are either the product of the author's imagination or are used fictitiously, and any resemblance to actual persons, living or dead, businesses or establishments, events or locales is coincidental.

Cast of Characters

Vermilion Blew: retired school librarian and teacher
MaryAnne Sanderson: resident of Five Points
Peter 'Fat Man' Gunn: resident of Five Points
Davy McDougal: resident of Five Points
Gail Dupres: resident of Five Points, friend of MaryAnne's
Ashley: employee of Five Points
Mr. Tom: long-time resident of Five Points
Becky Landrieu: resident of Five Points, friend of MaryAnne's
Darrell Pitts: Private Investigator, Very's business partner
Olivia Grainger: Darrell's new secretary/helper
Joey Sanchez: Very's best friend
Deputy Bobby Sanchez: Joey's husband
Cleopatra: Very's new cat
Gabriela (Gabby) Hernandez: young friend of Very's
Father Sullivan: parish priest well-known in Bakersfield
Frankie Monroe: Very's fiancé

Chapter One: The Ambulance

"You SOB. You're not going to get away with it this time. Pride goeth before a fall," screeched the short woman, blonde hair unchanged since high school, though plenty of wrinkles belied her age.

Vermilion Blew had just walked into the lobby of the Five Points Clubhouse, her second day in the new community. The group of people gathered around the woman and her object of vitriol seemed familiar to Very, but the scene of chaos, crackling with emotion and menace, was not.

"Watch what you say, be careful what you wish for, all is vanity," drawled the object of the blonde's abuse. The fat man, there was no other way to describe him, turned on his heel, stuck his chin in the air and carefully put one foot in front of the other. "Agreed, it's over?" He threw the comment over his shoulder as he made for the exit.

"It's not over. Not until I say so. Once bitten, twice shy. Hope for the best, prepare for the worst. You can't do this to me. Again." The woman lunged towards the man's shirt, grabbing a handful of the tail which overflowed behind him. She hung on, even as Fat Man Gunn headed for the door.

She knocked against the table of the foyer, full of flyers for future events, bowls of candies and a huge Chinese vase full of April fake flowers. A loud 'thunk' thundered among the group, followed by a screech of pain, a 'crack' as the woman hit the marble floor and slid across. Finally, she let go of Fat Man's shirt, as he continued to amble out the door. Very stepped aside to let him pass as she watched the round foyer table wobble, strewing goodies onto the floor. The large vase slid slowly and gracefully towards the edge and hesitated for a second before it leaped off and shattered with a resounding crack, sending shards skittering across the floor, inches from the injured woman.

"Whah, whah, whah!" wailed the woman. "Call an ambulance. I've broken my leg. The worst has come to me. Whah, whah."

"I've got it, MaryAnne. I'm onto it," said a voice from the back of the scrum. "Calling now."

Very recoiled as she realized that Fat Man had bumped into her as he left, leaving her smarting and perhaps bruised on her right side.

MaryAnne screamed again, agony mixed with anger, as a number of the women crowded around. One leaned over and said gently, "Can you stand up?"

"Nooooooooo. I've broken my leg, I'm sure. Prepare for the best, expect the worst. Look," she bellowed as loud as was possible from her awkward place on the floor.

Her nearest friend responded with a cry of her own, "Look at her ankle!"

Very edged a little closer, anxious to see the damage. One ankle was indeed bent at an incredibly awkward angle, twisted wildly around and backwards. Very drew her breath in, in sympathy and agony. It looked extraordinarily painful, resting in an unnatural position. MaryAnne continued to scream, as those around tried to make her comfortable, check on the ambulance or sent sympathetic noises throughout the lobby.

Very stepped back as a person with a broom and dustpan tried to step around her on his way to the dangerous mess on the floor. She recovered enough to ask, "Is there anything I can do to help?"

"Yeah," the man dressed in a green uniform shirt and pants grunted. "Keep them all out of my way. I've got this, just keep them back. Nobody should touch any of this, the boss will insist because of the insurance. Heads will roll, and it will be terrible."

"Maybe they should think of plastic or metal? Not this pottery!" Very said, standing guard with her arms spread wide.

"Ya think?" said the custodian as he swiftly swept the pieces up into a neat pile.

A newcomer swept into the lobby. Very recognized him from her aborted trip to the hot tub the previous day. Now he joined his voice to the general cacophony, a loud booming voice with a pronounced Aussie accent. "What did I miss?"

"Ah Davy, you missed the fight of the century. MaryAnne and Pete, having it out, one more time," said one of the bystanders.

Davy pushed his way into the circle around MaryAnne. "Ah, poor thing. Don't worry babe, you'll be right. Hey, listen. The ambulance is coming."

One of the women surrounding MaryAnne now stood and faced Davy. "Out of the way, Davy. Can't you see how hurt she is? She's not going to be all right, not at all."

"Excuse me, I was just trying to be kind to the little woman. Pete had better watch out, it looks as though he's gone too far this time."

One of the men in the circle cleared his throat. "Well, even though there were words, I can't say that Pete actually did anything. MaryAnne tripped and fell, Pete never touched her."

"So whose side are you on?" the friend of MaryAnne countered.

"Oh no, I don't do sides. Not in this case." The man slid into the background once more in the face of the demand to align himself.

"Becky, Becky, don't get upset. This is not so bad, really. Look, there's no blood, she's stopped screaming. Someone said that the ambulance was here. Wow, case almost closed."

Becky stood tall and looked around. Very recognized height when presented with it and this woman stood inches taller than Very. Tall. Her shorts revealed long, brown legs with not an extra ounce of flesh. The similarly brown face that turned to MaryAnne's other friend was long and lean, with a sharply pointed chin. Regal bearing. "MaryAnne, honey, they're here. The saviors are here," said Becky to the woman on the floor.

Behind her, Very heard the squeal of brakes, the noises of authority, and the clank of rescue apparatus. She moved to the side, mindful of her duty of protecting the busy janitor as he scraped the last of the big pieces of the vase into a pan.

"Where is he?" shouted the first of the rescue squad.

"Here, here, she's right here. MaryAnne is here," shouted one of MaryAnne's friends.

The man, dressed in dark gray pants with lots of pockets and special tabs, cautiously approached MaryAnne sprawled on the floor. He bent down and talked quietly. "So, what's the matter here? Heart attack, was it?"

"No, it's a broken leg or at least a terrible ankle," said a voice from the back of the crowd. "Look!"

The EMT bent down and cautiously looked at MaryAnne's face and addressed her again.

Her eyes flew open and she whimpered, her voice gaining strength as she talked, "I fell. I hit my arm and then my leg just went 'whoosh,' out from under me. It's broken, it's twisted, it's just all gone on me. Agony, death awaits me. Whah, whah."

The man moved down to look at the twisted ankle. Gingerly he touched it and then let go as MaryAnne set up another howl of pain.

"But you have no heart attack? Stroke? You can breathe?" he asked again.

"Well, maybe I will if you don't do something. You can't let him get away with this. There's no time like the present." MaryAnne shot back.

"Is he here? Is he okay?" the EMT asked, looking around for someone to answer him.

"Oh, he's gone. He walked out on his own two feet. No problem there." The same voice from the rear spoke up.

Within two minutes, MaryAnne was loaded onto a gurney and was being wheeled out. One of her friends snagged the purse with cards and phone and offered to go with her.

The circle of spectators spread but no one left. Very tried to catch a breath and remember what she had come here for. The small desk that served as the portal to all business beckoned her, but she felt reluctant to leave the scene. She struggled to pick out a few faces from the group that she had met the day before at the 9 am aerobics class. One woman near her seemed familiar, so Very leaned over and asked, "What was this all about? What will MaryAnne not let go?"

The woman looked at Very, "Oh, you're the new one, huh? Oh those two, just friends. Neighbors actually."

"They fight all the time, this was nothing new," added the man who had volunteered information to the EMT.

"But she said, 'You're not going to get away with it this time.' What's so different about this time?" Very said.

"Drama queens, both of them." The woman looked away, as if she was reluctant to say more.

The man looked at her, then back to Very. "Maybe she meant it."

"But does MaryAnne even know if she meant it or not? Well, some excitement today, at least."

"Is there often excitement? Are ambulances common here?" Very asked.

"Yeah, all the time."

"Not so much."

The answers came together and Very had trouble discerning which answer to respond to. "I guess, with retirees and all, that we might have a few calls," she offered.

"But this was small potatoes, compared to the murder. Remember?" Another voice chimed in.

"That was so unusual, though," countered yet another voice.

Very's eyes widened. "Murder?" she asked.

"Domestic," offered another opinion.

"But there were seventeen vehicles!"

"How do you know? Counted?"

"Well, I live across the street, I mean, there was nothing else to do that night."

"You counted, you really counted?"

"Oh, here they come, police and fire."

Very turned and looked out the plate glass doors to the traffic round. A single police car and a small red fire engine had stopped just outside, blocking the entrance to the clubhouse. One of the staff members slipped out the doors and was talking to the police man who stood, hands on hips that bristled with a gun, a stun gun, a wooden stick, handcuffs and other bizarre weapons that Very did not recognize. His clean-shaven cheeks shone with pink excitement. As he spoke to the slender young woman, he attempted to peer into the lobby to see what was left of the kerfuffle. Behind Very, the small crowd closed ranks and looked back at the young officer. Very felt a subtle shift as the group created a barrier, protecting their domain, and their members.

"Why do we need all three of these guys? Every time?" muttered a voice from the rear.

"It's the law," came the answer from another disembodied voice.

"Maybe MaryAnne can file a suit against Pete. Maybe the police should talk with MaryAnne," came another suggestion from somewhere in the group.

Very had determined that it was time to leave. The high-ceilinged lobby had created space for voices, but the atmosphere was confusing. She hadn't sorted the characters out, she was confused by all the comments, and all the action that had just taken place. She wanted to go home to her mess of boxes and find the TV. She wanted comfort food, mindless reruns on the idiot box and a chat with her best friend Joey. Yeah, and maybe she could ask Joey's husband, the sheriff's deputy, about the murder, the one that she didn't know about before she bought here, in bucolic Five Points, a 55+ retirement community. It was supposed to be safe here, gated, patrolled, protected, shielded from the masses. And now, she has just learned about a murder!

She turned to the group behind her, pasting a smile on her face and was about to open her mouth, with a quick goodbye, when a wail rose from behind the group.

"I heard them, I heard the sirens, where are they?" A short woman, a clone of MaryAnne, blonde hair layered carefully in a style 45 years out of date, pushed her way to the front. As she watched, the police car and fire engine glided silently out of the parking round, heading for the front gate. "Where's the ambulance?" she asked again.

"They've gone, Susie. They picked her up and took her off. It's taken care of." A woman tried to wrap her arms around Susie, who threw her off.

"Picked who up? Who was in the ambulance?" Susie stood, her voice creeping higher and higher, resisting the comfort of the group.

"MaryAnne. She was hurt during a fight with Pete. Again. Did a real number on her leg, ankle, whatever."

"MaryAnne is in the ambulance? She took the ambulance? No, no, she can't; that's mine. For my Bill." Susie said frantically.

"For Bill, your husband Bill? What's wrong with him? Why does he need an ambulance? Isn't he in the gym?"

"Yeah, he's in the gym. I was supposed to meet him here. When I got there, he was on the floor, reaching for his left arm. Oh, I knew what it was. It was his heart. He had been warned to take it easy, he had been told not to go to the gym and do all those stupid exercises. He's on meds. You know, he just can't take that sort of thing."

"A heart attack?"

"I called an ambulance. Quietly. I know that it is never quiet, but I thought maybe if I didn't panic, neither would he. But I waited and waited and then I heard it. But they never came." Susie began to cry, huge tears falling down her cheeks as she gave into her hysteria.

"We can call another one, they come really fast here, you know."

"No, no, no," Susie pulled away from the group and ran down the hall, heading for the gym.

"Quick, quick," someone urged the man with the telephone.

"Whoa, how did that happen? Two emergencies, one right after the other."

Very stepped back into the corner near the door of the foyer. Things had gone too fast, too much excitement for her. She could feel her own heart racing with excitement, or panic. She found a chair and collapsed into it. She knew her pacemaker regulated her heart, more to keep up with her activities, but could all this turmoil cause her 'little computer in her chest' to malfunction? Maybe she needed an ambulance.

Susie reappeared and screamed at no one in particular, "Who does she think she is? Drama queen, stealing my ambulance! That bitch, she has gone too far this time. Heaven will judge you and find you wanting!" Susie howled with pain.

"Blame it on Gunn, not MaryAnne," muttered a male voice.

"We'll get another ambulance, don't worry."

"You don't understand. It's too late. He's dead."

Chapter Two: The Ambulance Thief

Susie screamed again, her wails reaching high into the ceiling rafters, swirling around, and coming back. "Who did this? That bitch, that terrible bitch! She killed him, with her fake injuries, stealing the ambulance!"

"Susie, calm down. You really shouldn't blame MaryAnne. You know, it was Peter Gunn who started the fight."

"Yeah," another voice chimed in. "He was the one who egged her on. He manipulated poor MaryAnne into lunging at him."

"Who made her slip and sprain her ankle? That was Peter's doing, you betcha."

Very listened, but was confused as to who were the speakers. On the other hand, no one said anything other than what she knew to be true, as far as she could see. Best to keep out of it. She felt an urge to leave as she could do nothing, but noticed that no one else had left the scene. They were like little kids, hanging around to find out what was going to go down next.

Sirens began to wail in the distance. Silence fell as everyone waited for the orange van to pull up at the curb. The EMTs jumped out and pulled the gurney from the back. Everyone who stood near the front door moved back, a parting of the Red Sea, to allow the emergency crew to get by. Susie led the way down the corridor to the small gym in the rear of the clubhouse.

Before the small procession had disappeared, a police car and the same fire truck appeared. The fire crew waited outside as the police slowly came in through the whooshing doors. The tall Aussie man pointed down the hallway towards the disappearing ambulance crew.

"What now?" asked the woman standing next to Very.

"Out of respect, I think we wait," replied one of the women. Surreptitiously, she turned to her neighbor. "Have you signed up for the Ladies Luncheon yet? Are there still places left?"

A quiet whisper back was inaudible. At least they were polite enough to do their social planning quietly.

"Oh Susie," the erstwhile Ladies Luncheon attendee stepped forward. "Can we help? What can we do?"

The group watched the gurney, politely covered, be wheeled out. The policeman, dressed to kill, waddled past. He turned to the group. "Anything anyone want to say, need to report?"

"Just a case of mistaken ambulances, that's all," said a tall quiet man from the rear. The ladies around him nodded.

"So sad," said one and the others chimed in. "Yes, it is."

The police looked at the group, who seemed to close ranks, many seeking a companion to stand next to, touching at shoulders or forearms.

"Susie, how can we help?" One of the group detached herself and stood beside Susie, holding her arm and hand.

"I need to c-c-c-call my d-d-d-daughter in Visalia," Susie managed to say between sobs and hiccups.

"Where's your phone, I'll help you find the number. You just hang in there." The two women moved off into the fireplace area of clustered couches. Someone had turned down the TV that was permanently turned to FOX News, and now it was only a thrum in the background.

"That daughter in Visalia won't do much good, she'd be better off with the one in New York," said another of the gathered group. Very shivered at the thought that everyone here knew who had children, where they lived and how useful they would be in a crisis like this.

"Visalia is closer, it would take a whole day, maybe more, to get the other one here. I've met her daughter who lives in Visalia, she's nice."

"Effective is what you need in a crisis, not just nice."

"Martie has got her in hand, look at that, got a hold of the family. Yes, yes, taken care of."

"So sad, so sudden. Bill was such a nice guy. And besides, we've lost a couple at our table now. Can't carry on with an uneven number."

"You can't think of kicking her out of your table grouping, can you?"

"She could always go to the widow's table, what wrong with that?"

"She could try finding a single man to fill the slot."

"Single man, around here? Straight? Really? And besides, don't you think it should be her choice about the table?"

"She could try finding a female friend to be her partner."

"That wouldn't do, it would be uneven, we need balance!"

"Balance comes before your friend?"

"Balance is important, you know what I mean, the conversational balance, between the sexes."

"The men dominate the conversation, even if there is just one of them. I don't see what the big deal is. Three men or four men, what's the difference? Besides, I think another woman might improve the quality of the conversation."

Susie stood and her companion announced to everyone. "Susie's daughter is on her way, or at least really, really soon. But I told her that we are all here for her. Okay, everyone?"

Very drifted towards the front desk. She wanted to ask about clubs and schedules. But she also wanted to listen to the gossip, the conversations that twirled and twisted around her. The names and faces confused her, but the conversations were enlightening.

She smiled as sweetly as she could at the younger woman behind the desk window. "Hi, I'm looking for clubs and schedules."

"Here's the bulletin," said Ashley, or so Very deduced as the nametag on the desk said Ashley was on duty.

Very looked at the multi-page document. "Uh, do I sign up? Where? I was thinking about pickle ball."

"No, just come!" said a woman who was directly behind Very.

Very whirled and blinked at the fit-looking woman who stood close behind her. Her jet black hair somehow didn't look real. Dyed? A wig?

"Hi, I'm Shari and we'd love to have you join us."

"I'm sort of interested, I've heard that it is the newest, latest thing for the older crowd, a little like tennis but easier on the joints. Is that true?"

"Yeah, that describes it pretty well. Are you a tennis player?" Shari showed a magnificent set of even white teeth surrounded by lips that parted in a curving pattern. Like a shark.

"No, I don't play, I tried a few times when I was younger, but it didn't seem like my game. But maybe I could try pickle ball."

"Join us for the beginners. Here, it's in the schedule. Any day you can try it out! I'm sure you'll like it." Shari the

Shark sent a sparkling grin towards Very and then moved away.

"What about the Crafters Club? Does it meet every week?" Very moved closer to the window, bent on asking about more clubs.

"No, every other week. It's all about knitting, crocheting, quilting, things like that. Frankly, I've heard that it's just a gossip club, not much about crafts, just the ladies trading gossip about the other residents." Ashley smiled sweetly as she said this.

"Really? Just gossip, no crafting?"

"Oh, never mind what others say, I think they are just jealous. You join by just going along at the right time."

Very looked at the bulletin and found the page where all the activities were listed. "What about the pool? Is it open? I love to swim."

Ashley looked at the schedule. "Yeah, well, it's open, if you like freezing water."

"I thought it was heated, you know, in the spring and fall, when the water's cold."

"It's supposed to be open on April 15, but…"

"But what? Don't we pay for this? Sorry, I didn't mean it like that. I just moved here and I want to check over the facilities, the amenities. I guess I'm not used to people telling me that this or that doesn't work or isn't true or something. So, will it be open on April 15?"

"That's the plan. We've been having problems with the heater on the hot tub and we suspect the same is true of the pool. So, plan on that, April 15. Closer to the time, please do check back. That's a couple weeks away."

"I shall be ever hopeful. I guess that non-swimmers are not happy about the cost of heating the pool?"

"You got it there. You can also try the water aerobics group. They meet every morning at nine am. When it's heated. They are very particular about the temperature of the pool," her head wobbled in consternation. "But they are a very friendly bunch and I know that it has done a lot of good for some of the ladies. And gentlemen too."

"I'd rather swim laps, but water aerobics are good too."

One of the group that had not dispersed from the ambulance debacle sidled up behind Very. "Don't forget to join the book club."

Very twisted around to see her face. Familiar, but no name popped up in the menu of names she had heard.

The woman continued, "Every second Thursday. There's a list of the books on the bulletin board. You can mingle with the readers among us. It's enlightening."

Another woman sneaked in behind Very. "And the Ladies Luncheon every month. Sign up now. She can do that, can't she, Ashley?" The woman laughed, a restrained giggle.

"Sure, that one is a pay later." Ashley fumbled in a stack of folders, looking for the right sign-up sheet. She pulled it out and thrust it at Very. She whipped it right side up for Very to sign. And then watched closely as Very carefully printed her name.

"Oh, you're Ms. Blew, aren't you? How do you spell your name, your first name? It's Ver, Ver…"

"Vermilion, but just call me Very, it's easier. It means a red color, like Ruby or Scarlet. My mother picked an unusual name for me, and I've just lived with it." Very sighed deeply.

"Oh, it's cute and not easy to forget. Very, very nice name." Ashley beamed at Very. "Look, now that I know you are here, and signed up for at least one thing, you will benefit from this." She pulled out a large envelope with Very's name on the cover. "Here are all your papers and things, including your fob."

"My fob?" Very put a confused look on her face.

"To get into the pool area, and the courts, if you want to play after, or before, hours. It's here," she said as she pulled two small plastic disks out of the envelope. "Just swipe it on the key pad next to the gate and you'll hear a click. Then, voila!"

Very looked at the two fobs. Keys to adventure?

"Don't lose them, $50 to replace!" Ashley said. "Oh, so important for you if you want to go to the hot tub. You know, it's open even when the clubhouse isn't, so keep them handy!"

"The annual Pool Party, you need to sign up for that, for sure." The woman who stood behind Very spoke up again. Then she giggled.

"Oh, I'm sorry," Very said turning to face the woman, "Did you have business to conduct? I can come back another time. I've got a lot here, already. Need to read all of this."

"No, it's just that you need to sign up for the Pool Party now, because of the deadline."

"Sure," said Ashley, reaching for another folder. "Which table will you be at?"

Very hesitated, "I have to choose a table? I don't really know anybody. I don't know how to choose."

"No problem, put her down at my table. Gail is the name," she said giggling again. Giggling Gail, another name Very would not forget soon.

Ashley found the table with Gail's names and four others, Very was the fifth. Very tried to peek and see the other names on the list but could not make the scribbled names out, upside down and messy.

"April 11 and you are my guest!" Gail said and smiled at Very. "So nice to meet you! So glad you are here with us."

Very's alarm bells strummed quietly in her chest. There was a certain hesitation at the implied ownership of this woman. Who was she? What did it mean to be at her table and not someone else's? Had she signed up for the witches' table, the lonely divorcee's table, the widow's table, the group of old ladies that no one else wanted to claim?

Ashley watched as Gail drifted away and then leaned forward. "You don't have to sit all the time at that table. Usually people mingle a lot, don't sit down much, except if they've had too many mojitos. Don't worry, they're a good table. Now, any other questions I can answer today? You can call any time, you know."

"Thank you, Ashley, you have been super."

"Whoa! Whoa!" said a voice behind Very.

Very turned to see one of the group whispering to the collected crowd, who seemed to have swelled, rather than diminished, now that the emergency was over.

"So now who do you think Susie is mad at? She was very peeved at MaryAnne, but now, she says that she knows that it is Peter Gunn's fault, as she was advised to do."

The large man with the Aussie accent pushed his way to the fore of the group. He turned and faced the gathered crowd. "She should be angry with Gunn, the Hot Tub Hog. Someday, someone should hold his head under water in his precious hot tub."

He thrust his shoulders out and proceeded to exit through the door. A collective gasp followed him.

Chapter Three: Meeting Mr. Tom

Very stretched and lay back on her lounge chair. The blueness of the pool shimmered at her feet, the noise of the jets in the hot tub came from behind her, and she wriggled in pleasure as she reached for her cool drink in the tall glass on the table beside her. The sky was blue, the temperature today was predicted to be 90 degrees, an early harbinger of summer. This was the sort of thing that she used to do at her mother's house, minus the hot tub burbling, and a smile played on her lips. She reached for the last two sections of the Sunday paper that she hadn't managed to read the day before. Why did she feel so much more relaxed here?

Maybe it was the escape that she had made from the unpacking. All weekend she had holed up with the boxes. She refused the usual Sunday evening dinner at her friend Joey's house. She had missed the easy camaraderie with Joey's family, especially her granddaughter Clara and her husband Bobby, but she knew that she wouldn't have been able to talk to Joey alone. She had used the time to get the TV set up and she had watched the Sunday evening PBS shows that she had watched with her mother. She had woken up this Monday morning with a grudge against her mother, or really against herself. What had she kept so many things over the years? Why had she made the decision to put them in boxes and move them to her new house instead of throwing or giving them away? So many of them were her mother's old stuff. Why couldn't she get rid of the old potato peelers and chipped dishes? Never mind, now she was here, basking in the sunshine at the pool, taking advantage of her new amenities.

"Hello there, young 'un!" came a voice from beside her.

Very lifted her head and looked at who had called her young. He had a mostly bald head, with only a whisper of hair along the back and sides. His face was clean-shaven and round, giving him the appearance of a half-completed Mr. Potato Head. He had on a small swimming suit, the kind that was popular when she was young. It left nothing much to the imagination, only covering the naked essentials. His legs emerged from the miniscule Speedo racing suit as two long sticks. How could someone with such a magnificent belly have such skinny legs?

A pair of sunglasses looked at Very. "Hi, I'm Tom. I'm the grandad of all grandads. I was the tenth person who moved here, so I have bragging rights. I lived in a different house then. But I'm now the oldest inhabitant of Five Points. Pleased to meet you. I think you must be the newest here."

"Very possibly. It's only been a few days, not really unpacked yet. By the way, my name is Very. Easy to remember."

"Where do you live, how's your house situated. Do you like your back yard, or are you going to redo it?"

"Whoa, whoa. One question at a time." Very proceeded to answer all of his intrusive questions about her house, how big it was, how big the yard was, what and how she was planning to remodel in the near future.

"Roses, you need roses, they do so well in this climate. They don't do so well in the dirt out here, terrible stuff, but you can feed them and they are magnificent. I can give you the name of a good gardener. Oh, do you have someone to clean your house yet?"

Very answered all these newer questions with noncommittal answers, wondering why and how she could get rid of him and get back to her sunbathing. She laid back, closed her eyes and let him ramble on.

"You need to come and see my workshop. I've made a lot of furniture in my house. It's in my garage, it's my man cave workshop. You can't really do it inside the house in any case. You would be surprised how many garages are taken up with storage, or are workshops or have classic cars or old motorcycles in them. Some of them have been done up with tiles, or special flooring for garages. They have heaters and fans, couches and lounge chairs, trophy cabinets and TVs mounted on the wall. Do you actually park your car in your garage?"

Very laughed. "This is the first time in my life that I have a garage to park in and I am thrilled. And yes, I park in my garage."

"You know that the man down the street from you has two magnificent Corvettes parked in his garage. He has his truck parked in the driveway like everyone else, because his garage is full."

"So, you know where I live?"

Mr. Tom laughed, "Of course, everyone knows where everyone else lives. It's what we do here, know everything, like a village. Are you going to swim today? Kinda cold."

"Yes, it is. I felt it. I think I'll wait until the heater is on."

"You could try the hot tub. But you need to be careful of the Leeches."

"There are leeches in the hot tub? Ick, why doesn't someone do something about them?"

"No, not the little black blood suckers, the big ones. I never go near the place, but I've heard about the not so salubrious characters who can be encountered there nearly every day."

"Really? Anyone in particular."

In response to this, Mr. Tom started humming a tune that made Very squirm with familiarity. An old TV show, perhaps. She looked askance at Mr. Tom and shrugged.

"Peter Gunn, remember the TV show? And I think it's his real name."

"The one who was at the heart of the kerfuffle on Friday?"

"The very one. So, you have met?"

Very shook her head. "I have seen and heard him. And heard some comments about him and the hot tub."

"Maybe too much gossip around here. I mean it, you need to come and see my workshop and my furniture. I do secret drawers."

"Do you mean the hidden drawers that can only be opened by a cleverly disguised mechanism, like a little niche in the back or underneath?"

"Yeah, like that. I think you are a fan." He gave Very a wink. "I put a secret drawer in everything I make, even benches. Just a little one. My family thinks I'm crazy, that I've gone off the deep end. They can't wait to get at my stuff."

"What kind of stuff? Antiques Roadshow-worthy stuff? Valuable?"

Mr. Tom leaned forward, motioning to Very to lean towards him. He spoke in a whisper. "It's the stash of cash they are after."

"You have cash put away? Do they know where it is?"

"They think they do, but I've fooled them all. It's hidden away." Mr. Tom suddenly appeared coy, a look that went well with his bald head and elfin ears.

Very laughed, "In a hidden drawer. I get it. But why do you have cash? Wouldn't a bank account be a better place?

You know, they are going to get it in the end, in a hidden drawer or in the bank?"

"Oh, but this cash is…" Mr. Tom hesitated, looked around to make sure they were alone, and leaned in towards Very. "Not exactly the kind of cash that would do well in a bank account. Not strictly legal, you understand."

Very's mouth dropped open, but she quickly shut it, in an attempt to dispel the alarm she felt. What was this old guy talking about? He's got illegal cash stashed in some secret drawer? Does he have all his marbles? Very smiled. She had not had to deal with dementia in her mother and was not sure exactly what the manifestations were. But this appeared to come under the heading of delusion, dementia, disconnect from the world? Very smiled and leaned in, indicating her willingness to participate in the conspiracy. "And who are these family members so anxious to get their hands on the loot?"

"Two sons, twins, but only fraternal and very different. Except they do look alike. And when one cuts his hair, the other one does too. It's so annoying. It's some weird game they play about their twinship. I thought we had brought them up to be kind and generous people, but somehow we missed, the wife and I. They are greedy."

"So they want to get their hands on this cash you have. And you say that it is in cash because it's not strictly legal?" Very chose her words carefully, trying to get Mr. Tom to admit that the situation was a bit dicey at the best of times, but the fact that he was complaining about his sons being greedy, when he had hidden illegal money from them, wasn't exactly angelic on his part. More information needed.

"Tell me about this cash? Where'd it come from?" Very said, smiling and keeping her voice low and confidential.

"Oh, it's hard to say exactly. I can't remember much now, how it started. I was an accountant, you see, and I was trustworthy to a 'T'. It's easy when you are trusted and 'in' the company. Never too big a company, never too complicated books, but just enough to make a bit extra. It was difficult with two boys, wanting things all the time. Needing things like clothes, educational experiences like summer camps. And the wife nagging at me to ask for a raise blah, blah, blah. Well, I got my raise, my raises. It was always so small, never more than I needed and never enough to cheat the boss or anyone else at the company. Just a little extra for my boys. And it was always cash."

Very felt a strange twinge in her chest. This man was confessing theft to her. But nothing specific, so what could she say?

"It was in cash, you see. I think they may have suspected, some of them, but it was easy and it was the right thing to do. They were rich, I was poor. It wasn't fair, so I made it more fair. They never needed it. And after a while, I would move on to another place. A good accountant is always in demand."

"Always cash, and you kept it in…"

"A secret drawer. No one ever knew anything about it. I saved it for my kids, send them to college, or to get them a car. But they never liked college, a couple of years, and then they got jobs. So they didn't need any money for college or a nice car or to buy a house. It was useless. The money, I never used it. It sat in my drawers for years."

"If you had put it in the bank or in stocks, you could have earned interest."

"Oh, I used some of it. When my wife died, I took a trip, but it wasn't very much fun by myself. That's when I came here. Lots of people around, clubs, the pool. How much money can you spend on a car? You can only drive one car at a time, huh? You can only live in one house at a time. And vacations are no fun by yourself. So, I just left it. And now, I think they are just waiting for me to pop off and they will tear the place apart, looking for my loot. But they are too stupid to find it." Mr. Tom smiled.

"Surely they know about your secret drawers?" Very chuckled.

"Ah, there is this little thing about 'Dad's hobby' that they never understood. They didn't know or care about the woodworking hobby. They never helped me and they didn't know about the drawers. I didn't necessarily tell anyone about it. Just my customers, sometimes. I would show them how to open it and then I would say how special it was and it was one of a kind, so no one suspected that there were secret drawers in all my creations. They don't know about the money, the cash, and they don't know about the secret drawers. Stupid little boys."

"But why are you telling me this? If you don't need the money and your children 'shouldn't' get it, what will you do with it?"

"Hmmmm. Maybe that's why I'm telling you. I'll give it to you."

"But why me? If you gave me money, a windfall as it were, I would give it away. Charities of all sorts need cash."

"Then they'd find out. No, I can't do that. It's in cash, you see. Someone might recognize the old bills. But I've fooled them. Over the years, I replaced the old bills with new ones, so no one would find out. And then I would spend a little, just a little, here and there. No, those two useless boys will get none of my money. It's safe, it's hidden. Besides, it's diminished over the years. Shrunk. Like me." Mr. Tom leaned back in his chair and closed his eyes.

Very opened her mouth three times, but each time, she closed it without saying anything. She had just met this old man. He had told her a fantastic story, parts of it contradicting other parts. Was he all there? Was this even true? Parts of it, any of it? She looked at him, lying back in the sun, and everything he had said seemed too preposterous, too implausible to be true. This eccentric old man must have made it all up.

"If I may ask, how much is there? Left, that is, after all your expenditures?"

"Ohh, you would like to know, wouldn't you?" Mr. Tom lifted his sunglasses and stared at Very.

"Never mind, it's your money. You have just told me a secret and I have no right to pry." Very tried to backtrack gracefully. What a stupid thing to ask, how much. Obviously, this thing is a long time secret and he wasn't going to part with any more information.

"Last I looked, $43,000."

"Oh, a lot."

Mr. Tom smiled at Very. A secretive enigmatic wisp of a smile.

"One more thing you can do for me. Pray."

"I'm not much of a prayerful person, I'm afraid," Very ventured. How was she going to decline this request? Would it mean full novenas, or just some good will wishes?

"I'm having a procedure in a few days. Heart stuff. No big deal, but you never know."

"Oh, certainly I will send good wishes and, and, well, prayers for you. Good luck!"

Chapter Four: Exploring the Neighborhood

Even though Very had spent time in the sun at the pool, she had no intent of letting a lovely day go to waste, so she sat in the chair in her backyard, enjoying the baking sun. The fences kept out the prying eyes of neighbors and the bursts of wind but captured the warmth. This place would not be good in the depths of summer, but for now, a great place.

The packet from the head desk of Five Points lay on a table beside her. She leaned back and absentmindedly reached her hand out to pet a wandering cat. No cats here. She thought of her mother's dead cat and her backyard grave. If she had to find a place to bury a cat here, where would it be? The small patch of grass and a few bushes was not a replication of her mother's garden of rose bushes and flowers. What could she do to change this place into something more pleasing?

Very let her mind wander and thought about the community clubs. Why bother moving to a place like this, and ignore her neighbors? Wasn't the point of moving to a community to have common activities? Even if they were childish like bunco and scavenger hunts? No one said she needed to join those clubs, or participate in those activities. Choice, that is what it was all about. Finding your like-minded community members. But she loved the pool, so shouldn't she try finding others who swam or exercised in the pool?

A walk, that's what she needed to do. Explore the lay of the land. The decoration of front yards was strictly controlled, and she had heard a few comments about the 'front yard police.' The HOA here meant that she gave up control in order to have a limit on chaos, such as cars parked in front yards on dusty patches of unwatered lawn. But she had seen some potted plants, little flags and other detritus in front yards and doorways. Check them out, get ideas, plan her own brilliant front yard approach.

She pocketed her keys and locked the front door, as she had been warned to do. All the houses on her block had closed doors, closed blinds and could have been thought empty except for the cars parked in the driveways. In this development, as in much of the rest of California, the front of one's house was no longer a place to look out of, or to be seen, from the street. These houses consisted of driveways, entryways and one window to a front bedroom or guestroom. All the master bedrooms were at the back of the house, as were the great rooms where cooking, eating and socializing took place. The houses were not strictly all the same, but there was a color scheme and a monotony to the look. Every house had a patch of lawn, a small hedge and a tree, or two. The doors were different colors, at least.

Cars, that was the primary personal statement in the front of the house. Some had large garages, basically three car garages, and so the front had room for at least two cars, and sometimes three. Trucks, classic cars, golf carts and storage. The overflow landed in the driveways. So, what was inside the garages?

The answer came in the next block. A workshop. A collection of classic neon lights advertising Coca-Cola, Havoline motor oil, Harley-Davidsons motorcycles and gear. The floor was treated with a glossy paint or covering and two lawn chairs sat in the parking space, with a round table between them. Two empty beer glasses sat side by side. The back of a wall of board from which jutted hooks of all shapes and sizes held tools, electric and manual, and boxes of screws, nuts, bolts and the miscellaneous flotsam and jetsam of a home do-it-yourselfer. It looked like an advertisement for a home remodel project. This must be the envy of the community. Mr. Tom talked about this, and by his account, this was not the only one in Five Points.

Very turned the corner and saw a couple talking to a man across the street. The three turned and waved at Very, who waved back. She had learned that it was polite here to wave and say hello to everyone. It seemed to be the unwritten code of the 55+ communities. Getting along was more important than fierce tribal and political loyalties.

The three made a cozy group. The couple leaned forward and then the woman bent down to pet the dog, held on a leash by the big man that Very recognized as the one with the Aussie accent. He smiled and said something to the couple. The place was a veritable zoo full of dogs, all kinds, big and small, short and long-haired, barkers and non-barkers. The one they petted was a small, but not tiny, long haired…cat?

It was a huge cat, held firmly by a harness attached to a leash. The cat sat quietly as it was petted and cooed at. Very turned the rolodex of her mind and what she knew about cats. A bobcat? Certainly not, as a huge fluffy tail swung gracefully along the cement. No other wild cat that she had ever seen looked like this, so it must be domestic. Huge, fluffy, friendly, able to be persuaded to walk in a harness; it could only be a Maine Coon Cat.

Very stayed on her side of the street and continued on with her walk, checking out the front yards and porches. Many had small seasonal flags, which now featured bunny rabbits, eggs and fluffy chicks in soft pastel colors. When had Easter become pastel? Some houses had completely bare entryways, but most had a plant or two, a seasonal wreath or a wooden welcome sign. Very continued to walk, veering down interesting streets, checking out the front porches, lawns and trees. The tree in her front yard was pathetic compared to the others she found. Some were huge, over 20 years old, thick trunks, wide-spreading branches. Envy crept in.

Soon she realized that she had circumnavigated the community and was now walking on the back side of the clubhouse and grounds. She walked around the east end and approached the clubhouse from the opposite direction of her house. Why not drop by, check out the library, make sure the pool was still there and being prepared for her maiden dip in a few days time? She checked in at the front desk and headed to the library. She scanned the shelves and took two books. Were these to be added to the hundreds that already lined the bookcases in her front hallway? Bah, cannot have too many books. She followed the corridor past the gym, now cleaned, and ready for customers. At the moment, no one was running, lifting weights, or rowing phantom boats. Very would not feel comfortable in this room for some time to come.

She meandered outside and headed to the pool, for one more sit. She used her small plastic disc to enter the enclosure and wandered towards a small cluster of lounge chairs placed half in the sun and half in the shade. She sat, laid back into the shade and closed her eyes. She listened to noises of others coming to catch some rays. She heard women's voices and the rhythmic 'clunk, clunk' of a slowly moving orthopedic boot.

Very's eyes popped open. Three women, the middle one hobbling on an orthopedic boot, progressed along the opposite side of the pool. MaryAnne had obviously recovered sufficiently to venture out as far as the pool. She was being supported by her two friends. One, Very recognized as Giggling Gail and the other was a tall dark-skinned woman that Very thought was Becky. They spoke quietly and walked slowly.

Very closed her eyes again. The sound of a mocking bird exploded over her head, followed by the throaty caw of a crow.

Then she heard a man's voice, singing. It was melodic, but Very strained to hear the words.

"Boom, boom, boom."

Very opened her eyes to slits to see who it was. Where had he come from? He hadn't been there when she sat down.

"Down in the jungle lived a maid of royal blood, though dusky shade. A marked impression once she made upon a Zulu, from Matabulu. Boom, boom, boom."

Very sat up. She hadn't heard the song in years, but recognized it from an old movie. It was sung by Judy Garland. It was cute in the movie, but now?

"Argh! What do you think you are doing?" MaryAnne's voiced screamed across the water.

The man continued, "If you like-a me like I like-a you."

"Stop that," Giggling Gail's voice rose in anger.

"Oh, Gail doesn't like my singing, huh?" Peter Gunn taunted the three.

Very felt at sea. When she arrived, not more than five minutes ago, no one was here, now she felt surrounded by screams and unpleasantness. The three women must have come from the direction of the hot tub, while Peter could have walked in quietly from the barbecue area just around the corner.

"If you like-a me like I like-a you," sang Peter again.

"I do NOT like-a you. What has gotten into you? Why do you keep saying that I like you? And STOP singing that racist song. Do unto others as you would have them do unto you. Life is too short to sweat the small stuff. Being good is easy, being devilish is hard work. Never do such a thing like that in Five Points. We don't do things like that here." MaryAnne's tone was menacing now.

"We do not do things like that here, EVER." Gail joined in the condemnation.

"A leopard cannot change its spots," MaryAnne interjected.

Becky pushed both aside both and stood in front of the lounging Peter. "We can ignore this poor ignoramus, with his inadequate intellect, his lack of courtesy and profoundly distasteful choice in song. I am the proud granddaughter of an African princess. And I am supremely honored to be of dusky shade. It reflects my royal heritage."

"Unlike you!" spat Gail.

"You can go to hell in a handbasket," MaryAnne spat in the Fat Man's direction. "We go, ladies, we leave this pathetic excuse of humanity. We go with our feathers unfurled and magnificent. We go in dignity." MaryAnne hung onto Becky's arm as they made their way slowly out of the pool enclosure.

As they went, Very could hear Peter humming the song as they passed him. What a dork! How could someone, called out for their blatant racism, embrace it so publicly? Very was not usually the kind to walk into a dispute like this, and besides, the three ladies held up their dignity splendidly in the face of disrespect.

Very gritted her teeth and closed her eyes. What had she gotten involved in, coming to live in this place? Ah well, Bakersfield had a record of racism, home to a branch of the Ku Klux Klan, cross burnings and the like. It appeared that the kind of attitude still survived. Should she just lie here and tolerate it?

She sat up, with a resolve to say something. The pool area was deserted. The hot tub aerator pump suddenly ceased and a wave of calm pervaded the scene. Very sighed and got up. The day was spoiled. Go home.

But first, Very went around the hedge that enclosed the hot tub. Although the pump could be heard quite plainly, no one could actually see inside the enclosure, as there was foliage surrounding the tub, giving it a cozy feel. She peeked into the round space. There were three chairs lined up against the back fence, but little space to lounge. It seemed more like just a water feature. Very put her books down on a chair, slipped off her shoes and sat on the side of the pool. There was a sign saying 'no diving' and now Very contemplated the reason. It was almost big enough to dive into. Perhaps the sign was there because someone would be foolish enough to try? Another sign hung high up on a post. 'Occupancy 18.' Very casually eyed the pool, the water level and noted that eighteen people would undoubtedly cause a spillover. Ten, perhaps, might fit easily.

She sunk her feet into the water, gasping as the heat wrapped around her feet and ankles. "Ahhh," she said out loud. Immediately, she looked around to see if anyone was listening to her raptures. Such a quiet, isolated place. Anything could go on here, unnoticed. Surely, things did go on here?

Three minutes later, Very lifted her feet and placed them on the cement to dry. Bring a towel, maybe your swimsuit, do it properly next time. She picked up her two books and exited the hot tub. She went out of the pool enclosure and then exited via the side gate, simply pushing the gate open and watched it swing shut with a clang.

"I need to do some boxes today," she murmured to herself. She needed to be careful about this habit she had developed, of talking to herself. Others may think she was becoming looney, or lonely.

She slowly walked down the street. She took the shortest way home and noted a few more open garages and discreet lawn art.

She heard a car pull up beside her. She ignored it, until she realized it had stopped. "Very," a woman's voice called to her.

Very did not recognize the woman by name, but she placed the face as among those she had been introduced to the day of the debacle in the lobby of the clubhouse. "Yes?"

"You knew Mr. Tom, didn't you? I thought someone said you had met him at the pool."

"Yeah, such a sweet old guy, what a character."

"Well, I thought, seeing as how I ran into you, that you should know."

Very held her breath, waiting for the news.

"He passed last night, in his sleep, peacefully in his own bed. We are so sorry to have him leave us."

Very's mouth dropped open. "Yes, I had just met him, just the once. And now he is gone."

Chapter Five: Mr. Tom Joins the Marble Forest

It was too soon for him to go! "I hadn't really had a chance to chat with him. He was going to show me his workshop and all his furniture." Very stood stunned in the street, blocking traffic.

"We'll keep you informed about services, shall we?" offered the driver informant.

"Sure, sure, keep me in the loop." Very stepped back onto the sidewalk and allowed the car and the one behind to pass.

She slowed her steps as she walked home. The wide streets, covered with inky black tar, must be hot in the summer. Although there were many trees, they weren't tall or wide enough to provide deep shade, yet. But she had seen the gardeners out and about, whacking at bushes and trees, cutting all the new growth, and some of the old, creating neat boxy shapes. It made the whole complex look too similar, one house, one street to the next. Well, at least the HOA took care of the front lawns and she and other homeowners could concentrate on their own patios and backyards.

The sun beat down and by the time she had arrived home, she felt parched and warm. She fixed a tall glass of ice water and went outside to the patio. April first, OMG, April Fool's Day; was everything that had happened today real, or was it all a joke?

She sat in a comfortable chair and closed her eyes, reviewing the events of the day. A gentle breeze started swinging the wind chimes next door. They were deep melodious notes that threatened to lull her to sleep. Then, the bushes set up a rattle, a dusty clicking sound as leaves rubbed each other, adding to the chimes' noise. Within minutes, the air filled with dust and electricity, a phenomenon that Very recognized as a change in barometric pressure. Her mother had complained that this was the kind of weather that caused her arthritis to ache. Maybe it was the portent of more rain. The Lord knew that Bakersfield could use some more rain this year, indeed every year.

Mr. Tom died. Was it just two days ago that she had met him sitting by the side of the pool? Very tried to picture his face, his posture, other indications of his health. His mind had seemed clear. Although, Very had thought at the time that he was telling her a story, not quite true, maybe with sprinkles of truth, but full of holes, misrememberances, and lies. What is truth, anyway?

And when and where do truth and death meet? If a person dies, and their memory dies with them, does that mean all of their truths die with them as well? Is truth only facts that can be verified or does it include our feelings, our memories, our own consciousness?

Very thought of her mother's death, a quiet one, and not unexpected, but it had disrupted Very's life. A lot of her mother's stuff, both material and immaterial, had fallen into Very's life in a way she had not appreciated. The move to Five Points was a way of breaking away, cutting the strings, the ropes, the glue that had held her mother's life together. She had wanted her own life, not her mother's. And making a new home for herself was one way to move forward. But now, Very had to face death again. Her new friend's.

Very thought again of her mother's cat and the grave. Suddenly, she felt guilty for leaving the rotting corpse of the cat under the old tomato vine in her mother's house. Maybe she should have dug it up and brought it with her? No, no, no. Leave the little animal in peace. No, let the ashes fall into ashes and the dust into dust.

Life, she needed life. She rose from the chair and called Darrell. There was no answer, so she left a short message.

Darrell had entered her life about a year and a half ago as she began to search for her long-lost fiancé. She had thought his body may have been the one that had been found in an orchard, but it hadn't. In the meantime, she had worked with Darrell Pitts, Private Investigator, in a continued search for the man who had left her standing at the altar, pregnant. Losing the baby had meant losing all ties, or so she had thought. Becoming a partner in Darrell's business and another investigation had brought her closer to Darrell and together they had continued the search for Frankie Monroe.

Now, she sighed and left her seat in the sun for the indoor world of packed boxes that awaited her.

On Thursday, Very walked up the staircase in the 17th Street office building of Darrell Pitts, Private Investigator. The first time she had climbed these stairs, she had channeled the thought of Miss Wonderly visiting Sam Spade in his San Francisco office. She was the mysterious femme fatale bringing a case to the world-weary PI. Later on, Very laughed at her fantasy as Darrell was hardly a Sam Spade. Darrell was an accountant, a forty-something loner who had wandered into the business from the investigations of his accounting firm. With this bird watcher on the weekends, and an intensely private person, Very had forged a relationship of sorts. Now her name also appeared on the door, partners.

"Hey there, Darrell, long time no see." Very burst into the office with a renewed vigor. "Sorry it's been so long, weeks, I know. But not only have I moved into a new house,

I have moved onto a new stage of my life. I am an officially retired person now. I've given myself up to the decadent pleasures of lying by the poolside and am contemplating joining the pickle ball crowd."

"Pickle ball? Really?" Darrell laughed at Very's enthusiasm. "Tell me about your new house and your new community."

"Well, the house is way too much for me, but I had the money, so why not? Instead of my mother's little backyard swimming pool, I have a ginormous pool that will be heated soon. There's a hot tub, tennis courts, pickle ball courts, pool tables, even a little theater to watch movies in. But I'm not sure how involved I want to become. You know me, I don't always subscribe to Bakersfield political or religious leanings, and I'm afraid of joining some group, then finding out they are all rabid subscribers to something I don't like."

"Very, just don't talk politics. Stick to the weather! Didn't your mother teach you that?" Darrell laughed. "Glad to see you. Are you still looking for Frankie Monroe?"

Very sat in the chair in front of the computer that Darrell had designated hers. The tiny office felt crowded. "Naw, I think I'm done with that, actually. I have moved on, as I said. But if you have more work, maybe you could entice me back." Very laughed loudly, hoping that Darrell would get the point that she didn't really want to come back. Did she?

They chatted for a while and then Darrell suggested lunch. It was a meal they enjoyed having together, both ordering too much and then taking it home to eat a solitary dinner.

"La Costa Mariscos has moved; they are at the Ice House now. And I hear they have decorated it up," Darrell said.

"Then let's go." Very picked up her purse and looked around. Her personal things didn't belong here anymore, did they? Maybe she should pick up anything that was crowding the office, things that were hers, not the office's. She spotted an old coffee mug and looked inside. Had had tea in it recently, so just leave it. Oh, just leave everything.

At La Costa Marisco's, they were seated promptly and then turned to the menu. Their favorites were still there, although new items had been discreetly added, and the prices increased. Never mind, someone had to pay for the upgrades visible all around them. On one wall was painted a little Mexican village; multi-hued houses, a church, stores, restaurants, cars and trucks. Palm trees swayed in the wind. The rest of the restaurant was crowded with paper flowers and crafts from Mexico, giving the overall feelings of brightness, and a homey touch. Soft music played in the background, although the high ceilings bounced back the noise of happy patrons. Darrell ordered shrimp and Very stuck with enchiladas poblanas. Soon, they were both dipping warm chips into salsa. Before they were ready it seemed, huge platters of food were placed in front of them by a friendly waiter. He wore a short black apron and a black tee shirt with the restaurant logo. Very lifted her fork and dug into her enchiladas, soft tortillas swimming in brown chocolate sauce. She moaned faintly as she stuck the first bite into her mouth. "Oh, I have missed this."

Darrell leaned over his plate, using his fingers to lift a shrimp by its tail, preparatory to biting down on it. "Ah," he echoed Very, as he munched on his food. "I just love the service here. They are always so quick; I don't think I've ever waited very long for my food."

"It's one of the reason why we love it!" Very replied. Then she attacked her food in earnest.

The clang of dishes, ice buckets and the voices of waiters and cooks mixed with patrons' laughs and conversations.

When they neared the end of a feeding frenzy, Very caught a passing waiter and asked for a box. "Better make it two," she said as she eyed Darrell's plate, still piled with food.

Very filled her box with her leftovers, plonked $25 on the table and rose to leave. "Gotta go. Enjoy!" She walked away, then turned to wave at Darrell.

Was that a hang-dog expression on his face? Was he expecting her to stay and chat all afternoon? Did she leave too abruptly? But had she promised more than eating a meal together? Very had always suspected that Darrell had a crush on her, and as she neared her car, she hesitated. Should she go back inside, sit down and say - what? No, call tomorrow and be very nice to him.

She stopped by Smith's Bakery on Union Avenue and bought a dozen smiley face cookies. They were large with crinkled edges, covered with bright yellow frosting. Two chocolate blobs made the eyes. And then the decorator had taken the frosting cone and made a wide smile. Each cookie was slightly different; this one sported a smirk, that one a quiet smile, another an intense urge to break into song. Whatever, everyone loved these cookies, even though Very tried hard to reject them, not on her diet because of the incredible amount of sugar and fat. She bought them for Joey's family, for tomorrow night.

Friday, late in the morning a week later, Very gathered with others from Five Points in the Ball Room. A long table groaned with sandwiches, desserts, salads, and finger foods. Another table held lemonade, iced tea, cold water and hot coffee. More than a dozen large round tables with white table cloths were scattered around. Very saw a few of the women she had met and claimed a chair at their table. At the front of the room was another table with photographs of Mr. Tom in his heyday. Young, with a young wife. A family portrait with wife and twin sons. On a vacation cruise to Hawaii, in his workshop with his furniture. The two grown sons stood near this table and talked with the guests. One handed out flyers for the yard sale the following day. Tacky? Or just being opportunistic? Very took a flyer and made a note to go and see what was for sale. She needed nothing in her home as she had had all of her mother's furniture to choose from and had brought most of it to her new home. Waste not, want not.

Very collected a plate and put a reasonable amount of food on it, grabbed a plastic cup of lemonade and retreated to her table. She visited, listened to a few eulogies and then a short speech from one of the twins about Mr. Tom's woodworking hobby, along with another invitation to the yard sale. Then a man with a dark suit coat took over and began to intone a prayer. He praised Mr. Tom for being loving husband and father, an upright citizen and faithful accountant for many companies. Faithfully stealing profits, did he mean? "And now, we commend Mr. Tom to his eternal reward and to join his family in the Marble Forest Cemetery in his hometown in Ohio. He will remain in our hearts forever. Amen." A chorus of 'amens' ricocheted off the rafters.

"Goodbye, friend," Very said, as she stood.

Protests came from the other ladies at the table. "You're not staying for the music?"

Very mumbled about just moving in, things to do, new bedding plants to purchase and escaped.

At home, Very puttered and scratched items off her to-do list. She made a dish to take to Joey's that evening.

At Joey's house, she didn't bother to knock. Years of friendship meant that if you were expected, you didn't bother knocking, just came in. She walked through the front room, and the kitchen, exiting out the back where the family had gathered. Family meant Joey and her husband, Deputy

Sheriff Bobby Sanchez, three sons, three daughters-in-law, and a large and growing number of grandchildren. All were in attendance this Friday evening. Very greeted all and sundry and then managed to get Joey alone in a corner for a good chat, which she had missed the week before.

"So how is Five Points? When do I get to come and see your house? And the clubhouse and community? How's it going, living up to expectations?" Joey asked.

"Two deaths in the first week. One was a heart attack in the gym and the other was a quiet death at home, but I had just met him, so it was a bit shocking. Gone to join his ancestors in the cemetery." Very tried to explain about Mr. Tom's hobby of woodworking and the secret drawers, but was interrupted before she got to the stolen cash. Well, that was apocryphal, the $43,000.

Bobby Jr. stopped by to remind his mother of a babysitting job she had promised to do for him. Bobby Jr. was the most like his dad and Very occasionally wished that he had been her son. His wife was also much like Joey, a teacher, a down-to-earth mother and wife. They seemed to have replicated their parents' lives. Their middle child was smart, lively and charming. Her name was Clara and for her, Very was her 'Aunt Berry'.

She could have had a family like this. She could have had a granddaughter like Clara. Even though Frankie had left her the day before the wedding, the baby was lost, and she was free to marry. Why hadn't she? What had stopped her?

"How's the new place, Five Points, isn't it? What does Five Points mean, anyway?" Bobby Jr. slipped into a small chair next to Very.

"The points of the compass, North, South, East, West and the last, Heaven. Where we will all go someday, presumably."

Bobby met this explanation with a wide-eyed stare. "You're kidding right?"

"No, that's what I was told. And two of our members have already headed for the Fifth Point. The first week, two of them. I thought that I was turning over a new leaf, a new phase of my life. I thought I was retired and I could play all day. But instead I have been reminded that we are all heading for the marble forests, the graveyard. We are all going there one day. But we can't just line up, plan for it, because it is just one day, life goes 'whoosh' and we are out. We can't do much to stop or slow it down too much. It's fate, the great raffle, the roulette wheel of life. What have I done to prepare for it?"

"Very, don't be in such a panic," said Bobby.

As he rambled on about the vagaries of life, Very looked over his shoulder to where Bobby Sr. was manning the barbecue. Standing next to him was a man wearing a white Stetson, white shirt and well-worn jeans. He turned to look at Very and she saw a handsomely craggy face, a neat salt and pepper mustache and dark brooding eyes. He stared at her and then slowly raised a hand to the brim of his hat and touched it. A salute, a hello.

Chapter Six: The Yard Sale

The sunlight came through the slats in the blinds and woke Very. She glanced at the clock and almost jumped. Then she remembered it was Saturday, a very busy day. But not yet, she had a few minutes to loll in bed and review the past week. She reached across to fluff her pillow and felt a pull at her shoulder. The days of box emptying, crouching to put things away in the lower cupboards, the flowers put into the hard cement-like earth, all had taken a toll on her aging body. She needed a soak in the hot tub; maybe this evening. But the first order of business was the yard sale. Mr. Tom's sons were going to be selling a lot of his furniture. She had missed out on a private tour of his furniture workshop, but now, she could do it post mortem. Up and at 'em.

Tonight was the pool party, her first foray into 'society' at Five Points. She scrolled through the clothes in her closet. She had worn nothing but sloppy old khakis and holey shirts for the past few weeks. It was a party, she could wear something really nice. She had a good assortment and they all fit; thanks to her close attention to diet and exercise. But, they told her she should wear her swimming suit underneath it all so she could have a go at the hot tub towards the end of the evening. So, what went well over her suit? Or maybe she could just bring it and change? That blouse, the white one with embroidery.

She made a simple breakfast and then donned a nice pair of shorts. She walked the five blocks to Mr. Tom's house. As she neared it, she encountered cars parked along the street and a crowd in the driveway. Very approached, looking for familiar faces. She didn't find familiar faces, but she did find some familiar looking dinner ware. She picked up a piece and laughed, just like a set her mother had had. Gone now, broken, chipped and given away after her mother was gone. No, Very should not even think of buying some more of this.

"Do you think you need more dishes?" a tall gray-haired man leaned over to say to her. "Don't we all have too many? Gifts, an extra set for company or the Thanksgiving dinner with the extended family. I know we have too many." He laughed with a hearty chuckle. "But I know how it is. I'm a collector, so I suspect my wife will do this to my wonderful collections."

Very smiled. "Don't we all have collections of something? What do you collect?"

"I videotape movies. Actually, I have not done much of that recently, videotape is getting really old. But I have a collection of miniature bottles. You know, the little ones that you get on airplanes with whiskey in them?"

"Miniature whiskey bottles? Are they full? With whiskey?" Very looked at the tall man beside her. He did not give the appearance of a mentally unstable person, but what a collector! "How many of them do you have?"

"Last count it was about 15,000."

"You're kidding! What do you do with them? Where do you store them? Do you display them somewhere?"

"There's a room in my house. And there are others who collect. We have conferences and a newsletter. Did you know that the oldest miniature bottles for whiskey go back to the Civil War? You know, a little bit for one person."

"Wow," said Very, putting the unwanted plate down. "Tell me more!"

"No, I don't want to bore you. My wife says I can spend too much time talking about my hobbies. I'm here looking for more, but don't tell my wife!"

"I wouldn't dream of snitching on a cheating husband. At least it's just miniature whiskey bottles."

The man guffawed and stuck out his hand, "I'm John, really nice to meet you. Are you new here?"

"Yes, this is my first yard sale in Five Points, but it looks like other yard sales. Not much in the way of kitchen stuff like matching cloth napkins and table cloths."

"His wife died years ago, so I think he got rid of a lot of that stuff then. Have you met the sons?"

Very sighed, "Yeah, yesterday at the memorial. I was surprised that they had this sale so soon, he's hardly in the ground and they are getting rid of his life, erasing him as it were."

"You sound like you have experience of this?" John said gently.

Very spoke of her mother and admitted that she moved here to have a clean slate, take back her life.

"Actually, I believe that Mr. Tom himself had slated this day for a yard sale. He knew his time was coming and he wanted to sell some of his furniture. He was a stable, honest, very practical person."

Very blinked and looked closely at John. He appeared to be telling the truth as he saw it. What Mr. Tom had revealed at the pool seemed even more implausible given all the close friends and family she had met.

"Have you seen his work?"

"No, he himself told me about it. He invited me to come and look at his collection, but he passed just two days later."

"Come, I'll show you." John indicated the garage which was full of simple tables, end tables, cabinets, desks and a bedroom set that had a sign on it, "Not for sale."

Very approached the bedroom set and smiled. "I guess that maybe his sons want to keep this. Magnificent." A queen-sized bed with a towering headboard and footboard was the center of the set. Two night tables, two chests of drawers and a man's suit stand clustered together. Very reached out to touch, slowing stroking the elegant, simply finished wood, which brought a smile to her face.

"Oh, I see you are a fan," said a man behind Very.

She turned and recognized one of the sons. He looked a bit like his father, only a generation younger. His smile was a bit lopsided. Was it a reflection of his personality? Lopsided?

"Are you interested in buying something? I have lots of other things, smaller, over here."

He pointed to a cluster of chests of drawers, side tables and a clever three-legged corner chair.

Very approached and then realized John had disappeared on her. She turned to the furniture. Before her stood a five-drawer chest of drawers, divided into two tiers. The son reached over to the second drawer, opened it and stuck his hand into the interior, pressing some hidden button. The third drawer popped and sprang open slightly, allowing access. "See, a locked drawer. Looks normal, but can't be opened unless you access the secret knob. My dad did this to a lot of pieces of furniture. This one," he indicated a desk, "has five secret drawers."

"It's lovely, but I don't think I can afford it, and don't really need it. I met Mr. Tom just a few days before he…died, passed, at the pool."

"Oh, just say died. We all die. And pass what? The test of life?" came the quick riposte.

"I see your point. But what I was trying to say was I enjoyed his company and I was sorry to hear he had gone, or rather, died. And he bragged about his secret drawers. I would love to have something, maybe something smaller."

The second son approached and smiled at Very. She remembered that they were twins, but not identical twins. One was slightly heavier, and had a deeper tan, but they were incredibly similar. "We have a few lovely smaller pieces, and very reasonable. Here's a side table, everyone can use another side table, can't they," he smiled, smoothly symmetrical.

Warming to his attitude and smile, Very approached the cluster of smaller pieces. She looked at a bedside table, two tiers, with a drawer in the lower level. She touched and admired the wood, craftsmanship and asked, "How much?"

"$25. Is that okay?"

"Sure," Very said, looking at her new purchase. So, where was the secret drawer in this one? She crouched down and opened and closed the drawer and felt around the edges.

"Oh, no secret drawer in that one, I'm afraid," said the second twin.

"We've looked," said the first son. "He made a few things without, but he bragged as if everything was secreted up."

Very looked again and eyed the distance between the bottom of the edge of the drawer and the bottom of the shelf. She turned her head and smiled to herself. No secret drawer? We'll see about that. "$25?"

The first brother shot daggers at the second, who smiled sweetly and said, "It's used, not special, just a well-made specimen of my father's craft." The second twin smirked in return to the daggers.

"Not really, technically, used," shot back the first brother.

"Never mind him," said the second twin. "He will soon be awash in all these treasures, plus all of his own, plus his partner's, so he won't have much room. If you want to get rid of some of this," he turned to address his twin, "you'll have to price it more reasonably. After all, this place isn't the big city."

Very pulled out her purse and extracted $25. She held it out and the first brother grabbed it. The second pulled out a small notebook and wrote something. An accountant like his father?

"He's moving in here, you see," said the second brother. "But, of course, our father, the redoubtable Mr. Tom, left everything to both of us. Share, brother, learn how to share. And, like I said, when you move in, you'll have far too much stuff! Maybe I'll just move into the extra bedroom." He gestured to the double set of windows in the front of the house. Lovely positioning, this room." He turned to his brother and smiled slyly again.

"I'll just go get my car and take it off your hands." Very turned to leave.

John materialized and smiled at Very, "Bought something?"

"Yes, could you keep an eye on this little beauty here while I go get my car?" She lowered her voice, "Just don't let them sell it again."

Within minutes, Very had returned with her car. She and John loaded it in and she slammed the back hatchback shut. "Sure I can't help you," John offered. "It's not heavy, but awkward."

"You are so sweet, but I can manage. See you tonight at the Pool Party!" she said as she drove the few blocks to her house.

Once in the driveway, she remotely opened the doors of her two-car garage. Contrary to her usual habit of parking smack in the middle of the space, she pulled over to the side.

After struggling with the table to get it out of the back of her red Prius, Very closed the door to her car and also the automatic door to the garage. She smacked the light switch to the overhead light in the garage to the on position and turned to look at her new purchase.

She squatted and looked at her new table. She reached up to grab a cloth and lost her balance. She turned to the shelf unit to balance herself. "Careful, girl," she said aloud. She slowly got up and opened the small side door of the garage which opened on to a narrow side yard where she stored her garbage cans. The light flooded in and she turned once more to her newest purchase.

Very owned six 'magic boxes' acquired in different parts of the world, each with its own cleverly hidden opening. Madagascar, Kenya, Kashmir, Uzbekistan, Costa Rica, North Carolina. Some were simple, but a couple were too clever for all but her most intelligent and creative friends. She knew what she was looking for.

With the extra light from the open door, Very was able to grasp the rag and begin an overall dust. She pulled on the drawer, but it did not give easily. She slid it shut and tried again. Again, it was stiff and did not give easily. She carefully looked at all sides of the front, noting the larger than usual space below the drawer. She got closer and noted thin lines that denoted a break in the wood. She ran her fingernail along them, showing a definite outline. She breathed out and sat down on the floor next to the table. She opened the drawer again, but once again, it stuck, this time it opened a centimeter more than before. Was it stuck, or was the secret lock somewhere in the front of the drawer. She bent her head to look, and feeling for anything that wasn't in the right place.

"Yoohoo, hello there," boomed a voice from outside the door.

Very gave a frightened squeak and dropped the table, making an awkward clunk onto the garage floor. She looked up to see her next-door neighbor standing at his fence, peering through the open door. "Hi," Very said breathlessly.

"Just wanted to say hello and ask if you're going to the pool party tonight. I know that the tickets were on sale, but you were busy moving in. Did you manage to get a ticket? Have a table?"

Very stood and tried to conceal the table behind her. "Yes, I did get a ticket. I'm all set. Thanks for asking."

"Need any help with that?" A neighborly smile appeared. "Looks like you have some new furniture?"

"Yeah, just a little side table. No, I'm good. Just needs a swipe with a cloth, no problems with it." Very tried to use the dirty cloth to hide the opened drawer.

"Looks nice. Well, see you at the pool tonight. Take it easy." He disappeared from Very's view down the side of his house.

Very looked down at the table. She found a big black plastic bag and put it over the table. She cleared a space behind two old suitcases and shoved it into a dark corner of the garage. Another time; away from prying eyes.

Chapter Seven: The Pool Party

Even though there was a name for the party, something about spring or Tuscany or islands or magic, everyone was just calling it The Pool Party. Very sat in the chair in her backyard, enjoying the afternoon sun. She thought of what she might do for her back yard to bring color and life to it. At the moment, it was green grass and a few shrubs. There was also one little plot of bulbs she had hastily planted. She had brought them from her mother's house, although she felt sure it was too late for them to bloom this year, or maybe any year. Most had already started sticking their green swords up, but she had extracted them anyway. They weren't looking good, but they were Dutch iris of many colors and guaranteed to bloom year after year. Leave them be.

Suddenly, she jumped up. No more laziness, get ready. She had prepared a nibbles plate and bought a couple of wine coolers for herself. Although only an occasional drinker, she thought it best to get a slight buzz on tonight, as everyone else would be three sheets to the wind by sundown, or so she had heard. Bringing your own drinks was a custom here, it appeared. Very remembered a friend of her mother's who came to any dinner or party with her own drink; a can of Diet Pepsi and a half bottle of Jim Beam, which she proceeded to drink herself, never even offering it to any other guest. She was a happy guest, so why rock the boat, was her mother's comment.

She checked her email quickly to see if there were any changes for this evening. Nikki had emailed. Who was Nikki? Very checked her menu of names and faces to try and hone in on Nikki. Was she the one with blond-white hair, cut in bangs and with a slight curl under her chin? In the days of her youth, this hairstyle would have been accompanied by a heightened pouf of hair at the crown. Very never understood why this style had been adopted. She herself had resisted the style of backcombing or 'ratting' her hair to achieve this dubious hairstyle, as she had fine hair that hadn't taken well to the violent manipulation. It simply broke off and left a balding spot there. Better was the surfer girl style, long and straight, although that style, too, was beyond Very's capability. Her hair was just too curly. Instead of lying straight and smooth, it fluffed up, especially if Very left the bone-dry desert of Bakersfield. At college in Santa Cruz, she had let her hair become long and flyaway. So, Nikki was one of those who had kept her youthful hairstyle, minus the ratting. A little plump, giddy and cheerful, owl-like eyes behind giant glasses. What did she have to say, one hour before the grand kick-off?

"Pool is still unheated for tonight's party, and the heater for the hot tub is a bit dicey for this evening. But we go ahead. PARTY TIME!"

Very decided to wear clothes and throw her towel and suit into the bag she was taking. She chose a bright blouse and a long skirt that fell in gentle folds and would swish gently as she walked. Feminine. The party might be at the pool, but was not, it seemed, going to include the pool in the festivities.

At five Very headed out the door for the seven-minute walk to the clubhouse. There was a circle in front of the clubhouse planted with colorful flowers. A tall flagpole stood in the center, a flag fluttering in the breeze. Large parking lots flanked the clubhouse, with an overabundance of disabled parking spots. There were also a few golf cart spaces, or spaces for very small cars. A bicycle rack sat next to the large gate off to the side. Tall bush-like trees grew in the grand entryway. Very breathed deeply. Yes, a lovely place to live, like a resort. Very entered.

A woman stood with a clipboard blocking entry until checked off. Nikki accosted her, "Very, isn't it? Such an unusual name. You've paid and you're at table 8. Now, you have brought drinks and hors d'oeuvres, haven't you?"

Very stared in panic. Was she supposed to bring enough for the whole table? Or just herself? Very looked into her bag. There were two canned wine cocktails and a series of plastic containers with various nibbles. She looked up.

"I'm sure what you've brought is more than enough. And between you, me and the gatepost, there is always waaaay too much, especially of the alcoholic type. Have fun."

Very stepped outside to the patio. Music was spinning, old 50's and 60's songs. Of course, it was a type of music that all here could relate to, none of this 90's hip-hop or blaring dance music. Elvis, the Platters, Brenda Lee and of course, the Beatles. Yeah, yeah, yeah.

She spotted someone waving at her. What was her name? Cindi, Candy, Sandy, Barbie, Joanie, Susie? She waved back and headed for the table, which she saw was labeled #8. Was this the table she had signed up for? It didn't appear to be the one, but what the hell? There was a name card and Nikki said this one. Never mind, she snagged a chair and dumped her bag in it. The pool was just a few feet from where she stood. She bent and stuck her hand in the water, letting it swirl through her fingers.

"What did you expect?" asked someone behind her.

She turned to find John, with drink in hand, smiling at her.

"Ever hopeful. It must be my middle name."

"I trust you got your table home?"

"Yes. It's bit dusty, so it's still in my garage. I'm waiting to find the right spot in the house for it."

John leaned closer and whispered, "Have you found the secret drawer yet?"

Very felt John's knowing eyes on her. "I was told there wasn't any in that piece. And no, I haven't found anything; I don't expect to." She looked at John with steely eyes and a warning writ on her face.

John smiled, gave a chuckle and walked away.

"Hello, Very, come and meet my hubby." One of the group Very had met in the last two weeks waved her over to Table 5. Her husband stood beside her, red-faced and already slurring his words. Better be introduced now before he became totally sloshed.

Another woman thankfully pulled Very away and introduced her to some of her friends. Very recognized that she had already met two of them, but had forgotten their names. This had always been her nightmare as a teacher, names. It took her at least two months into the semester to get the names down, even after doing everything she could think of to jog her memory. Smile, Very; smiling will ease all.

"Have you joined any clubs yet? You must come and do water aerobics with us in the mornings. We have to wait until the pool is warmer, but it is great exercise."

"I love to swim, and I might do that, but I prefer doing laps." Noting her new friend's look of horror, Very softened the blow. "Oh, aerobics is such good exercise, why not do both, huh?"

"Pickle ball? We can always use another good player," said another in the group.

Very smiled, "Good player, I am not. I've never played, but I'd love to try."

"Oh, another beginner. Well, we have lots of those, but we could really use some more experienced players. Do come, though, who knows, you might be a natural."

"Sounds good, what time do you play?"

"Seven."

Very gasped, "AM?"

"The heat, Very, the heat. In the summer, it's the only time."

"Oh, some of us have taken to doing warm ups at 6. Well, 6:30."

"I will definitely give it a try."

Very wandered back to her own table and extracted a can of wine cooler. She looked around for a glass and then realized she was supposed to bring her own, plastic glass that is. No glass at the pool area. She looked towards the hot tub area. No one seemed to be there. Was now the time to check it out? She meandered over to the enclosure. The pool bathers could not see the hot tub bathers, nor the other way around. She marveled at how cozy and isolated it all seemed to be. Thick bushes surrounded the hot tub area, maybe for privacy, maybe to keep the kids out. She followed the hedge around to the side of the circle and then saw the two steps up to the tub, which sat in its own floral splendor. There was an overhead fretwork canopy and on a post, the controls for the jets. She glanced at the sign again, the capacity of 18. If 18 large sized Five Points residents got into the tub, it would surely overflow. Twelve, maybe.

Suddenly, the music blared and Very recognized that a live band now gave them music, instead of a turntable. She abandoned the hot tub and walked back towards the pool, her table, and the rest of the gang from her special community.

She suddenly bumped into a woman. "Mary Anne, isn't it? You have recovered well, haven't you? The last time I saw you, you were still limping around."

"Yes, I'm better, thank you. Have you been checking out our renowned hot tub? There's no time like the present. If you can't beat 'em, join 'em. How's the water?" Mary Anne pivoted towards the party.

"Oh, I forgot to check it out."

"Later, there'll be time later. Food has arrived you know; better join the line. The early bird gets the worm. Time is money, waste not, want not." Mary Anne hobbled, more than before, towards her table.

Very watched the line form and held back. The sun was setting and the sky was turning a darker blue, with the clouds picking up the pink and orange of the setting sun. She breathed in deeply. This was her favorite time of day. The smell of food coaxed her to reluctantly join the snaking line that headed for the long tables of food.

Before she arrived at the plate and cutlery station, a large man wearing loud red shorts and no shirt pushed in front of her. Fat Man Gunn put out his substantial elbow to create a space. Very could hardly elbow past him without being rude. The couple who had been in line in front of Very found themselves being pushed from the rear. Both turned to look at the pusher. The man's eyes bulged, "YOU."

Very stepped back and gave the person behind a bump. She turned to apologize and found Mary Anne on her heels. "If it were me who had been shoved like that, I would have knocked the man over. Give as good as you get. When the going gets tough, the tough get going. Mistake to turn the other cheek." Then she said it louder, "KNOCK HIM OVER."

Behind Mary Anne was Gail, her giggling friend. "Don't worry," she said to Mary Anne and Very, "someday soon, he will get his." She smiled wickedly and gave a giggle.

MaryAnne turned and said sotto voce, "Oh, he will, he will; don't worry about that. The boomerang always returns. What's good for the goose is good for the gander."

Very smiled. Their voices were sweet and feminine, non-threatening, even as their words were threats.

"Hey Petey!" called Becky to Peter Gunn. She had been in the line behind Gail, but now she stepped out of line and stood next to Peter Gunn, aka Fat Man Gunn. "I've got something for you, a peace offering as it were. After dinner, I'll bring it over to you. We can't continue feuding if we all live here, can we?"

Why were they being so nasty and then so pleasant? Did they have plans?

"Okay, darling!" Pete said, half turning to answer her. "Peace!"

From somewhere behind her, Very heard a muttered, "When pigs fly." When she turned to find the speaker, she only saw faces turned away from the fracas.

Then it was Very's turn at the food and she concentrated on choosing dishes for her plate. There were so many salads that even if she took just one spoonful, she would have no room for meat, or the fried potatoes she saw farther up the table.

She sat and ate with the other seven single, widowed or otherwise unattached women at her table. They were fun, sharing their wine and stories of other Pool Parties.

Soon, the music became even louder and a few couples got up to dance. One couple did an energetic twist for a minute, then retired with red faces and heaving lungs. Someone noticed that Very had finished all her own drinks and found a glass and filled it with white wine. Oh no, the reason why Very had brought the light-as-air spritzers was to keep her consumption down. She feared that she would imbibe too much and make a fool of herself, dancing with inappropriate men, talking too loud, worse, vomit up her dinner. She smiled and sipped the wine. Cheap, the best kind for stretching it out for the rest of the evening.

She watched the other guests, noting who was with whom, who was talking with whom. She saw Gail and Becky approach Fat Man Gunn sitting at a table. There was no way to hear what was being said, but Becky had a cocktail in her hand. It was in a big plastic martini glass with a little umbrella sticking out of it. The color was milky, green or turquoise perhaps. A grasshopper? Some new-fangled recipe? Becky bent over Peter, and Very could see her smirk and coo to him. He took the glass with a wide grin. Becky watched him sip, then gulp half of the drink. Giggling Gail was on the other side and handed him a small plateful of cookies. Very read the body language, and then she was startled to be able to read Gail's lips. She smiled and opened her mouth with exaggeration, "They are all for you." She shook her head, no, no, no, don't give them to anyone else. I baked them myself. The two women backed away and Very craned her neck to see if Peter Gunn would consume his special snacks. They were making up to Peter, but with a snarky attitude.

Suddenly, Peter Gunn stood and grabbed a microphone from one of the band members. He sang the lyrics of the 50's era ballad, a boy misses his girlfriend, summer away, he's jealous. The nerve of the man to butt into the performance was colossal. The band kept playing, the singer, whose microphone had been hijacked, hung around near the edge of the group, singing along with Fat Man Gunn. Soon, Peter lost the lyrics and the beat, causing the audience to stir and begin catcalling to Peter Gunn to sit down and shut up. The band wrapped up the song, then they all applauded. They were used to catering to the man who thought he could sing and had too much to drink.

Very had to concede that Peter's voice was good, and that he had the experience and the nerve to perform with professionals. But others knew him better than she and they knew that it was not the time for encouragement.

Very looked at the clock on the wall. The party was to be over, finally and with the place picked up, no later than 10. There was time for a quick dip in the hot tub. Forget what else the band had in store.

A splash sounded behind her. As she turned in her seat to look in the direction of the pool, another two splashes in quick succession were followed by a hearty bellow of rage.

"Oh, what the hell!" screamed one inebriated female voice, followed by a splash and a scream of surprise and pain. Before someone could find and add her to the pool party dunking bodies, Very grabbed her bag and moved quickly to the changing rooms on the far side of the table area. Time for her suit and the hot tub.

"Cannonball," screamed Fat Man Gunn as he launched himself into the pool with a resounding boom.

Alcohol and pools, especially cold ones, do not mix, ever.

Chapter Eight: The Hot Tub

As she entered the toilet block and changing rooms, Very looked over her shoulder. As she expected, the crowd was all on its feet, shouts were heard from the pool, the poolside, from the tables, from every direction. More bodies could be heard splashing into the pool. Thank goodness the depth of the pool at this point was very shallow. Even though it was theoretically possible to drown in a bathtub, the big danger here was an accident on the way in. Shouts and shrieks reverberated from the water as the band played on. Soon, the lead singer announced one final song, but before they could begin, there was a flicker and the lights went off. Groans and muffled shouts came from the pool. The band's singer, in a powerful voice, urged caution and restraint. Most took this for a warning to pack it in, get out of the pool and head for home.

In the dark and only starting to change, Very paused. Should she continue getting on her suit and go to the hot tub, or should she abandon the attempt? Were the lights coming on soon? Was this just a signal or was this a major power outage? She was determined. She proceeded carefully in the dark to take off her clothes and slip on her suit. She made sure that all of her items were neatly stowed in the bag, with her towel on top. The lights sprang on again. The noise outside began to abate and Very hurried out to help with the clean-up. As she emerged from the changing room, she was met by an almost deserted pool deck.

The band had managed to pack up everything and take it away. Perhaps they had experience of parties gone wild, even in supposedly sedate circumstances like a retirement community. Teenagers, maybe, but these old goats? Very walked over to the table she had been sitting at, but it had been cleared and a huge trash bag occupied the place where she had been sitting. A few people still wandered around, cleaning up the last-minute items, and Very tried to help. But it had mostly been done. She attempted to fold a chair, but someone chided her, "Leave it for the morning."

She looked towards the hot tub and saw three figures slinking away. She recognized MaryAnne by her limping gait, Becky by her height and Gail by a soft giggle. They glided away quietly, skirting the pool area and exiting by a gate near the back of the toilet block. None looked wet. But had they gone to the hot tub to soak? And then changed their minds? They certainly hadn't been in the changing room while Very was there.

Then, it was quiet, eerily quiet. Very heard some insect noises, but the human noises had gone with the crowd. She found herself alone. Noises from within the clubhouse told her that someone was still around cleaning up.

Wow, the hot tub to herself. She walked towards it, but found herself moving chairs out of her way to get to the entrance. She heard the jets bubbling in the water and grinned. A soak and a massage. As she turned the corner and was about the mount the steps, the lights went out. Again.

She waited, sure that this was another warning by the staff of the clubhouse to indicate the end of the Pool Party. She turned to retrace her steps back to the pool area, when she heard a noise. "Hello, who's there?" Very said to the darkness.

She closed her eyes to force them to dilate so she could see better in the dim light. She opened them, but still found only deep shadows. She stepped back towards the pool. The lights should come on again soon, it wasn't time for the clubhouse and environs to close yet. The lights off was just a warning. Wasn't it?

She heard a peal of laughter in the distance, cars being started and moving off, someone walking through the mix of discarded tables and chairs. She waited and turned towards the clubhouse. The lights suddenly blazed on inside. But not here.

She was not going to be cheated out of a dip in the hot tub, lights or no. By now, her eyes had adjusted to the dim light and she managed to find her way to the steps to the small pool. Light from the nearby street lights gave enough illumination to see the tub, the shadowy shapes of the chairs surrounding it and the high handles indicating the steps. She put her things carefully on a chair, slipped off her sandals and gingerly stepped towards the pool. The water jets had quit. Good, probably the timer had timed out or perhaps someone had shut the timer function off, or had it gone off with the lights? Ah, never mind, she didn't need them anyway.

Slowly, she stepped onto the first step. The hot water burned her skin, causing a slight painful sensation. She knew this was not real heat, just the shock of the difference between the air temperature, her skin temperature and the pool water. She moaned in pleasure. She lowered herself gently and slid around to a place to sit. She felt the hot water of the tub heater output and she moved in front of it, letting the hotter water massage her back. She moaned again.

The darkness infused an aura of solitude and naughtiness. The water swirled around and Very hung onto the seat to keep from moving with the current. Then she allowed herself to float momentarily as she repositioned herself. She let the heat seep into her whole body and capture the sense of self, body and soul. "Ohh," she said aloud.

With a sudden jerk, she sat up.

She sensed something or someone else here, in the pool enclosure, in the pool even. She squinted her eyes and tried to see in the darkness. She knew that it was not pitch black, so she should be able to see something. A dark shape floated by in front of her. She breathlessly moved away from it, but the current created by her movement brought the dark thing closer.

Very thought of the dead raccoon found floating in her mother's pool one morning. It moved like this, with the whirring pool pump slowly making the corpse float gently around the pool. Maybe it was a skunk, they too had been known to seek water features. She raised her body up and sniffed deeply. No skunk smell, no smell of putrid dead animal.

The shadows shifted with the current and the wind. Very gently tried to scoot over to the steps and get out. But when she moved, the swirling object moved closer.

It was not a skunk or a raccoon, it was much bigger. Human-sized big. But much bigger than that.

Fear muted her and she moved quickly to the steps, or what she thought were the steps. The huge floating object chased her as she grabbed for the rail to exit. She missed and splashed into the hot water, causing hot water to rush into her mouth as she opened it. She pushed towards the steps, spewing water from her mouth. She coughed, then spat again. She reached once more for the steps, and then overshot them, the huge bulk chasing her even faster.

Finally, Very grabbed the handrails and shot out of the pool, slipping on the deck as she exited. "Oh, damn," she cried.

She turned to look at the pool, half expecting the blob to rise with her and join her on the edge of the pool. Too much to drink. Alcohol and pools do not mix.

"Help," she screamed. Only the sound was a mouse squeak, rather than a cry. "Help," she tried again.

She stepped away from the hot tub, looking for her towel as the cool night air had hit her wet skin, causing a cold pain over most of her body. "Help,' she tried again.

She found the chair where she had placed her bag and grabbed at the topmost item, which was her towel. Quickly throwing it over her shoulders, she attempted the cry for help again, "Help, help, help." Each attempt became louder, and more insistent. Finally, she bellowed, "HELP, HERE, NOW."

She tried to find a dry spot to stand, as her feet were now getting cold. She daintily stepped from spot to spot, but then she stepped on a squishy mass. "Oooooh," she said quietly. A pile of wet leaves? She soon realized that it was a towel, left by someone too lazy to take with them. She stepped in the opposite direction, cold cement meeting her bare feet.

She turned her face toward the big pool, still unable to see what was there in the dark. Noises in the distance, maybe from the clubhouse, answered her. "Coming, emergency?"

With a clunk, the lights sprang on, momentarily blinding Very. She covered her eyes for a few seconds, trying to readjust from the dark. When she opened them, she saw what had floated in the hot tub with her.

His thinning hair no longer covered his scalp, which was revealed as his face was in the water. No shirt covered his back, but voluminous red shorts swirled in the gently moving water.

Peter Gunn, Fat Man Gunn, floated face down in the hot tub.

Behind her, a small contingent of the staff and residents, who had planned the party and stayed to help with clean-up, rushed into the enclosure and up the steps. Murmurs of, "Oh my god," "Look at that?" "Who is it?" "Call an ambulance." "Is he…?" burst from the gathered onlookers.

Two energetic men waded into the pool and attempted to pull the large man out. They only succeeded in dragging him to the steps and turning him over. Very averted her gaze from his obviously lifeless face. That didn't mean he was dead, just that life no longer showed there.

"Quick," one of the men said, "get the ambulance here. It's going to be difficult to get him out, he's dead weight."

Silence met this comment. The second man started preparing to do mouth to mouth resuscitation right in the pool. The first man held onto the body which tried to slip away with every movement. One of the younger women got into the pool and tried to hold Peter Gunn's body still, so that he could be saved. The small group stood silent while the three in the pool held the large body still and continued with efforts to revive.

Sirens could be heard in the distance and coming closer. Two of the residents on the committee looked at each other. "Gate code," said one.

"Gosh, I hope the emergency services have it this time. It hasn't changed. Not since before… before they called for Bill."

At this point, the three in the pool began to flag in their enthusiasm and energy. The young woman jumped out, dripping water as she headed back to the clubhouse, to alert the emergency crew where to come, this time. The two men made half-hearted efforts to keep Peter Gunn's body floating face up. They drew him close to the steps and tried again to drag him out. An older man, one Very thought was married to one of the friends who had tried to recruit her to pickle ball, spoke. "Gently, gently, just be respectful, it's all that's required. We are all here, together, waiting."

One of the women said, "Too much alcohol, too much water, especially hot water. It's a lethal mix. A pool party is always fun, but what a way to have it end."

They waited as the noise of emergency personnel crossed the pool area.

True, pools and alcohol don't mix, but in Very's head, the murmured curse ran and ran. It was the third day after her arrival, and she hadn't taken much in yet. But she remembered the words, spoken softly, but clearly, as MaryAnne had been taken away by an ambulance after the altercation with Fat Man Gunn. The implications were that no one would miss him, and that he would receive the punishment he deserved because he was such a dislikable man.

And now, the prophecy had come true, Pete Gunn had died in the hot tub.

But was it an accident, or was it homicide?

Chapter Nine: Meltdown

Very stood on the edge of the crowd and watched as the body was taken away. The emergency crew had declined to do any more resuscitation, but had also not declared him dead. Was this some sort of legal thing? There was no doctor here, or on the ambulance crew, so who was going to say, 'Dead?'

Suddenly, Very reacted to the cold and began to shake. She felt someone drape another layer over her shoulders, but what she really needed was to change out of her wet suit. She tried to grab her belongings before the police cordoned off the area, her bag with it. The young woman from the clubhouse helped her towards the changing room, even as she shivered with the cold, dripping in her clothes. She stood guard as Very quickly changed. Her hair was still mostly dry, although half of it had gotten a brief soak when she slipped on the steps getting out of the hot tub.

"Are they going to question us?" Very asked the girl. Was it Ashley? She needed to start remembering people's names better.

"Maybe. And I need some dry clothes too. And you look like you could use a jacket or sweater. I'm sure there is something in the lost and found. I'll escort you. Then the police or whatever can have you. I mean, question you if they want. Really, all you did was get to the hot tub and find a dead resident. Nothing to do with you, huh?"

As the two women exited the changing room, they met a young policeman waiting for them. "You need to come with me," he said.

"You need to let us get some warmer clothes, otherwise you will be responsible for another death from cold. This elderly lady needs to get a sweater. Come with me and we can go to the clubhouse. We can talk there." The clubhouse staff member grabbed Very's arm in a firm movement and headed for the buildings just a few yards away. The young policeman followed.

The policeman was joined by an older colleague, but both were brushed aside by the younger staff member. She kept a hand on Very's arm as she stepped into the office and dug out the box for the lost and found. As promised, there were quite a few extraneous items of clothes. Very took a large man's jacket, hoping it did not belong to the Fat Man, and draped it over her thin blouse. She burst into tears. The attendant scooted behind a door and pulled off her jeans, as she wrapped a sweater around her waist, artfully concealing her skimpy underwear. Very tried to wipe her tears, but then began to blubber with laughter.

"We're waiting," came a command from the hallway.

"We're dressing," came the reply. The young woman turned to Very, "Are you okay now? Ready for the big bad men?"

Very wiped at her nose and turned to her rescuer, "You have been great. And yes, I'm ready."

Soon Very was seated and the younger policeman took out a notebook, while the senior officer began the questions.

Very listened for a minute, then began to softly cry again. "I don't know anything. I saw nothing. I didn't even know anyone was in the hot tub, I thought I was alone. I didn't see anyone anywhere near the place. Everyone was jumping in the pool and I wasn't going there. So I went to the hot tub. Then the lights went out, and I couldn't see anything."

"Why did you go into the hot tub with no lights?"

"Why not?" Very shot back.

"Did the victim speak to you?"

"What a stupid question. He was dead, or at least almost. He said nothing, I didn't hear him say anything. I didn't hear or see anything. Until I realized that there was something floating in the pool. I thought it might be a dead animal, you know they like getting into swimming pools, animals that is. But I couldn't see anything. Then I realized that it was big and lifeless and that's when I called out. That's all."

The police looked at each other and shrugged. They got Very's address and said if she remembered anything else to contact them. She got a card.

Very did remember things, noises, persons near the hot tub, murmured threats, but she was never going to reveal these things until she was certain about them. She was going to think carefully before she said anything; she needed to make sure of what it was she saw, and heard, and was willing to reveal.

As Very was preparing to leave, Giggling Gail appeared at her side. "Oh, you poor thing," Gail said, taking Very's arm gently. "I'll give you a ride home. You walked, didn't you? You always walk. But you can't go out there now, not alone and walking. Nosiree."

Gail took over the job of looking out for Very from the clubhouse staffer and steered her out to the parking lot. Gail opened the car door for Very and made sure she had her bag with her before slamming the door shut. "As a matter of fact, I'll take you home with me. You can sleep in my spare room. That's much better than you being on your own tonight. Too much to think about and maybe you will feel a little afraid?

I would. Yesiree, I would feel downright scared to sleep by myself tonight. I'll make sure you have a nice hot shower and some hot chocolate, or a brandy, whichever suits you. Then we'll just pop you into a comfy bed and give you a little pill. I have this go-to pill when I need to sleep. It's got just the slightest hint of this wonderful little chemical…"

Very tuned out the rest of Gail's wandering commentary on what she was going to do with Very. Not wanting to go back to her own empty-of-humans house, she allowed Gail to be a good Samaritan. As they entered the house through the garage, a loud 'meow' greeted them.

"Oh, you're not allergic to cats, are you? I only have the one and she is a short hair, but…"

Very laughed and assured Gail she liked cats.

A shower, hot tea and the acceptance of just one teeny sleeping pill, found Very welcoming the comfort of a bed, and the cat. "She just wants to make sure you are comfortable. She likes giving comfort; she's an empathetic cat, a little like a dog, really. Oh, she likes you!" Gail said as Very reached down to pet the cat, who purred in return.

Very woke with the sun pouring into her eyes, and a feeling of displacement. The cat, who had been curled at Very's back, gave a soft meow purr as Very stirred. Very's mind did tricks on her as she reached around to pet the cat. What was she doing in a strange room with a cat? Then she remembered.

Before she got up, she oriented herself. The little pill had done a surprising job. Very felt rested and ready for the day that lay ahead. She remembered the corpse in the hot tub, and the inquisition of the police. Yes, she did remember things, but she still needed time to sort them out.

She heard no noise in the house, so she got up, threw on her clothes, gathered her things together and leaving a note on the countertop in the great room kitchen, she quietly let herself out. She was just a block and a half from her own home and she went home quickly, meeting no one else at this time of day. The dog walkers had either come and gone, or would be out in force later.

Over a fresh cup of coffee, Very took stock. The third death in three weeks. No, read the newspaper, peruse the obits, check emails, forget the dead. Very fixed herself a whole wheat muffin and cut up some fruit. The idea of greasy eggs or anything heavy caused her stomach to lurch. Gently gently.

She went to her home office and turned on the computer. She went straight to her emails. Five from friends at Five Seasons, one leaving her phone number and a plea to call and reassure the sender that Very was okay. Very called, and heard laughter in the background, the clinking of ice in cocktail glasses and voices of others. "Well, I just wanted to call and tell you I'm fine. You guys sound like you are starting early." Very laughed.

"Glad to hear you're okay. Yes, it's our regular Sunday morning group. We pray for a good week ahead, and coordinate our calendars. You must join us sometime!"

Very murmured a pleasantry and said goodbye. Leave the other emails until later. If this was an indication of concern, let them be concerned. She grabbed another cup of coffee and went out to her patio. The birds cried overhead and two hummingbirds had a fight in midair. A fight, or was it mating season?

At 11:30, Very called Joey. "Hope it's not too early, I need to talk."

"Talk lady," came the reply. "I heard via the grapevine that you had a little incident out there last night."

"Heard what, exactly?"

"Oh, accidental drowning, but what a scene. A bunch of old folks making merry, being naughty."

"Joey, I found him."

"You were involved in the drowning? You, yourself?"

"No, I didn't drown him, I just found him. Floating, face down in the hot tub. He, he, bumped into me."

"Very, you were in the hot tub with a drowning victim?"

"I thought it was a raccoon. You know how they loved my mother's pool. So when, when I realized there was this blob, too big for a raccoon, well…"

"Let me get this straight. You went into the hot tub with a corpse that you thought was a raccoon?"

"It was dark. The lights had gone out, I couldn't see anything. You know, I've never been afraid of the dark, so I thought it would be fun, cool, different. I didn't mind that it was dark out there, but then there was a body. I knew him, he'd been at the party. He was kind of obnoxious, nobody liked him."

"So you got into a dark hot tub with him, and then you discover he's dead?"

"You make it sound really awful. I guess it was. I'm still a little shaken. Dead bodies are not my thing."

"Nor mine. I like them old, in a casket, with family and friends mourning them."

The doorbell rang and Very held the phone while she continued the conversation. "Oh, it's the police again. I'll call later, Joey." She punched the red button to hang up.

She stood at the door and waited for the officers to tell them what they wanted, to ask some more questions, and to be allowed inside. Very stalled. She wasn't ready for them. Not yet. She offered them coffee and when they declined, she insisted on making more for herself before she got down to business. When the smells of fresh coffee began to drift around the room, Very managed to entice the police to have a cup with her. She delayed, reaching for nice cups, pouring creamer in a dainty creamer. She emptied some sugar in a matching bowl and put it all on a tray.

When the policeman opened a notebook, Very thought the place very stuffy and insisted on opening the sliding door to the patio. "It's nicer out here, are you sure you wouldn't like to sit out here? Oh yeah, only one chair, so I guess it's here." She sat down and waited for someone to start the conversation. She sipped coffee. She commented on the coffee.

The senior looking officer started by asking details of her name, address and then a request to tell them again what had happened the night before.

Very sat up straight, took a deep breath and began to tell her story. "Well, a few months ago, I decided that it was time to get out of my mother's house. You know, sell it and move on. Well, I was born here and I really haven't lived anywhere else and all my friends are here, so I decided to buy here. Here, as in Bakersfield. And this place is for retired, or sort of, kind of going to be retired people. It's called an active retirement community. It's not for everyone, but I like the locked gate and the fact that there are lots of people like me here and I can find friends, and activities. Because you see, I'm single and this is just a good place for me.

"You know, the pool party was just about the first thing I did, well, there was the yard sale, but the gathering at the pool was the first biggie for me. It was the annual pool party and everyone gathered at the pool. We had drinks, dinner, music and then there was a thing in the pool."

"Could you explain more about that?" the officer asked.

"You mean the free-for-all jumping and pushing into the cold pool?"

"Yes," the answer came, "that part of the evening."

The doorbell rang. Very sat up and looked in the direction of the door. The bell rang again. Like a zombie,

Very stood and walked towards the door, ignoring her guests in the living room. She pulled the door open.

"Very," Joey said, out of breath. "I came as quickly as I could. Are they still here?"

"Yeah, come in and join the party. Coffee?"

"What have you told them?" Joey asked in a whisper.

"Just started, so nothing much."

"I'm here, don't say anything more than you have already told them. Carefully, just the bare and simple facts. I'm here," Joey repeated.

They continued into the living room. The two police stood and Very said in a louder than necessary voice. "I'd like you to meet my friend, she's here with me. This is Mrs. Robert Sanchez. Maybe you know her husband? Works for the sheriff's office?"

The two police smiled, but made no comment.

"Now, I know you need to question her, and that's fine," said Joey. "I'm just here for moral support. She's had a shock, a big shock. She's not used to dead bodies and she needs support. But I'm not here in a legal capacity or anything. Just a friend, to help Very stay calm and collected and on track." Joey gave the two men her toothiest smile.

Very went back to telling her story. The abbreviated one that left out possible noises in the bushes, others who might have been around and any extraneous information. Just the facts.

Soon the police were thanking Very for her cooperation and bid her a good day.

When the door closed behind them, Very leaned against it and sighed.

"Was that the whole story?" Joey asked.

"Not really. There was more that I could have said, speculation only, you understand."

"Very, come for dinner tonight, I need help."

"You need help? Well, okay, if you ask like that."

"Good."

"I didn't tell them about the raccoon. I forgot. Dashing off into the bushes."

"Really, Very, a raccoon? Into the bushes?"

"Maybe that was a dream?" Very looked askance at Joey. "Did I tell you about the little pill I took last night to help me sleep? Ooooh, and I don't know what it was. Dreams?"

Chapter Ten: Gabby Has a Problem

Very awoke with the sun shining in her eyes. Early, too early. It would help to close the blinds. Privacy and blocking the morning sun. She dragged herself up and closed the blinds.

Before the blinds blocked out the view, Very noted that the sky was blue, deep blue, which meant that the day would probably be HOT. She dressed quickly and drank some water. The pool wasn't heated yet, so she put on her walking shoes and headed out to do the circle path. This was a mile-long walk that took the walker around the inner circle of the whole development of Five Points. It was a favorite of dog walkers, runners and the slow shufflers alike. It was calming.

After her walk, Very showered, changed and had a quick breakfast, while attempting to read the newspaper that had gotten wet yet once again by the sprinklers.

She called Darrell, her Private Investigator partner. "Sorry I haven't been in for a while. And you know why, the big move. And the last time, sorry the visit was so short. But you understand, boxes, boxes, everywhere."

"Well, yeah, I was about to call you. You've had a phone call." Darrell said.

"No, don't tell me, I'm coming in. Now. It can wait fifteen minutes, can't it? Or maybe it will be twenty, now that I live further from town."

Very quickly changed clothes so that she was wearing nice clothes; just in case she had to see someone, or go somewhere. She managed to put aside the tragedy of Saturday night with the expectation of a new case. Or at least something other than the affairs of the inhabitants of Five Points. She got into her car and drove slowly out of the compound. Before she turned onto Hwy 178, she glanced towards the hills, just a few miles away. She could see faint patches of green on the hillsides. They said that in the winter when it snowed, the hills became blanketed with the white stuff, at least on the tops. Living this far out of town meant the air was cleaner, the traffic lighter and the shopping possibilities fewer. The developments in Bakersfield had been almost all confined to the west side of town, which now boasted of traffic jams at rush hour and more oppressive air. At least, the people who lived on the west side had shopping centers, restaurants and a choice of supermarkets.

She sped up and within minutes she was driving down Chester Avenue to turn onto 17th Street, where Darrell's office lay tucked in between accountants and bail bond offices. It had character, this part of downtown, even if the rents were modest. Very looked for a free parking space. She bristled at paying for the privilege of parking on the wide streets of her hometown. Did the city use her parking fee to do any improvements to the streets, the sidewalks or anything else? The homeless population grew year by year, so why couldn't they spend some money on homeless shelters? Don't go there today. Concentrate on what Darrell needed. Reluctantly, she parked in a space that needed payment. As she slipped the money into the machine, she said, "This had better go towards making my hometown more beautiful!"

An older woman, dressed in three sweaters and pushing a shopping cart full of her worldly possessions, carefully maneuvered around Very, the crazy woman talking to a parking meter machine. As she walked by, she averted her gaze, careful not to engage with Very. At the last minute, she turned to Very, "Any spare change?"

"Sorry, I just put it into the machine," Very smiled and shrugged.

Going up the stairs to the second-floor office that Darrell rented for his small PI business, Very laughed. She remembered the first day she had climbed these stairs. Now she hesitated outside the door. In gold stick-on letters were the names of the detectives, 'Pitts and Blew, Private Investigators.' Since she hadn't been here very often in six weeks, or maybe more, was it still appropriate to have her name on the door? When she had decided to move, she let her involvement in the business lapse. She needed to get rid of her mother's stuff, pack up her own, do all the running around necessary for buying a house and this was the thing left behind, her part-time job with Darrell. Or as he saw it, her partnership in the business.

She walked in. Darrell was on the phone, but immediately turned his back to her and whispered, "I'll call you back." He looked up at Very with a strange expression. Was it a guilty secretive look?

"Hi, what's happening," Very said, too brightly.

"Nothing much."

"Have you had a lot of work? You know you could have called me. I could have put off some of the unpacking to help out."

"I didn't want to bother you. No, I haven't had too much work. You know it's easy to put off some things. And besides, you have a new life, new friends. You don't really need to do all this work." Darrell waved his hand around the office.

Very followed his waving hand and thought the place look remarkably clean and neat for Darrell's office.

"Anything interesting lately?" Very asked, her voice lifting with the question.

Darrell's mouth clamped shut and he opened his eyes wide. He missed a beat, then said, "You and your place, death in the spa."

"How'd you find that out?"

"I have insiders in law enforcement, as you do."

"I found the…the person."

"The body? The dead body? Very, it was you who found it? Him."

"It was awful. Terrible. I spent all day yesterday in total meltdown."

Darrell's expression morphed into one of awe. "I've never seen a dead body, except all prettied up in a casket."

"So what do your informants say?"

Suddenly Darrell was coy. If Very knew more than he, why was she asking? "That he wasn't well liked."

"Hah, what a lame thing to say. Lots of nasty people are disliked, but that does not mean they don't die in their beds. But for this guy, I guess dying in the hot tub was the equivalent of dying in his bed. He loved the place. It seemed as though he was always there. So I've been told. He drank too much, and slipped under. You know that it was at the end of a great party? A grand party, with too much alcohol and jumping into the pool."

"That's not what I heard. Suspicious, they say."

"How, suspicious? Who says so?"

"I'm not at liberty to divulge my sources." Darrell sat up straight and looked at his computer screen. "I don't know any more than that."

"Darrell, you can't leave me hanging like this. I'm involved. I was the last person to see him, well, the first to see him dead. I mean, the police have been questioning me. I have nothing to tell them, but I'm in this too deep. And now you tell me that you can't tell me anything. Is it because I found the body?"

Darrell sat still, not looking at her, cutting her out. In a way, it was lying to her. He knew more than he was willing to tell. The stillness got under Very's skin. Was something bothering him today, in particular? Very always knew that he had a crush on her. She liked him for it, but was unwilling or unable to reciprocate. She liked to tease him, without saying anything about how she knew he felt about her. But now, he was not just cool, but cold. Had something changed? She thought back to the phone call, the secretiveness of the conversation and how quickly he had hung up. And acted as if Very had better not ask who it was.

Or was it just the taint of finding a body? Could Darrell be the kind of person who was superstitious and not want to be near someone who had discovered, and maybe even touched, a dead body? Some people were ultra-squeamish about death, dying and decay. There were reasons why some didn't want to go to funerals, especially of people they knew. But Darrell didn't know Fat Man Gunn. Or did he? Very vowed to be respectful when talking about the dead man. What had she said so far, was it polite and respectful enough?

"Oh, I almost forgot," Very shook herself out of her reverie. "You said there was a phone call."

Darrell had regained his equilibrium and good humor. "Oh, listen to this, mighty PI Very." Darrell chuckled as he played with the phone to listen to the recording.

"Hi, Very, this is Gabby. Remember me? I hope I have the right number. Anyway, I need to hire you: I need a detective. And I have money, don't worry about that. It's about my family, so it's got to be confidential. Don't tell anybody, promise! Here's my number." And then Gabby rattled off a number. Very copied it down. Then she listened again. She sat back, thinking of Gabby.

The last time she had seen her was at her sister's and her brother's funerals. A joint affair, attended by the whole family, Very hung out at the edges of the crowd. That was almost a year ago. Gabby sounded much the same, a precocious, lively thirteen-year-old. Very reached for her bag and dug inside. She found the key chain Gabby had given her. It was a small set of wings that belonged to a Harley-Davidson motorcycle, Gabby's brother, Javier's motorcycle. The machine itself had been destroyed in the murderous foray by the gang from LA. Only the wings had survived. An uncle had fashioned them into a keychain, which Gabby had given to Very as a memento. A wash of sadness for the loss of life, of connection to family, for the trauma that she had witnessed, passed over her.

Darrell let Very sit quietly, in respect for the incident that had affected all who knew her.

"I didn't keep in touch. Was that bad of me? I didn't want to remember the horrors of the drownings in the Kern River, and the cold-blooded murder. I think I was always afraid that they may have blamed me, and that showing my face was bad form. Stay away, let them deal with it. What could I do anyway?"

"Very, it wasn't your fault, you know that."

Very fingered the key chain. "Okay, funny, priceless, wonderful little friend, you may hire me, for the family business."

"Oh, so you are doing private cases now, cutting me out?" Darrell asked.

"Darrell, I will not be charging Gabby anything. There's no money in it for me or you, no billable hours, so don't worry about it. I have time you know."

"Soooo," Darrell began. "If you are going to be busy with Gabby's case, then you won't be here much? Because I do need some help. I'm getting behind on paperwork, nobody likes it, so I've let it go a bit and, well, I need someone to do this filing and well, I was thinking, maybe we could get another person to do that. Especially if you are busy like with Gabby's problem and…"

"Darrell, you want to hire someone else?"

"Like a secretary, not an investigator, like you. Not to take your place or anything. This would be to do some of the clerical type of things. No, no, no, no one could replace you. You are so smart, so bold, so…"

"Wild, unpredictable, hard to control, secretive, unsteady, volatile and in the end, maybe unreliable?" Very looked at Darrell.

"Well, you said it, not me. I mean, look at what you've done in the past? Go off looking for some crazed drug dealer with a gun, that chased you…"

"I didn't know he had a gun, that wasn't in the plan at all. I was just looking for Frankie, the disappearing fiancé."

"In a homeless encampment with no telephone access?"

"I tried to call you. You didn't answer. You're supposed to be my partner."

"And what about the midnight visit to the scary neighborhood in East Bakersfield with the gang from LA?"

"It was NOT midnight, and I wasn't expecting the gang. And remember, it was little Gabby that got me out of that one, not my partner. So I owe her one." Very sat in the chair and swung the seat around from side to side, creating an annoying squeak.

"And now, the dead body in the hot tub?" Darrell said with a tiny smirk.

"That had absolutely nothing whatsoever to do with me. No, you cannot say that I was doing anything untoward."

"Untoward?" Darrell asked. "What does that mean? You were just minding your own business and going for a dip in the hot tub in the pitch blackout at close to midnight?"

"Oh, so you do know more about this than you let on! Who else knows? No, don't tell me. I'll bet that every PI in town as well as law enforcement, the DA's office and every criminal lawyer knows every last word about the incident. Well, you don't know, none of you."

"Very, are you keeping secrets again?"

"It is my prerogative. I get to choose what goes into my statements. Besides, aren't they saying it was an accident? Alcohol and hot tubs don't mix. End of story. I'm leaving that one behind me. So, if you want to hire another person, great. This desk is seldom used anyway and if you can find someone to help with the paperwork, so much the better. I'm calling Gabby, leaving a message."

Very looked at Darrell and saw a grin on his face. Sly dog, he probably already had someone in mind, maybe the person he was on the phone with when she came in.

Very punched in the number on her phone. She shook her head; she remembered party phone lines from her childhood. How technology had changed the world.

"Very!" Gabby's voice came over the lines clearly, not a recording.

"Oh, sorry, are you at school? I was going to leave a message."

"I'm on a break right now. Perfect timing."

"The answer is yes, I'll take your case. We need to meet somewhere, do you have a suggestion?"

Gabby said firmly, "Beale Park. Do you know it? We moved, and it's real close. After school today?"

"Yeah, I know Beale Park, very well in fact. Sure, what time?"

They firmed up the time and when Very hung up, she heard Darrell on the phone.

"Olivia? Sure, yeah."

Very knew that tone of voice. And here she had always thought that Darrell was pining for her. Obviously not, as there was a new softness and intimacy in his terse words.

Chapter Eleven: Meeting at Beale Park

At three that afternoon, Very drove to Beale Park, not far from downtown. Waves of nostalgia met her as she parked her car along the street on the north side of the park on Dracena Street, much quieter than Oleander. She remembered coming here as a child. Her mother had grown up in a house on Eye Street, just a few blocks away. And her dad's family home was just a few blocks north of here as well. She had never lived in this neighborhood, but when she was a child, she had spent many hours in this neck of the woods, visiting her grandparents.

Beale Park was the first city park in Bakersfield donated by the founding father Truxtun Beale. The amenities had included a swimming pool, now sadly filled in, and a gracious Greek outdoor theater, now sadly in need of repair. Would it too, go the way of the pool, which had been replaced by a spray park? What could substitute for this elegant flight of fancy? Very walked to the theater and stepped down into the cemented forecourt. Cracks ran in all directions in the cement and paint peeled from the columns and side walls. Very sat in one of the few places left for the audience, dirty and crumbling cement. Concerts were still held here in the summer, but today only a few neighbor kids were using the playground equipment or wandering around. Quiet spread over the theater.

Without warning, a squawking flock of green birds flew low over Very's head. Instinctively, Very reached up to shield her head from presents from the sky. Very had often seen these runaway tropical parakeets near her mother's house in the La Cresta neighborhood, and she knew they had taken up residence here, as well as other suitable habitats in town. Why was it that what Bakersfield could brag about was just plain weird, such as having the largest colony of 'naturalized' parakeets in the world? Very knew that the start was the very day that stuck in her memory as the day of the 'Big Wind'. In December of 1977, a huge dust storm descended on the area, leaving an inch of brown muck in the bottom of her mother's pool. It also destroyed the aviary of the small band of tropical parakeets. A couple of breeding pairs escaped, and resisted all attempts at recapture. They had thrived in Bakersfield, all wild and free. They had found Hart Park, the La Cresta neighborhood, Beale Park and a series of tall palm trees on the corner of California and Union Avenue. Ornithologists speculated that they had done so well because the climate was similar to that of the part of India they had been imported from. Lime green, big and noisy, they had not been welcomed as neighbors by some, but by now, it was hard to get rid of them. They had become 'naturalized' citizens of Bakersfield.

Very looked up and shook her fist at the birds, "I love you and I hate you."

"Verrrry, I'm here." Gabby's voice drifted across the park.

Very turned and watched Gabby run towards her. She looked the same, but older, much more than would be expected for the one year that had passed. Traumatic events could do that. When she got closer, Very noted that she looked like the pictures of her sister Maria, the one who had drowned in the Killer Kern. She had filled out, combed and styled her long dark brown locks, and looked taller as well.

Very stood and accepted the bear hug from Gabby. Very didn't get many hugs from anyone any more. "Wow, you've grown," Very said in greeting.

"Yeah, I'm three inches taller and look," she threw out her chest. There was a slight bulge in the right places.

"Grown, all grown-up." Very smiled at her.

"Not quite all grown up. They still treat me like a little kid. I'll be fourteen and I'm going to high school next year."

"Congratulations. Now, sit here and tell me what's bothering you. Why do you want to hire me?"

"The problem is secrecy. There are secrets and they don't want to tell me. It's Charlie, Carlos, and my parents. Something's happening and they won't tell me. They keep whispering behind my back. And then, when I ask, they change the subject. They tell me it's not my business, I shouldn't concern myself with it because it has nothing to do with me. I don't get it, I don't know what else to do. And then I thought of you. You can find out. Make them tell me."

"This sounds big. Maybe it's dangerous. No, they wouldn't do that. They will take good care of Carlos. So, can we start at the beginning?"

"Well, we moved, that was last fall. To this neighborhood. The house is a little bigger and the neighborhood is much more diversified. We have all races and religions and even some rich people in this neighborhood. You can see some really big houses, there's one there." Gabby pointed to the deeply shaded corner of Oleander and Beale. "Maybe it will become gentrified, who knows?"

Very was taken aback by the use of such academic words. And also puzzled by why the family moved. Or maybe not. It would seem natural to find a place that had no memories of the terrible tragedy of the drownings and the gang-related fight. Also, the house must have sustained some damage from the fireball that gutted the garage and destroyed the motorcycle. On the other hand, Very knew that family lived just up the street, so it would seem natural to find another house in the same neighborhood.

"Do you know who helped us? Just guess?" Gabby tilted her head in a coy question attitude.

Very turned to look north. The church's bell tower wasn't really visible from where they sat, but the direction was a subtle hint as to who was being referred to. "Father Sullivan helped you? Why?"

"He's nice, he helps everyone."

Very gave Gabby a quizzical glance, "He helps everyone in your neighborhood, everyone on your street? Are they still living there?"

"Well, maybe he knew we needed it more."

"Fair enough."

"So, maybe this has to do with Charlie too, that he needs it more."

"Okay, tell me about Charlie."

"Something is happening this summer. Charlie is going away, something good I think because he is happy. But they won't tell me anything. The more I ask, the quieter they are."

Very hummed and Gabby interrupted. "Did I say that right? Is that how you say it?"

"Yeah, perfect grammar. But why? What's the problem?"

"It's for Charlie, not for me. We always do things together. And this time, I'm not in on it. There's nothing for me. They keep telling me that it is none of my business: that it is Charlie's business. But maybe, Father Sullivan knows something about it."

"Why do you think that?"

"Visits. Pastoral visits. That's what he calls them. Lots of visits and lots of talking behind my back."

Very looked at Gabby. She was distressed, anxious, genuinely worried. But why be so concerned about what was happening for Charlie? Was she feeling left out? Obviously, but what was Very supposed to do about it?

"Can you find out for me? Investigate? I'll pay."

Very laughed, "No need to pay, I'll take the case. Do I have permission to ask your parents?"

"No, you can't say anything to them. They would be very unhappy if they knew I was going behind their backs. This is family business."

"Can I talk to Charlie? I mean, if this is about him, isn't that the logical place to start."

"No, you can't. He'll want to know why you are asking. No, you have to find out another way."

"Do you want me to investigate or not? I have to find out somehow, I have to ask questions."

Gabby looked down and wiggled her feet.

"Do I investigate or not?" Very demanded.

"You investigate."

"Ice cream at Dewar's, my treat." Very stood and looked around. A few more children had appeared in the park, bringing life to the more than 100-year-old park. A skateboard noise alerted Very to the use of the theater for more than barbershop quartet or Mariachi music concerts. Another followed and two youngsters spun and ground their way through and out the other side.

"I'll drive there, it's only a few blocks."

Gabby squealed with pleasure and ran towards Very's red Prius, parked on the far side of the park. How did that kid know Very's car so well? She had ridden in it for a few short blocks while escaping the gang that blew up their garage. They did need to move out of that neighborhood, and this was better.

On the way to Dewar's, Very made a short detour along Eye Street and pointed out the house where her mother grew up.

"Wow, what a coincidence. We live there." Gabby pointed across the street and up a few houses.

'Really close to the church." Very slowed and looked ahead to the tall, simple but modern Catholic church that stood on the corner ahead. "You know, there used to be a school there, but it was damaged in the earthquake, so they pulled it down. Then they built the church there. My mother went to that school."

"What earthquake?"

"1952. The big one." Very put on a solemn face.

"I've heard of it. Last century. Do you remember it?"

"No, I was way too little. But of course, everything was different afterwards. People talked about it all the time when I was young. And I know that a lot of old buildings were destroyed and had to be torn down. Like the old Lowell School. And the Beale Clock Tower. Building codes changed, everyone was conscious of disasters like that."

They pulled into the miniscule parking lot of Dewar's. Very couldn't walk into the place without feelings of nostalgia as memories crowded in. Gabby raced to the end of the shop and said hello to the animal heads on the wall. Very took in the red padded seats that lined the counter and the menu written on a board mounted on the far wall above the serving area. And then she inhaled. Dewar's had an odor that marked it as an ice cream shop. Sharp, metallic, cold, sweet, not exactly pleasant, but unique.

They took seats at the counter. It wasn't a luxurious seat. The area was small, the padding lumpy and higher in the middle than at the edges, threatening to dislodge the unwary patron who wiggled trying to become more comfortable. One sat at the counter for the privilege of doing so, not for the comfort.

"Oh, Very, what shall I get? It's all great, super great." Gabby's voice cracked with the emotion of decision.

"Well, are you watching your waistline? Do you have any allergies, flavors you hate? I always start there. If I'm feeling fat, I just get a scoop. If I'm feeling like I could eat a horse, hot fudge sundae. With a cherry on top. Be my guest, whatever you want."

They ordered and waited for the scooping and drizzling. "Ah," they said together as their dishes were put in front of them.

After a few spoonfuls, Very turned to Gabby. "Did I ever tell you about my father's story?" Very waited while Gabby shook her head, mouth full of ice cream and chocolate sauce. "Well, he said it was true, but my mother says not. Every Saturday morning, the owner would come to the back door with tubs of old ice cream. They had made new and needed to get rid of the old ice cream. So, for a nickel, the kids could eat all they wanted. For poor kids who didn't get to go inside often, it was such a treat."

"I wonder if they still do that?" Gabby murmured, eyes full of hunger for 'eat as much as you wanted' ice cream. "The good old days, huh?"

"I'm sure the department of health would have something to say about that. No, certainly not. But, you're right, the old days were not all bad."

"Can I come to your office sometime? Now that you're hired by me. I'm a client, aren't I?" Gabby looked sideways at Very.

"I don't work very often, so I'm not there most of the time. Call me before you start trekking down to my office."

"Okay, that's sounds fair enough. When can I get a report? I mean, will you be starting right away, seeing as how you don't have much to do?"

"Retirement is funny. I was always so busy before I retired. Classes, and students, and parents, and teacher conferences and planning vacations. But now that I'm free all the time, I'm too busy to do anything. Funny, what time does to us; getting old puts things into perspective. I'm not sure how long I'll be a detective, a private investigator." Very shook her head, mumbling to herself.

"Oh, Very, you're not old. No way. And besides, I can help you. I can work on cases with you. Yeah, I can be your Watson, your sidekick. Like, because you're Sherlock Holmes."

Very laughed out loud and dug into her ice cream, suddenly feeling much younger. Yeah, a Watson would do.

Chapter Twelve: Asking Father Sullivan for Help

Very turned away from her ice cream and looked up Father Sullivan's phone number. It was in her phone already, strangely. The phone rang and after the third ring, Father Sullivan himself answered.

"Oh," Very said, before identifying herself. "Sorry, I didn't expect you to answer. I wondered if I could talk with you sometime. I have some delicate questions for you."

The phone went silent for a beat, then Father Sullivan answered. "Yes, as a matter of fact I have some time right now. At the church? It's always open."

"I'm at Dewar's right now, so I will be there shortly. Thanks."

Very looked at her bowl of ice cream, only partially eaten. "This is too much." She shook her head. "What was I thinking?"

"Can I have it?" Gabby's dark eyes sparkled at the melting mounds of yellow and pink ice cream.

Laughing, Very consented. "Let's have the girl put it in a box for you and you can take it home, eat it later. You've already had a hot fudge sundae."

"Yeah, you're right. The only thing is, if someone finds it, it'll be gone before I get to it. You know my grandma is living with us now and then there is Charlie. My cousins often come over after school, so trying to hide a carton of ice cream is iffy at best. But I'll do that. Thanks."

Very paid, picking out a small box of assorted chews for Gabby's family. She remembered how much they liked them. And also, like the loaves and fishes of the Bible, how they proliferated. She still wondered how one bag of chews could create hundreds of papers in the streets of East Bakersfield. The generosity of neighbors? The receipt and then the giving back of gifts? Or the largesse of a powerful person, to buy influence? Don't be ridiculous, buying influence with candy?

Very and Gabby parted ways, with a promise from Very to keep in touch.

Very hesitated at the parking lot. There was only room for a few cars, and at the moment they were all taken. But the church was just a short walk away. Should she leave her car here and walk, or vacate the parking space for a real customer? As she stood pondering this dilemma, a car pulled up in the street and with a short 'beep' called attention to Very's conundrum. Very smiled and indicated that she was about to leave. The car waited while Very backed out. She went around the block and parked at the church.

Very entered at the main door. Monday afternoons were not a busy time at the church. She stood at the back and looked towards the altar. She thought of the many Sundays she had darkened this door. After her father's death, there was no sense in going to church, as it was he who felt the need to go to church every Sunday and Holyday. The place looked empty. Emptier than she had ever seen it. Sundays, weddings, funerals, graduations, school masses. Those were always well attended. But the emptiness of worshippers was a condition she had not experienced.

She sat in a pew at the back of the church and waited. There was the faint odor of incense, of candles burning too quickly and leaving an acrid smell behind. The light coming through the stained-glass windows gave color to the air, and the stillness within contrasted with traffic noises outside along H Street. Very closed her eyes and tried to channel some goodness into her heart, which still hadn't forgotten the dead body that she had found floating in the hot tub. Although she had not spoken nor thought much of it today, the direness lingered just below the surface, threatening to pop up and spoil anything good the day might bring.

The slap slap of shoes on the stone floor caused her to open her eyes. She turned, but saw no one. Then she saw Father Sullivan's bulk approach from one of the side altars. Had he been here all along? Waiting for her to come? He genuflected towards the main altar, then walked down the main aisle towards Very. She stood.

They greeted one another and then he motioned to the pew where Very had been sitting. She slid in further and Father took a seat beside Very. He hooked his arm over the back of the seat and smiled at her. "What can I do for you today? Delicate questions, you said."

Very smiled. "Not so very delicate. Gabby Hernandez wants to know what Carlos is doing this summer that excludes her. No one seems to want to tell her and because it's a secret, she is upset."

Father Sullivan smiled, forbearing to laugh out loud in church, but he might have if he had been somewhere else. "That's an easy one to answer. I am trying to get a place for Carlos in a boys' camp for the summer. It will mean that he can learn what it means to be a man, positive masculine skills in a modern world. So far, he's seen his father, an immigrant with little education and few skills be consigned to farm work, or back-breaking work that has undermined his health. His brother Javier could have been a good influence, but you know all too well that he is gone, as you were in the midst of it all. And his other brother Pedro, well, he was the one involved in the gangs. And he is currently out of the scene, which is a good thing. But Carlos has few role models. That's why the camp. I have some influence, and am trying to raise the money needed. Carlos needs this."

Very sat quietly. "I realize that. It really is too bad about Javier, I am sure he was having a good influence on him."

"I thought that there would be no problems with Javier around. Here was a man who had joined the Navy, used his G.I. bill to go to college, was set to make something of himself. Then, the goings on with the gangs; I was disappointed in him. I can't even say to them, 'Remember your brother Javier, a great man, he went too soon.' No, his involvement with the gangs was his undoing."

"But he didn't belong to any of the gangs. He had nothing to do with it. He was only defending his family, his sister." Very stopped. There was information that she had never told anyone. She had believed that keeping this information from the police was in the best interest of the family, the ones left behind. The persons involved were all dead, or in jail, or had gone away, so why drag Maria's name in the mud? And Javier's? Javier had killed his cousin Hector because Hector had been molesting Maria, Javier's younger sister. He had found Maria at the beach in Hart Park, with Hector attacking her. Enraged, Javier had struck out, killing Hector and while he was doing so, letting Maria drown. The fatal attack by gangs had taken his life, but Javier had made sure to secure the safety of the rest of his family. He had confessed to his part in the drownings of Maria and Hector just minutes before he died, but Very had never revealed this to anyone. She knew that Javier was an honorable man, albeit a hot-headed one. What good would it serve to reveal this to the police? Or to Father Sullivan? Very had thought long and hard before she had decided, a year ago, to keep this to herself. The only way now to convince Father Sullivan that Javier was a good man was to reveal the contents of the last conversation she had had with him. Should she tell? What good would it do now? Water under the bridge, and let the past be the past?

In the space of Very's mute voice, Father Sullivan continued. "I'm concerned that Carlos doesn't have a lot of men in his life who can give him good examples. To be an upright Christian man is not always easy in these days of too many temptations. To avoid the pitfalls of modern life, he needs some good role models, good men, in his life."

"But what about his twin sister, Gabby? Doesn't she deserve any chances? Does she go without this summer while her twin, the same age, the same situation, gets a summer full of camping, excitement, fun? What will she do all summer? Sit at home, do chores for everyone else? Maybe she'll find some trouble to get into? We wouldn't want that, would we?"

Father Sullivan sighed deeply. "No, I certainly don't want that. That one is too smart, and she could easily find danger."

"She could soar, she could do so much, given the chance. But I fear for her, just as you fear for her brother. The quagmires of modern life, huh?"

They sat in silence, each thinking of a solution to the problem of what to do with Gabriella.

"Maybe I could ask around, find out if anyone needed a volunteer for something, a summer camp, a tutorial situation," Very said at last. "I do know a lot of teachers, after all."

"Ummm. The new Catholic Boys and Girls Club is set to open next weekend, just on weekends until we get it finalized. But there may be an opportunity there. She's too young to take a paid position, but she could certainly volunteer." Father Sullivan sighed. "I see I have dug a hole for myself. I can't help every youngster in town, but you are right, helping one twin and not the other is not a good show."

"So, I can tell Gabby what is happening with her brother Charlie? And that we are looking very hard for a position for her for the summer?"

"This has never been a secret, but I did tell Mr. and Mrs. Hernandez that we must not say anything until it was certain. So maybe that was the confusion. Sorry."

"Whew, that case went easily." Very wiggled, her backside beginning to go numb sitting on the hard wooden pew.

"A case?"

"Oh, Gabby was going to hire me. Even offered to pay. She was in a tither, angry and feeling left out. And the secrecy part was really bothering her. Secret part solved, now the solution. That's harder. By the way, what's this about the Hernandez family moving? Did you have anything to do with that?"

He laughed. "They had to get out of that house, you understand that. And I thought it best that they get out of the neighborhood. They have family there, true, but the neighbors would always be twitching curtains whenever anyone came or went. No, best to find a new place altogether. Besides, I know the landlord. He's someone to keep an eye on them, let me know if there seems to be a problem, a threat to the family. I didn't want old troubles following them, you see." Father Sullivan leaned forward, his full mouth creating a smile, or was it a leer?

"Hum, I guess so." Very's hackles had started to rise when Father Sullivan had said, 'I thought it best' and a tingling feeling started running up and down her spine at, 'I know the landlord'. Nothing he had said or done was illegal or out of bounds, just a parish priest helping a family in need. But Very knew of the gossip of pedophilia and forced herself not to shiver.

Joey and her family were great supporters of the priest, trying to counter the rumors by denying the whispers, saying it was jealousy. They maintained that those in power were out to get the priest by brushing him with the taint of scandal. He had done so much good for so many, the Sanchez family said, that he had made enemies. But that he was on the side of God. Very remained skeptical.

"Oh, I have one more question for you. You may think this a bit silly, but there were a lot of papers on the streets that night. You know, the night of the great shoot out and fire-bombing. And I just wondered where they had come from?" Very tried to remain positive and smiling.

"Papers?"

"Dewar's chew papers."

"Well, I love them, who doesn't?" He patted his well-padded belly. "I keep a bunch at home. I even have an account with Dewar's."

"Do you give them away?"

"Yeah, quite often. I hear that you do too." He smiled again, a grin that bore a devilish turn to his lips.

"But where did all of them come from? I had given a few away that day, but not that many, there were thousands of them. Flying everywhere. It was like it was snowing chews papers."

"Don't look at me. Thousands you say? But you know, snow comes from heaven. Maybe they were a gift to the people of that street. They had to put up with so much, the least they could have were a few sweets to counter the sourness in their lives. It's not easy to live on a street that has seen so much evil."

Very tried her most incredulous look. "Thanks for your time. I'll be talking with Gabby, letting her know about Charlie's good news. I won't promise her anything, but let her know the lay of the land, that we are trying."

Very stood and walked out. Outside, away from the church walls, she took a deep breath and let it out. She was abrupt in her leave-taking, she acknowledged that, but she could feel the sweat and her pounding heart. The niggle of the gossip, hearsay, whispers, tittle-tattle, the whiff of scandal. She hoped it wasn't true. But feared anyway.

Chapter Thirteen: The Crafters Club

Very sat in the sunshine just beyond her patio, soaking in the warm April sunshine. This was the best time of year, so Very maintained. The winter was cold, the summer way too hot, the autumn dusty, but the spring time held the promise of the warmth of summer, but the morning cool of winter. She looked at the garden, a rather bare mish-mash of hardy bushes, and grass. Four rose bushes, the kind that lined the old freeways, grew and bloomed in the back, but there were no flowers, bright multicolored wisps of seasonal brightness. There were the few Dutch iris she had planted, but they had seemingly all died back. She made a note to buy some flowers and plant them. Did she miss her mother's colorful roses and perennial irises, lilies, and daffodils? No, this should be her garden, putting in what she wanted and needed. Not the busy, fussy, always needing weeding type of plants, but one of tidy bushes and trees.

Monji, that's who she needed. Get Monji to do her garden. Then she remembered the cost of a truly beautiful landscaped space. A few of her friends had forked over the big bucks to create a peaceful living space in their backyards. Could she afford it? It would mean forgoing a vacation or two, but in exchange she would get an enhanced value on her property and more importantly, a space that would be as good as any inside the house. Think about it.

Very closed her eyes and listened to the birds, the call of a mocking bird, the buzz of a hummingbird, and the tweets and stirrings of LBB's. She had learned to call those birds that one couldn't identify as Little Brown Birds, courtesy of Darrell, the Audubon Club man. Oh, also the LGB's, the little gray ones.

"Meow," came from the bushes, or the yard next door. A cat? Where? What kind? Very sat up, opened her eyes and looked. Stirrings in a pile of leaves under one of the trees alerted her to the possibility of mice, or a neighbor's cat. The little jungle that was her backyard hid mysteries in the nooks and crannies. The metaphor of hiding swerved her mind back to the body in the hot tub. What was he doing there alone? Even though he had lots of enemies, no one seemed to like him; they had all engaged with him on occasion, on the occasions when he turned on the charm. Charming he had been, clever even in his meanness.

"Meow," answered Very. "Here, kitty, kitty."

No answer came, no more stirrings in the leaves. What was she thinking of, trying to entice a cat into her life? Wasn't she trying to divest, not invest? Leave the animal alone, let him go home undisturbed.

Very puttered in the garden until the sun was high, then she moved indoors. This house had two bedrooms, an office or study and two bathrooms. Perfect for one person and a guest. But the rooms were big, the ceilings high and she felt as if she were rattling around. Things on the walls! Carpets on the floors! Make this a place to live in, not an empty space, that's what she needed to do.

A few hours of busy work and a quick lunch brought her to the time of the Crafters Club meeting. She had talked about the other clubs, met some of the members, but she had yet to join in any activity. She scrambled to find an old crocheting project. Oh well, she knew how to do granny squares and she could always tear out anything she did later.

She slung the bag over her shoulder, grabbed her large purse and walked out the door.

The stroll to the clubhouse was a pleasant one of seven or eight minutes. She was able to glance at house fronts to see what others had done to their entryways and front gardens. Even though the HOA fees paid for the upkeep of the front yards, it was possible to personalize parts of them. And the entryways were fair game. Colorful seasonal flags on small stands gave color to the small yards, while trees, bushes, flowering plants in pots adorned the bare cement entrances. A few larger ones sported iron furniture, although Very couldn't imagine any one sitting on the small pieces. Decorative only. Some yards boasted large trees that were beginning to throw patches of shade. In another twenty years, these streets would be lovely to walk along, and the individuality of the houses would become more apparent. What a lovely community it would be then.

But for now, the houses looked too much alike, the landscaping was patchy at best, the trees were still struggling with the poor soil and the flowers were hit and miss. But spring was in the air and made promises of green in the future.

Very entered the clubhouse and wrote her name on the list near the front door. It was a bit intrusive, who was using which facilities, and coming in, and going out. But it was a good way to check on who was where and if anyone had been left somewhere. Very twisted her lips in a grimace. It hadn't helped find the wandering Peter Gunn last Saturday night. If Very hadn't found him, would he have been left to float in the hot pool all night? She shivered. It was not the time to think of these things. Think of crocheting again.

She entered the crafts room. Four long tables were placed in two rows with chairs tucked under them. Room for 16, but only three women sat there.

A tall slender woman, carefully coiffed hair in streaked shades of brown and blonde, rose to greet Very. She sported a warm welcome smile and tried to disentangle her right hand to extend to shake, but couldn't throw off the long strands of multi-colored yarn. "Hi," she managed. "Very, isn't it? Or Vermilion?"

"Very is fine." Very racked her brain. She had met this woman before, but her name slipped and slid in her mind. Kathy, Barbie, Terry, Chrissie, Connie, Annie, Bonnie, Lindy, Margie, Shari, Judy, Sandy, Marty, Patty, Lynnie, Nancy? "Nancy," she said.

"You remembered, great. Let me introduce you." Nancy introduced the two other women there, both of whom Very had met previously. It was a small community, the circles of which were made smaller by the interests of those who were young and healthy enough to get out. Someone had told Very that half of those who lived at Five Points still worked and so that left even fewer to 'club' together.

For fifteen minutes, the other three women continued their chat about the previous week's ladies' luncheon. Then they turned to Very. Joanie asked, "What project are you working on?"

Very pulled out a half-finished granny square of various colors that she had started at least ten years before. For what purpose, she could not recall. "Umm, I haven't done any crocheting for years, but now that I'm retired, I thought I could take it up again."

"Good for you. It's like riding a bicycle, once you have learned how, you never really forget. You might need a little practice but the basics don't change."

Just then the door burst open. A small, well-dressed woman entered. She wore a fashionable blouse that had an off-kilter cut and flowed smoothly around her as she walked. Silk, high quality. Her pearl gray slacks matched the blouse. Tiny ballet slipper shoes peeked out from underneath the wide legs. Her hair was lacquered into a tasteful version of the 1968 ratted hair style that was the rage when they were all in high school. This denizen of Five Points could have been on the committee to abolish bad taste in the community. Hopefully not, Very would find herself with a string of fines for bad hair, tasteless clothes, and lack of make-up.

The new arrival looked around and spotted Nancy. She ignored everyone else and sat down opposite the club convener. She folded her hands on the table and leaned forward. Her nose twitched and wiggled, like a dog finding his favorite stick. Her body trembled with excitement.

Nancy leaned forward and smiled, "What's up?"

"You'll never guess! A sign went up." The newcomer leaned her head to one side and a coquettish smile cracked her face.

"Oh, where?" Nancy humored her, playing the adult version of a knock-knock joke.

"Guess!"

"Next door?" Nancy hazarded.

"Oh, but you are a clever one."

"Now, you are going to tell me that you are surprised."

"No, not them. Me." The newcomer giggled.

Nancy gasped, "You're selling? They've forced you out?"

"No, of course not, never. I'd never let them do that to me. I've found a better place. Actually, it's near my daughter and she wanted me to come and live closer. And I will maintain to my dying breath that it had nothing to do with them. I'm going to a better place."

"But what about the dogs barking, and the newspapers in their bushes, and their noisy parties, and the horrible comments they made about you on the Neighborhood Watch website? You can't let them get away with that!"

"Well, Nancy, you and the others can help there. You can let the new people know about them. Nasty men. But as I said, I'm off to greener pastures."

"Ohhhhh, we will miss you," Nancy said, leaning over the table for a hug.

"No need for that, I won't be leaving for a long time yet. Lots of time to sort those boys out! Another thing, one of their dogs ran away yesterday. Serves them right!"

"Oh, that's awful," said Nancy. "I'd be very sad if my dog got lost."

"I didn't say lost, did I? Ran away. Undoubtedly, they mistreated him. Good for the dog I say. Gotta go, I'm going to see the movie, Romantic Tuesday."

"Bye" they said in unison. Very never got her name. Never mind, this woman was leaving soon, so better to use her brain power to remember the names of people she would see again.

They all set to work and quiet reigned for five minutes.

Nancy broke the silence. "You do know that it was Very who found the body."

"You don't mean it was you who actually discovered the corpse, in the hot tub?" one of the other women said.

Very looked up and faced the woman. "Yes, I did. I was the stupid one who got into the hot tub, in the dark and found the man, floating, dead." Very gritted her teeth. Talking about this with a stranger, or rather a new friend, was difficult.

"So what happened? Did he have a heart attack? How awful it must have been for you. Once I saw a dead person at the scene of a traffic accident, and of course, the friends and relatives in their caskets. But up close like that. Was it an accident?"

"I don't know anything. But you know what they say about alcohol and hot tubs, they don't mix. All I do know is that he had been in the cold pool and then in the hot tub. Puts a strain on the system, especially the heart. Heart attack, maybe. But I don't know. I really don't." Very's voice held a slight whine. She did not need to say anything, she was only there at the discovery. That was the extent of her involvement. Why did these others think she knew something, or that she could add to their knowledge? They knew him better than she, they could draw their own conclusions.

"That man took chances. He felt no shame in saying anything he wanted to anyone. He could cuss someone out one minute and then expect that person to be his buddy, friend-for-life, the next. He was so contradictory."

"And unkind," said Nancy.

"That party and the hot tub were just two accidents waiting to happen. You know how people get at that party. There is always too much drinking. 'Everybody bring drinks to share.' No, we don't need that. What are the organizers thinking? One or two drinks must surely be enough. And that jumping into the pool. You know that happens, every single time we have a pool party, we end up in the drink, drunk. And then someone gets a scrape or cut or comes down with a cold, or sprains their ankle, or…"

"Gets pneumonia. Remember, Toni got pneumonia from jumping in the pool. She went to the hospital with it."

Very looked up with alarm. "Pneumonia from a dip in the pool?"

"Toni can be a bit…sketchy on taking care. She walked around for half an hour in sopping wet clothes, three sheets to the wind, and resisted anyone taking her home. Old ladies, not always so bright, huh?"

"Well, our Peter Gunn must have had an accident. Heart attack, stroke, whatever. Or we would have heard, wouldn't we?"

The three women looked towards Very. Very had no answers for them and simply shrugged. "Accident obviously. Misadventure, I think is a term used for something like this."

"Unless it wasn't. What if it was deliberate? Is there such a thing as hot tub homicide?"

Chapter Fourteen: The Crafters' Gossip

"Homicide, that's murder." Joanie declared. "I realize that the guy wasn't well-liked. No, no Julie, let me finish," Joanie held up her hand as if to halt Julie in her attempt to get a word in edgewise. This was obviously a common occurrence as neither Nancy or Julie made any move to continue while Joanie had a point to make. "Okay, I know no one who liked him. But we were all more or less pleasant to him, even when he was unpleasant to us. But just as I can see someone spiking his drink or tipping him into the pool or the hot tub, I just can't see someone pulling out a gun and shooting him."

"He was shot? I didn't know that," Julie looked at Joanie in surprise.

"No, I don't think so. Did I say that?" Joanie looked confused.

"I think you implied that homicide is violent and premeditated," Very intervened, "and that homicide in this instance, of Peter Gunn, was as if someone had pulled out a gun and shot him. I don't remember any blood, at all, anywhere. I never said that to anyone. I don't think he was shot."

"Yeah, yeah, that's what I meant, really deliberate like pulling out a gun."

Julie jumped in, "And that's why I don't have a gun. Besides the fact that it doesn't seem useful at all, I'm afraid that someone will use it on me. I'm pathetic that way. I'm a woman who lives alone and I just try to stay safe by locking my doors. I'm petrified of the things, guns that is."

"I think you have the best idea, but I do know there are guns out here. Lots of people must have them, for sure." Joanie sat back in her seat.

"It might have been really easy to get a gun and shoot him," Nancy said, "but that's not what I have heard."

The three other women turned to Nancy who inexplicably looked down at her knitting and started counting stitches. Knowing that it was incredibly rude to interrupt a knitter counting stitches, they waited for her to finish, the atmosphere becoming more and more tense as Nancy reached 150 and then quit, crying out in frustration. "Oh, God, I must have dropped a stitch!"

They all groaned in sympathy.

When they had all gone back to their projects, Very ventured a timid response to the last bit of gossip. "What have you heard?"

Nancy looked up from her knitting and said, "I heard that he died, but didn't drown."

The ladies looked at Very, "You were there," Joanie said. "Did he drown?"

"Well, it's hard to tell if someone drowned as opposed to having had a heart attack, or stroke, or a fit of some sort. All I know is that he wasn't covered in blood and was totally unresponsive."

"I heard that he wasn't declared dead until he got to the hospital."

"I am not a pathologist or a forensic scientist, so I don't see and judge dead bodies." Very tried to pick her words carefully. If it was homicide then she was the one to blame.

"But you were there. You must have some idea of what happened." Julie joined the conversation. The three women looked to Very.

"It was dark. I just found him, I didn't do anything. Well, I screamed."

"Then you must know something. I've heard gossip too." Julie shifted uneasily in her seat.

"From where, from whom?" Very's voice in pitch.

The atmosphere in the room froze. Then, when it began to thaw, it rapidly began to burn.

"I haven't heard any gossip, from anyone. I've hardly talked with anyone," Very protested.

"Gail. She took you home, didn't she? You stayed in her house until the next day. Maybe it came from her."

"Did you hear it from her?" Very asked, alarmed at the idea that she had told Gail something, anything.

"Ladies, ladies, enough. Crafts, crafts! We're here for the crafts. Julie, that is a lovely shade of green, just fabulous. What are you making? What is it for?" Nancy bossed the rest of them back to the topic of crafts and away from the hot tub incident. "Baby blanket? Sweater or shawl?" Nancy stood and walked to Julie and started feeling the project that Julie had on the table in front her. "Ohhhh, so soft."

Very rose in a spirit of reconciliation and solidarity with moving away from the dangerous topic and joined Nancy at Julie's project.

Julie tried to snatch her bundle of lumpy yarn from the inquisitive crew, but understood the gesture. Joanie leaned over the table to check out the shapeless project.

Very soon tired of trying to be conciliatory and sat back at her sat. She picked up her pathetic start of a granny square. Concentrate, the best thing at the moment. Gossip will be here, no matter what we say or do. The best thing for tittle-tattle was to ignore it. Do your part and that's what any of us would do. What color was best for the next round? Green, no green. Very didn't do green. That green of Julie's project was the most hideous, bilious shade of green-blue-black. Like leftover… Also, it was never good to be unkind. 'If you can't say something nice, don't say anything at all.' Where would discord get us, if we all tried our best to one up every other person at the table?

Very lifted her head and smiled all around. Nancy smiled back.

The door flew open and standing there was a short woman, her long gray head tied back in a loose bun. Glasses perched far down on her nose and she wore a smile that made the corners of her mouth turn up in an exaggerated grin. "Hi, am I in the right place?"

"If you are looking for the Crafters, you've come to the right place. Are you new here?"

"Yeah, just moved in."

"Where do you live?" Julie asked.

"Oh, down the street," the newcomer waved to the west.

"What street would that be?" Nancy added.

"Oh, I don't know the name of the street, but it is just a few houses down, the first one after the stop sign, on the main street here." She gestured again.

"I know where that is," added Joanie. "Is it a big place?"

"I think it's really nice. Bigger than my last place."

"What's your name?" Nancy asked. "And if you let me know your email address, we can send notices of the club meeting. If you want."

"My name is Samantha. But before you get all excited about that one, I just have to tell you. Everybody calls me Sweetie." Sweetie sat at a place in the nearest table to the door.

"Welcome Sweetie," said Nancy. "What kind of craft do you do? Knitting, crocheting, needlepoint, quilting? Or something else?"

"I do a little of everything, but mostly quilting." Sweetie pulled out her phone and for the next ten minutes they all looked at photos of Sweetie's projects. The sense of camaraderie returned.

"Are you from Bakersfield, Sweetie?" Nancy asked.

"No, I just moved here. Not my first choice, but there it is. Actually, I was living in Santa Maria."

"Nice place, and you moved here?" Julie exclaimed.

"It's a story, a rather interesting one. You see, I met someone, a man, online and well, we thought we would be good together. We met and got along and he asked me to move in with him. So I sold my house and moved here."

This story met with stunned silence and then the questions came. "You sold your house? Just like that? Are you married, or planning on it?"

"He's my fiancé, yeah. He's having some heart issues at the moment, but when it's all straightened out, we'll probably get married."

"Surely not the first?" Julie laughed.

Sweetie laughed heartily, her smile with the turned-up corners bringing merriment to the moment. "We've got five marriages between us, already, so we're both experienced."

Very looked at the very gutsy lady. She was at least ten years older than Very and she had up and sold her house, moved in with some old geezer with health issues, and was now trying to remake her life. Make a new life. Impressive will power and imagination.

"Welcome to Five Points," Very said. "I'm new here too. I used to crochet, and I almost chucked out all the old yarn. I'm glad I kept it. I still don't know what I'm planning to do with it."

"And your name is?" Sweetie smiled.

"Very, short for Vermilion. I know how I got my name, but Sweetie, how do you get from Samantha to Sweetie?"

Sweetie launched into a long story of adoption, or almost adoption and no one liking the name Samantha and Sweetie's adamant refusal to answer to 'Sammy'. So everyone called her Sweetie because she was such a sweet girl. Except for the name fiasco. So, Sweetie stuck. They all traded stories about how they had arrived at their names. Grandmother's names, mothers who didn't like their own names, so chose something modern and cute.

"Oh, I think that crafting anything is such a good hobby to have, anything to do with your hands, can carry it around with you, makes nice gifts." Julie bent over her bilious green project, mumbling platitudes. "Sweetie, such a cute name, did you work? What did you do?"

They all exchanged what they had worked at, when they retired and what kinds of activities they were pursuing in their leisure years. Very recounted her years as a school librarian and English teacher. She felt shy about mentioning her summers traveling around the world, the 76 countries she had visited, and the interesting summer volunteer jobs she had had. From experience, Very had long ago learned to keep these things private; she had been told she sounded like she was boasting and putting others down for being stay-at-homes. Her world view had been shaped by the experiences of helping out at orphanages in Thailand and Peru, teaching summer courses in English in Vietnam and Taiwan, and archaeological digs in England and Poland. She had helped out at food banks, supported doctors who performed eye operations in Madagascar, cleft palate support services in Mongolia, helping fit prostheses to land mine victims in Cambodia. She could talk about these things another time. Right now, light conversation was needed.

She sat back and looked at other's projects, trying to decide what she might try to do with her limited skills. She discussed this with the others and they all said she should start with a scarf or an afghan. "Nothing too complex," advised Nancy. "Use variegated yarn for color and brightness, but a simple pattern for ease of crocheting."

Before they realized, it was time to go. Very and Sweetie were encouraged to return. "We're such a wonderful group, don't you think?" Nancy said in bidding goodbye. "See you in two weeks."

Very, reluctant to go home to boxes and more unpacking and decorating, wandered outside to the pool. The hot tub area was still blocked off with official tape, but it had drooped into long hanging loops. Very had no desire to go any closer at the moment.

She dipped her hand into the pool. The water felt frigid, although she knew it couldn't be less than 65 degrees. "Ice cubes floating in it," she said out loud.

"Yeah, I think that's what they must do to keep it cool," said a voice behind her.

Very turned quickly to see a man standing near the pool with a forlorn look on his face. His hat and sunglasses obscured his face, but he had a wistful smile for Very. "I've been told it's soon, very soon. The guy from the heater company was here this morning. But of course, the hot tub is another story."

"Are you also waiting to swim?" Very asked.

"As soon as. I, too, do not like iced swimming pools. I don't know what is holding all this up. I pay my HOA dues like everyone else. Why can't they keep this running properly?" He turned and walked away.

Very at first thought he might be a nice person to have in the pool, but his snarky remark about paying HOA dues put her off. She had already started feeling that way and she feared this was a recurring story. She might feel that way after a while when she saw mismanagement too. Old-timers' complaints.

At home, Very had frozen food, a salad and sat in front of the TV. As she watched some rerun of a program she had seen five times already, she realized that she was doing what her mother had done. She turned off the program before the end.

She read a book before turning off the light. She lay and listened for the night sounds. They were few and far away. She heard some dogs yowling, and then she realized that it was more likely to be a pack of coyotes. After all, this development was on the very edge of the city, with wild fields on three sides.

She planned her walk for the next day. She would go all the way around, maybe twice, and get her legs exercised. As she was drifting off, she thought of her mother's cat, killed by the pit bulls from up the street. She heard a soft 'meow'. She sat up, listening more intently. It had sounded as if it was inside, at the foot of her bed. But that couldn't be.

She got up, threw on her robe and went to the back patio door. She slid it open. The moon bathed the grass in a soft white blanket. She listened again. She called, "Here, kitty, kitty." There was no answer.

She stepped back inside, and then she heard it again. "Meow," came drifting on the moonlight. It was a sign. She knew what she had to do tomorrow.

Chapter Fifteen: Cleopatra, the Egyptian Mau

She woke early and lay in bed, listening to the outside sounds. She heard cars heading off to jobs, and a rumble of a work truck, not the right day for garbage collection. She knew that she had promised that today was a day for getting a roommate. Her resolve engendered a mild panic attack, but she pushed the thoughts aside. There had been too many signs the evening before. She muttered to herself, "Don't get cold feet. Don't let the daytime brightness influence you. You know you want a cat. Go get one."

She had a quick breakfast and then got into her car. What did she need to get for a new cat? A license? She knew that the humongous pet store had cats for adoption; she had seen the advertisements in the paper and read about the cat rescue places that partnered with this store. But, could she just go to Hart Park and pick up a cat? They said that there were hundreds of feral cats who needed homes there. Feral cats, that's what she did not need. But it sounded so awful, to buy a cat. No, it was to support the services of the agencies that rescued cats, cleaned them up, socialized them and then offered them to good homes. Was hers a good home? If the fate of her mother's cat was any indication, then, no, she was not a good steward. She sat in her car for a fleeting minute to remember her mother's cat, attacked by pit bulls that lived down the street. The discovery of her lifeless body in the driveway, and subsequent burial in the yard, had caused a major meltdown. She couldn't even remember the cat's name. A new cat, that was what was needed. A fresh start.

Very parked in the parking lot of the pet store. Even this early, people were walking their dogs to the front door. As one of the few places that could not afford to turn away a patron with a dog, the pet store allowed pets inside. Obviously, ill-behaved animals were required to leave, but Very cringed at the thought of dogs walking around inside a store. On a leash, well-behaved, what did she have to fear?

But then again, coming to a store to browse and 'buy' a pet cat seemed somehow too commercial. If you needed a new frying pan, or a vacuum cleaner or a new pair of jeans, or a ream of paper for your laser printer, going to a store to buy these things was normal. But a pet? A companion? Someone that would sleep on your bed and sniff at your privates? A purchase of such a living creature should not be treated in the same vein as a new vacuum cleaner.

She locked her car, and headed for the front door. She had never actually been inside, so the vastness and completeness of the goods for sale was temporarily disconcerting. She strolled down the aisles and stopped to see birds, lizards, chinchillas and gerbils for sale. Inside their cages, they ran, chirped and leapt onto their spinning wheels in joyful abandon. Such small spaces!

A saleswoman approached Very. "Can I help you with finding anything?"

"A cat, I'm looking for a cat to adopt."

"Right this way. Do you know what kind? Male or female, a kitten or an older cat? We have lots, right here." The woman spoke as she walked and stopped in front of a small glassed in area. On the other side were a series of cages, most of them full. Adult cats lazed in their spaces, leisurely raising their heads to survey the customers. Kittens leaped and played. One little black kitten saw Very and reached out a paw through the bars of the cage at her. His mouth opened, but Very heard no sound.

"Would you like to come in and meet who we have today?"

Inside the cat showroom, Very looked down at her feet, so as not to step on a tail or paw. The smell was not unpleasant, but held the faint odor of litter and cat food. Fur seemed to float on the air and Very felt a tickle in her throat.

"Do you know what you want? We have this lovely guy," she bent down to pet a large ginger cat who sat and stared at Very. "Would you like a kitten, we have a few, but of course, they have the kitten playfulness and energy. That may be too much for you!"

Very almost choked on the thought that this young woman was insinuating that energy and playfulness were in her past and therefore, a companion with these traits could not be tolerated. Too old for a kitten?

"I don't think it matters much, neutered of course, but a kitten would be okay." Very stifled a sneer at the young woman. Too old for a kitten!

"We have a very sweet kitty who came in just last night. Bigger than a kitten, but young. I think she'll go real fast." She reached down and unlatched a cage.

A small striped cat stuck her head out and then emerged in all her colors. Black and gray striped with undertones of warm earth orange. She lifted her head to Very and showed off her stripes on her forehead. "She's sort of an Egyptian Mau. You see, those markings on her forehead. They say you can see the 'M' for mau, but others say it is a scarab, because they come from Egypt."

The cat looked directly into Very's eyes and pleaded, "Meow, meow." Then she wrapped her body around Very's ankles in a sinuous rub that used her whole body. Very could feel the soft brush of her fur on her ankles. The cat repeated, then repeated again the ankle rub and greeting. Very reached down to pet her. The cat arched her head to get the full weight of the head pet as Very reached around to her ears. She began to purr. Very squatted down to get a better grip on her ears and the Egyptian Mau purred louder, reaching up to meet Very's hand.

"Do you like her?" the woman asked. "I'll leave you here together for a while and then we will get you some others to look at."

Very and the little Egyptian Mau began a soft conversation, the cat lifting her tail into a question mark. She continued to purr and rub against Very as the human and animal conversation continued.

"So, would you like to look at some kittens, we have a new litter of calicos that have just become ready and then there is this little black one." The store clerk stepped back and looked at Very. "Or do you want our little princess here?" She smiled. "If you don't want her, I'll bet she goes within the day to someone else. She is a real sweetie."

"Yes, I'll take the little princess. Does she have a name?" Very stood, but kept her ankle close to the purring feline.

"Yeah, but you can change it if you want. Cats don't come when you call their name, so it's up to you. But she is a real regal one."

"An Egyptian queen. Cleopatra. Does that suit?" Very looked down at the cat and said, "Cleopatra, do you want to come home with me?"

The answer came with another round of purrs and ankle rubs.

Very filled out paperwork, paid for the adoption fee and then accepted coupons for all the other things needed for a cat. A litter box, as this little princess was going to be an inside cat, unlike her mother's feral Cat. Food, food dishes, scratching post, catnip, toys and a small carrying box.

Cleopatra objected to being pushed into the small carrier, but eventually went in and turned around and scrunched down facing out. Very's credit card took a hit, someone helped her out to her car, putting the bulky things into the trunk and the cat carrier on the front seat beside her. As soon as Very started the car, the wailing began. Very spoke to the bewildered cat all the way home. She left her in the carrier until she had unloaded the cat accoutrements and locked the door. Then she opened the small carrier.

Cleopatra leapt out and then stopped. She began the enormous job of orientation to the new place. Very gave her food and water, fixed the litter box and put Cleopatra in it. She sniffed and dug a small hole, but leapt out as if to say, "Yeah, yeah, I know what this is, but I don't go on demand."

Very put away the cat food and fixed up the scratcher. Then she went looking for Cleopatra. She found her curled up on her bed, sleepy until Very petted her. She woke then and began a series of cat sounds. She murphed, she chirred, she purred, she meowed, she produced a strange wheeze-purr when Very hit a particularly sensitive spot behind her ear. When Very tired of the petting, she got up and so did the cat, who followed her out of the bedroom and down the hallway. Very felt surprised to feel a distinctive bat at her ankle. She stopped and looked at Cleopatra, who put on an innocent face, even as she raised her head to be recognized.

"You naughty little thing. Your food is here, box there, water over there. What more do you want?"

"Meow," she said nosing her food.

Very looked at Cleo's side. She didn't have stripes that were quite like other cats. She had a few large black spots, a little irregular, like a leopard, or a giraffe. Very laughed, "It says 811, it really does. Is that your birthdate, your weight, your address?" Very walked to the other side and chortled again. "Of course, you are a mirror image. Nature's way of camouflage. Now the real question is: Are you 811 or 118?"

Very took a warm drink and went outside to the patio. A gentle breeze was blowing and the air was clear and sweet-smelling. She encouraged Cleopatra to come out, which she did very tentatively. Maybe she had not previously been an outdoor cat. Very had not thought to ask where she had come from, perhaps preferring not to know why and how she had been abandoned. How would she react to the freedom?

Very sat and encouraged Cleo to come sit beside her, which she did as long as Very's hand was somewhere in her fur. Then, Very began to talk to Cleopatra. "You are such a beautiful girl, who could bear to give you up?" The one-sided conversation went on in this vein for a good five minutes. Cleo seemed to understand that it was all for her and she jumped up onto the neighboring chair and settled in, purring and listening to Very's murmurings.

Very leant back and closed her eyes. She stopped talking out loud, but continued the conversation in her head. Did Cleo have a solitary existence, or did she have brothers and sisters or roommates? What kind of food did she eat, only cat food, or an occasional bite of freshly grilled chicken, salmon bits and hamburger? Where did she sleep at night? On a person's bed, or did she have a favorite spot on the top of a climbing tree?

Very veered from questions about the cat to those of her own life. Had she been lonely these past few years, since her mother had gone to her heavenly reward? Did she want, as Joey continued to insist she must, a roommate, boyfriend or companion of some sort? Was this part of the insistence on getting a companion, even a small furry one, to stall Joey's questions? Surely, the acquisition of a cat did not mean the barrier to a human relationship? Or did it? What kind of men liked cats? Liberal ones, if one interpreted the literature on who liked or owned cats versus dogs. Well, would Very want a conservative male companion? A dog man?

She jerked upright. The dog next door had set up a barking contest with the two behind her house. The three dogs gathered at the corner and yapped and barked as if an intruder had barged into their domains.

Cleopatra! An intruder. Very jumped up from the chair. The cat had quietly left her perch opposite Very and could not be seen anywhere. "Here, kitty, kitty!" Visions of her mother's cat's dead body flooded her brain. "Kitty, Kitty," she screamed. She stepped out onto the lawn and called again. Then she saw the bushes in the corner twitch.

Cleopatra's coloring had meant that she was superbly camouflaged in the bushes. Very ran to where she had seen the bushes move, and sure enough, hidden among the leaves was one small cat. "Queen Cleopatra, come out of there!" Cleo moved further in. Very bent down and encircled the cat, who allowed herself to be grabbed.

Very hauled the cat indoors and shut the sliding door. She gently lowered the cat to the floor, and began to berate her in honeyed tones. "You can't do that, bother the dogs. Dogs are not friends of cats, despite the YouTube videos on social media. You need to stay inside."

Cleopatra curled around Very's ankles, meowed and purred, then went to sit at the door, facing outward. Longing to return outside. What could Very do about a disobedient cat? Was confining this little animal inside what she must do to keep her safe? But what about her longing for the outside, the grass, the bushes, the fresh air, and the chance to tease the dogs next door?

Chapter Sixteen: Pickle Ball

Very dressed for a sporting activity. Her newest pair of walking shoes appeared appropriate. Short pants, but not the ultra-short shorts; loose shirt, but Very almost never wore a tight shirt, not wanting to show off her aging bosom. Was there a uniform, like for tennis? Did she need whites or a particular length of shorts? She had neglected to ask. As she prepared herself for going to the lodge to check out pickle ball, she told herself that she needed to mix more and although she might feel unready, she knew that getting back into the saddle was important. She needed to learn a new sport, get to know her neighbors and participate in the community activities. Last weekend's fiasco needed to be put in place. She needed to go to the clubhouse, socialize with people, go out and walk around the pool and spa.

And pickle ball was a good compromise. Someone had explained that it was like tennis, which she realized early on she was hopeless at, somewhat like ping-pong, another game Very felt inadequate at playing, but with an easier ball to hit and a big paddle. Very suspected that she had wonky eyes as she had always been prone to car sickness, but her glasses, not terribly strong, had served her adequately for years. She needed to give it a try, not reject it out of hand.

The beginner's pickle ball team was currently still playing in the late afternoon. Someone told her that by the beginning of May, they would move the time to a later one, given the heat in Bakersfield in the afternoon. Or perhaps they would aim for an early morning time.

At 4:50pm, Very left her house and headed for the clubhouse. It was still a little warm. She had forgotten a bottle of water and immediately knew that she was unprepared. Inside, she checked in, writing her name with a scrawl which seemed de rigueur, judging by the names ahead of hers. "Umm, are the pickle ball players here yet?" she asked.

"Oh, didn't you get the message? They pushed back the time from five to six. They said it was just too hot. No fun if it's too hot to play. We don't want any more accidents or disasters, do we?" The young woman behind the window smiled too brightly at Very. Did she recognize Very, the one who was prone to being around at accidents and disasters?

Instead of going outside to the courts to wait, Very decided that she would take advantage of the air conditioned lounge to relax for a few minutes. She meandered over to the small cozy area that had overstuffed couches and armchairs clustered near the fireplace, now mercifully cold and abandoned. She sat in the middle of the couch that faced the big screen TV. Too late, she realized it was turned, permanently, to FOX News. The volume was on low, so Very could ignore it if she wanted. All the news men and women had subtitles in any case. What was the purpose of that? Dueling news consumers who couldn't stand their partner's choice of news, so they could turn down the volume, but their spouse could still read the nefarious news? Come to think of it, all news channels did that these days. Walter Cronkite with subtitles?

Very looked out to the broad lobby area where she had gotten a welcome just two days after she had arrived. It was here, just ten feet away, where MaryAnne had the argument with Fat Man Gunn and had fallen, prompting the summons of an ambulance. Very scrunched lower in her seat, trying to block the view of the lobby. A large armchair stood in the way of a view if Very sat low. She watched the almost silent TV for a few minutes, until she realized that others were in the lounge area as well, behind and towards the back of the room. She couldn't see them, but could they see her?

She heard muffled steps and the scraping of chairs as at least two, or maybe three, people seated themselves behind her. She sat still and eavesdropped on their conversation.

"We can sit here, nobody's around. Now, what did you hear? You know this is important." A husky voice, one that Very could not identify, but she felt as though it might click if she saw the speaker, whispered.

"You know what he said. I heard it distinctly. Peter Gunn called her a…" The second voice dropped the volume on the epithet, so Very couldn't hear what it was he called her.

"But they were an item, I mean together, weren't they? It was a good six months ago, but I thought it was going along smoothly."

"We thought so. But somewhere around the New Year's Eve Party, things started getting a little rocky."

"Thanksgiving, they were together, by Valentine's Day, they were old news." This came from a third voice, again, familiar but unidentifiable.

"They didn't just come to dinners together. They were lovers, I could smell it!"

Very was lost in trying to identify the speakers. Who said what? She could clearly make out three voices, vaguely familiar, but faces or names?

"Then the fights began. Oh, it was embarrassing!"

"People should just keep their dirty laundry in the laundry basket. I mean, we are all grown-ups here…"

"Speak for yourself. I've seen a lot of juvenile behavior from a lot of people. And those two, childish. The names they called each other, and in public! Shameful."

"It's really hard to live in a place like this after you've broken up. It's small, too small for hiding from the gossip mongers. It is a place where some people want you to choose sides. 'It's either him or me, whose side are you on?'"

"Oh, then don't choose!"

"But it's hard not to when people come to all the parties. It's hard to avoid one, and not the other, everyone knows and can see who is talking with whom."

"But he was a total jerk. I never understood what she saw in him in the first place."

"A charming jerk."

"That's an oxymoron."

"Oxy what? Don't use those big words in front of me. Just because you know lots of them doesn't mean you need to use them all."

"I just meant that being a jerk doesn't go with charming, you can't be both."

"He was very funny sometimes, you have to admit that."

"Yeah, but it was almost always cruel. MaryAnne was a fool to ever get involved."

"But it's over. Did we ever find out exactly what happened?"

"Accident, obviously."

"It's not obvious to me. Shhhh, look who's coming. The Gossip Princess." There was a reverse scraping of chairs and the small group moved, up and towards the door.

"Candy, how sweet of you to join us," trilled the one who had called her a Gossip Princess.

Candy's strident voice greeted them.

And then someone asked, "So, what's up with you?"

"Oh, more trouble with my evil sister-in-law."

"What now, more stealing of your mother's mugs?"

"No, the leather chair, the lounger that my father gave to me. She wants that now. She said that it was promised to her. The nerve!"

"Oh, don't worry about it, Candy. We all have an evil sister-in-law. It comes with the territory. Are we all ready? Shall we go?"

Very sunk even lower and waited until the group had departed. Because she had laid low, she had heard the conversation, but what would have happened if she had been found out? Lurking in the depths of the couch, listening to private conversations, participating in the gossip. No, she didn't participate. But keeping a mouth shut and remaining silent was a tacit assent to the things said. Or was it?

Very twisted around and spotted a clock. Good, it was a good time to head out to the pickle ball courts, she might find someone to talk to, get some introduction to the sport, manage an orientation so she wasn't a total idiot. With a pounding heart, she stood up and looked around. Empty, for the moment.

She walked out of the clubhouse past the gym and looked in. A few older men were grunting with their efforts. Why did these old men pretend to be able to lift weights, or run on the walking machines? They didn't need to exaggerate their strength or make believe they were twenty again, did they? Couldn't they just do what they knew was possible, and leave the vigorous grunting behind? "Huh, huh, huh," accompanied her exit out the back door to the pool and athletic courts area.

She walked slowly towards the courts, but speeded up when she saw a few gathered already. "Hi," she greeted the two women and a man. "I've come to learn pickle ball, I hope."

"Very, isn't it? We've met. Welcome to the club." The woman smiled.

Very smiled back. Name, name? Peggy, Shelly, Lindy, Connie, Bonnie, Lizzy, Margie, Cheri, Patty, Annie. "Annie! Nice to meet again. I'm hoping that you all can give me some help. I am a total amateur." Very tried to be as upbeat and chipper as possible.

The three crowded around and murmured happy welcomes.

"You've come to the right place. We are all amateurs here, just trying to have fun. Stan." He thrust out his hand and shook Very's with purpose and vigor.

Stan stepped back and checked out Very's height, weight, musculature and general physical condition. "You'll do well, I'm sure. Never played before huh? Ever play tennis?"

Very's voice threatened to betray her. Could she just say 'no' and let it go at that? Did she have to say she was a total flop at tennis? "I've played a little ping-pong, does that count?"

"Helps with the idea, at least. So, here is a paddle and here's the ball." Stan proceeded to give Very a brief rundown on how the game was played. He demonstrated some techniques to her and then he stopped, "Let's just play." And they started to play.

Very conjured up any knowledge of tennis, and doubles, which was what they were playing now. Did she 'go for' a ball, or did they have to take turns? She swung at the ball that came directly at her, and missed completely. This performance was greeted with mixed emotions. A few 'bad lucks' mixed with suggestions of how she held her paddle incorrectly flew around. Very was unable to pinpoint who said what. "Ah," she said, shaking her head. "Let's go on." She laughed brightly to show she was a good sport.

They played some more, each exchange more vigorous than the last. As the play went on, they ignored any attempt to include teaching moments, words of encouragement, or acknowledge that they were playing with a total newcomer. Swings became vicious and catcalls greeted poorly played or missed shots. The others played faster and faster.

Suddenly, the rubber ball came at high speed directly at Very. At the very last moment, Very was able to blink as the ball hit her squarely in the forehead. "Ow," she cried, bending over, dropping her paddle.

The others stopped and stared at Very. "What happened?" Annie asked.

"The ball, my head, my eye," coughed Very.

This explanation was greeted with silence.

"How could the ball get your head?" Stan asked.

Very bent over in pain and let the tears well from both eyes.

"You're not supposed to put your face in front of the ball, just your paddle." Stan whined.

"Is it bleeding? Did you cut it? Here, let me look," Annie gently pulled Very's hands away from her face. "Oh dear," she exclaimed at the reddened area on Very's face. "I'm going to get her some ice. You two, find her a seat somewhere."

Very was led to a bench, and then Annie returned with a towel full of ice cubes which she gently applied to the reddened spot just between and above her eyes. "You know, it doesn't look too bad. Here, let's go to the clubhouse and you can sit comfortably and let it sort itself out."

As Very was led away, she heard Stan grumble, "How do you get a ball in your face anyway? You look with your eyes, not put them in the trajectory of the ball. Humph!"

Annie led Very to the same seat she had occupied just minutes before, where she had listened to the gossip. Annie took the ice pack away from Very's face and asked Very if she could open her eyes. Very did, and Annie was relieved to know that she could not only open her eyes, but Very acknowledged that she could see just fine.

"That's why we have thick bones around our eyes, to protect them," Annie commented.

"And keep speeding balls from blinding us," Very murmured.

'Listen, I'm going to join the rest of them and finish the game."

"I'm going to go home," Very said, pushing herself into a standing position. "Maybe pickle ball's not for me."

"Oh, no, no, no. You have to come back. You can't let this one little thing put you off. That's what the game is all about, not letting anyone or anything defeat you."

Very smiled at Annie and murmured her thanks. How was it possible to say that someone defeating you wasn't the point of the game? Someone wins and someone loses. Always.

Very went home, and after an hour, when the swelling had failed to materialize, she fixed herself a cold drink and went out to the patio. At first, she thought it was warm enough, but went inside to get a sweater. Cleopatra followed her out.

"Okay, little girl, but only if you stay here, by me. Don't get lost."

Very sat back and closed her eyes and let the evening descend.

"Meow."

"Kitty, where are you?" Very's eyes snapped open and she looked around. "Kitty, kitty, kitty," she called, panic mounting as no answer came.

Very walked around the garden calling again and again, every breath more frantic than the last. Then she saw a bush quiver. Very looked and watched it quiver again. She bent down and pulled up a branch. Underneath was a very well camouflaged cat with a grin on her face.

"Cleopatra. Princess. Naughty cat." Very bent and picked her up. She purred in Very's arms as she was carried inside. "You scared me. You can't go walkabout on the first day."

Chapter Seventeen: Opening the Table

Very slept extremely well and decided that she would tackle the new table she had bought. She had a quick breakfast, then went out to the garage. She turned on the light, but decided she needed more light, so she opened the side door to the garage. Cleopatra had followed her to the garage and then proceeded to cry to be let out. When the garage door opened, she took the opportunity to dash into the back yard. Very followed and scolded her on her disappearing act.

The side door opened onto a narrow walkway between her house and the one next door. She chased Cleopatra into the back yard, and saw her disappear into the bushes. She needed to make this place home, so climbing into the shrubbery was part of the fun. Very needed to let the cat explore and make herself at home. She had seen other cats roaming the grounds and maybe Cleo could find some friends, or were they to be enemies? Very left off the cat prowl and went back to the garage and her new side table.

She tried opening the drawer, which appeared to be stuck. Very pulled and then went back into the kitchen to find a candle. A little wax might help. She rubbed and pulled and rubbed some more. Finally, the drawer came out more than halfway. There was nothing in the drawer, and no indication anywhere that there was, or had ever been, a secret drawer. "Where are you?" Very murmured as she stuck her hand far into the drawer, feeling for the latch, the mechanism that would expose the secret hideaway.

What would she do with the money if and when she found it? Forty-three thousand dollars was a lot of money. Would she give it back to the sons? Very's mouth turned down at the thought. Rather greedy, unpleasant people shouldn't get windfalls like this. She could get a new car, but her own car was just a few years old and she didn't need another one. It might cause comment if she suddenly came up with a brand-new car. She could take a vacation. No one need know that she was going first class on a cruise. But that would mean being alone, no one to share the fun of spending money. Spending money had never been important to Very. Maybe she could give it away, find a charity that would be happy to have $40,000. Whoops, did she mean that she would keep part of it? Why not give it all away?

First, she needed to find it. "Damn, where are you?"

"Did you lose something?" a deep voice came from next door.

Very looked up, startled. Her next-door neighbor was once more leaning over the fence and staring into the garage. She slammed the drawer closed and righted the small table. "No, not unless you can say I lost my money buying a used table."

"That looks like a nice one. Mr. Tom's, isn't it?" The man smiled at Very, his eyebrows traveling up and down on his forehead.

"Yeah, how did you know? Can you tell his work?" Very's voice betrayed her nervousness. Did everyone here know everyone else's business? What they sold and who bought it? Was the gossip network that extensive?

"As a matter of fact, I do, or rather I did. It was a small box, a birthday present to my wife. She took it when she left.

But I felt cheated; it didn't have a secret drawer." The man leaned farther over the fence.

What was it about men and their shirts? Shirts are not optional, even if only talking over the fence to a neighbor, are they? Very bit her tongue as it suddenly wanted to tell the man to put on some clothing.

"I was thinking about painting it, or maybe just revarnishing it. I was checking it out. This drawer seemed stuck a little, but I've got it now. Thanks." Very stood, put the table upright, and brushed herself off. Smiling, she strode over to the door and slammed it shut in the neighbor's face. She locked it. She re-covered the table with a plastic bag and stuck it back in the corner behind two old suitcases.

Shaken, she went back inside, but then thought immediately of her little cat still outside. She fixed a drink and went outside to the patio. Cleopatra came running when she saw Very and for the next few minutes happily sat in the shade with Very, who stroked the cat with her free hand. She listened to the hum of hummingbirds and the coos of pigeons. Then she heard the unmistakable 'snick' of a sliding door unlocking, and the 'swoosh' of the door opening. The air was so still she couldn't tell from which direction it came.

"You have a lovely backyard, what is there to complain about?" came an unidentified female voice.

"Monji, that's who did it, not me. All the landscaping, everything. They even come once a quarter and trim everything. Marvel of marvels, they replace scrubs if they aren't doing well. It's simply wonderful, isn't it."

"I'm sure it cost a lot."

"Yeah, well, at my age, what am I going to spend my money on? Leave it all to my greedy nieces and nephews? My dog? Certainly not my worthless son. No, spend it on my garden. Flowering shrubs, wandering walkways, cool corners to sit in. I love you, Monji."

"Yes, yes, stunning and comfortable. Mosquitoes in the summertime?"

"Oh, they take care of that as well. Plants, you know. Then I use citronella candles when it's really bad. But I don't want to brag too much in front of my friends, so don't say anything. You can tell them I have a great garden, but not about the cost!"

"Your secret is safe with me. Do you have any other secrets you're not telling?"

Very looked around and spotted the yard the conversation must have been coming from. Directly behind her was a shady, colorful back yard. Also, it hid anyone having a conversation.

Then she heard the sliding door open again and another voice joined the two women, a man this time. "Ladies, a drink," and Very listened to the clink of ice in glasses. She licked her lips in empathy. "Now, tell me, what can we do to get rid of him?"

"Bar him from joining all clubs, and then the clubhouse."

"That's pretty extreme, don't you think?"

"We can't bar him from living here, can we?"

The first woman spoke again, "What we really want to do is get him to move away."

The man answered, "Don't you mean 'pass away'? That's the easiest way to replace a neighbor."

"Haven't we had enough of that recently? The number of funerals has been more than the baby showers recently in the clubhouse ballroom. The last one was nice, though, wasn't it?"

"Ha, ha. The dirty drinks cart outside was the star attraction." The man laughed again. "Are you ladies ready for another?"

"That man is a disgrace to have living here. He is fat and ugly, wears terrible clothes, and is extremely annoying at all times. I want him out of here. I want him out of my sight."

The man laughed again, a big hearty guffaw that was somehow lighthearted. "I know that you are not the only one, there are others that agree with you. I might even include myself. He said something the other day, really nasty and way out of line. I'm not sure what we could do."

"Well, you know what they are saying about Peter Gunn, the accident in the hot tub? Well, some say it wasn't an accident at all."

"Maybe just fortuitous, right man in the right place."

Very leaned forward and listened intensely. All she heard were whispers and murmurs and then the swoosh of the sliding back door.

They had obviously been talking about two men, only one of whom was Peter Gunn, the body in the hot tub. Who was the other? Who else was fat and ugly and unliked? Obviously more than one man fit that description. And who were the speakers? The one who lived there with the lovely garden by Monji had a familiar voice, but Very had never been good at putting faces to disembodied voices.

They had gone in, so Very got up and went to her back fence. The fence was just at the height that it took someone taller than she to see over. Standing on tiptoes only gave her a view of dense vegetation and a red umbrella through the foliage. Who were these people? Who were they talking about? They seemed a bit cavalier about Peter Gunn being found in the hot tub, almost joking about it. What would they try to do to force someone to move away? Or was it all talk? Would any of them try action? As they insinuated happened to Fat Man Gunn? Very made a note to talk to Darrell or Joey about the police department whispers in the case. After all, she had a right to know, she had found the body.

When she found herself bored, she went back to the garage. Keeping the side door closed, Very reached in and pulled out the covered table. She spread an old sheet on the floor and then sat down next to the small table. She armed herself with the old candle, in case she needed more wax, and a small mallet, used for whacking wooden or plastic pieces into place.

She opened the drawer again, as far as she could. She used the mallet to force it further out, and then she applied more wax and elbow grease. Carefully working the drawer out, Very finally had it mostly pulled out. She turned the table over to look at the bottom of the drawer. Finally, she used the mallet to force the drawer out onto the floor. The last whack sent her backwards so hard she lost her balance and hit the floor. "Ouf," she said.

But she smiled as she had now separated the drawer from the table. Excitedly, she stuck her hand deep inside the drawer space. Feeling carefully around the five sides of the drawer's innards, she pulled out her hand in disgust. She went to the kitchen and found a flashlight. She repeated the search with the light, turning the table in all directions, banging her shins, forearms and knees in the process. "Damn! Where are you? I just know there is a secret space here. Maybe no money, but a secret drawer."

She sat back and took a deep breath. Thanking the weather for not making the garage hot or cold, she picked up the drawer and looked all around the outside, pushing and plucking at anything that stuck out, or in. She held the drawer up and then turned it upside down, shaking and listening for any movement.

It was then that she noticed the tiniest of hairline cracks across the bottom of the drawer on the inside. Instead of being one piece of wood, it was made of two. She turned it over. The bottom was one solid piece. Here was the hidden drawer, here on the inside. But how was one to access it? Very shone the flashlight onto the edges of the two pieces, carefully running her fingernail along the joints on either side, and at the ends.

Then she used her finger to slowly slide along the back of the drawer. The nail suddenly dipped and came up on the other side. Here it was, slightly caulked with wood colored paste. Looking did not show it, only feeling for it revealed the slight fingernail-sized gap. Very tried with a fingernail, but was unable to get enough leverage. She dashed inside and retrieved a nail file from her purse. Using the pointed end, she cleared away the caulking until the finger space was clearly revealed. Very tried her fingernail again, and jumped when the wood pulled away, but only an eighth of an inch. Using the nail file, she inserted it deeper into the slit and tried again. The wood groaned and then came up further.

Very was able to use most of her fingernails as grippers. Luckily, she had strong nails. Thank you, Mom, for making her drink all that milk as a kid. She carefully inserted six of her nails into the now wider space and scrabbled. The wood opened, but not without a protest. Very grabbed the wooden piece and yanked it up.

Then she saw it. An envelope. Old, dirty and open on one end.

Very reached a hand out to touch it. Her hand shook. Trembling fingers met her gaze. So, 'with trembling hands' was not just something that happened in books. And it could occur even when it didn't involve one's long lost love. Very shook her right hand, commanding it to just behave and take the envelope out of the drawer.

She reached in and pulled it out. Brown, wrinkled, torn open at the end. Very could see the green bills sticking out. She licked her lips and grabbed.

They were all flat and neat, but there weren't a lot of them. Very pulled them out and spread them open in a fan. Neatly placed, larger ones and then smaller. She counted.

Three tens, two fives and three ones. Forty-three dollars. Only. She laughed. Mr. Tom, you have the last laugh of all.

What was she going to do with this now? It was hers, she had bought the table. But hardly enough for a dinner for two, if you included the wine. What could $43 do for her? Not much. Not much good to anyone.

Very threw her head back and laughed and laughed and laughed.

Chapter Eighteen: The Sex Offenders Index

Very secreted the envelope in the old oak desk that she had brought from her mother's house. There was a deep drawer, not exactly hidden, in the back of the front desk drawer. She kept check books, money and now, the old envelope with $43 in it in this hard to reach space. She sat at the desk and checked her email. Junk, junk, junk, then an email from her realtor.

"Forgot to tell you, and I think it's important, that you need to check the Sex Offenders Index. I can't remember the exact URL, but just google it. I think that some of the horrible things that have happened to young children, and even law-abiding citizens in the last few years, prompted the setting up of these indexes. I don't think there is a real and present danger, but maybe you'll want to know who is living near you. Then again, maybe you don't want to know. You need to trust your own judgement about the friends you make. I don't think any of the active sex offenders will bother you at all and maybe you don't care, but I just had to tell you."

Very was certainly aware of the sex offenders who have to register, but she never thought that anyone like that lived in her own neighborhood. Who would sell their house to someone like that? Then again, if you are leaving, why should you care? Except that your neighbors might not be too happy to have someone on the register living next door.

She quickly went online, looked up the register and then entered her address. Whoops, there are some living in Five Points. She shut the lid down, firmly. No, don't look there.

She got herself a cold drink, went outside to the patio, found her cat and petted her for ten minutes. The thick fur slipping through her fingers was soothing and comforting. It made her think again about looking at the website. Dispassionate, don't take things personally. You don't know the whole story, don't prejudge. Let your heart be kind. She ran out of platitudes, but they pushed her back inside to look one more time at the Sex Offenders official website.

The map of Bakersfield showed up with a series of tiny paddles, or miniature bubbles arising from the addresses where sex offenders had listed their homes. She made the map closer and closer to Five Points with her mouse, until she could see the streets laid out neatly in the neighborhood. She saw three paddles within the community. She sat, fascinated by the placement of sex offenders just down the street.

She quickly switched to her old address, the tony and up-scale La Cresta neighborhood. What would she find there? At least on the street where she had lived, there were no paddles attached to the houses on the block where her mother's house had been. But a few blocks away, a paddle sat. Very hovered over it and finally she clicked.

A file sprang up. There was a photo, a mug shot, full front, bust photo of a man. He had gray hair, receding, and a neutral expression on his face. Very didn't recognize the man. It's not the sort of thing you use as a way to introduce yourself to newcomers to the neighborhood. How long had he been living there? Did his neighbors know? Although it was only a five-minute walk from her mother's address, it was down the hill and in a different socio-economic neighborhood. She didn't live there anymore, so why should she be bothered?

She went back to the Five Points map. Her mouse hovered over one bubble just two streets away. She hesitated, then with determination, clicked.

Again, the file sprang up. A man's face, somewhat like the previous one, stared back at her. This one was old, easily the 55+ needed to live at Five Points, and obese. His eyes were slits, barely visible in the folds of fat in his face. His gray hair appeared as a comb-over. Very looked at his offense. Oh no, sex with a child under the age of ten. How disgusting. Shivers ran up and down her spine, causing her to physically shiver. He lived just down the street, there on the corner, not far from the clubhouse. How could we allow this? Who allows a monster like this to live in our community?

Very clicked to return to the map. Two more in the village. She looked at the map and then saw a bubble on a street corner that she seemed to remember. Was that the house with the gray peaked roof, and the interesting crepe myrtle in the front yard? She had passed by one day and wondered what color it was going to be when it bloomed.

The thoughts of the morning, just a few days after she moved in, came back. She had walked to the clubhouse, and right past the first sex offender in the neighborhood's house, and gone along the back side of the clubhouse. The bushes were so thick, she couldn't tell where the pool, tennis courts, gazebo and hot tub were. Then she came out to the older houses on the far side of the development. This house was on a corner, and Very stopped to admire the mature front yard bushes. The front screen door suddenly opened.

"Hi," said a male voice from the shadows.

"Hi," Very answered tentatively, with the thought that Five Points was a very friendly place. Total strangers were quite happy to greet the new people, even if they didn't live on the street.

"New here?"

"Yeah, I was just doing an exploratory walk." Very chuckled.

"Would you like to come in? Have a cup of coffee? Or maybe hot chocolate? It's a bit chilly this morning."

Very stared. She couldn't see into the entryway, but she had the impression that he was wearing pajamas, or some sort of casualwear.

"Oh, gosh, how sweet of you. But I'm in a bit of a hurry. Some other time, okay." She waved vigorously and turned her back and walked away from the house.

She had never gone back to walk that way again. And she did not know what the man looked like. Now she knew, as she gazed at the stubble filled face that stared back at her. He looked normal, but when the knowledge of his crimes came up, signs of decadence, evil and loathing, came to the fore. Maybe some primitive instinct had kept her from engaging further with this man? He was on the sex offenders' list, so maybe not the best 'friend' for Very to make. But was her avoidance of him, and his house, justified? How did she make that decision?

Her telephone rang. Hastily, she deleted the Sex Offender's file. She looked at her phone. A number had come up, one that she didn't recognize, but as she stared at it, the phone rang again and again. She swiped at the green circle. "Hello."

"Vermilion Blew. Did I get the right number?" The male voice was familiar, but in her confused state, Very was hesitant to say anymore.

Finally, she managed a squeak, "Yes."

"Why, this is Father Sullivan, Clarence Sullivan. I'm calling on a different line. Sorry about that. Your phone might not recognize me. I just wanted to tell you I have good news."

Very breathed a huge sigh of relief. She found her breath coming in short spurts, as if trying to come to an equilibrium. She closed her eyes and willed her heart and lungs to return to normal. "Yes, what good news?"

"Gabby is set. I have found what I think will be a good fit for her. If she is available, she can go on Saturday, when the center has a soft opening. She will be my guest. But it is more for her to meet the director and assistant directors and to get a feel for the whole place. I think what I have arranged will be good for all. Here it is.

It's a volunteer position, for now. There might be some compensation in the future, but because she is too young to work officially right now, she can't make money. But maybe we can arrange to give her guest passes and she can invite friends to come. And then, she can participate in all the activities herself, which is a good deal. She can work in the office, doing filing sorts of things, in the game room, checking out equipment for the other kids, and so forth. She will have a little uniform, a center tee shirt and help out where needed. She will be a valued member of the staff. Now, how does that sound?"

"Oh, that sounds great, just the thing for a young girl. She'll be around the other kids all day, but in an assistant position. Thanks so much for arranging this. I know that it must have entailed pulling some strings. A position like this would be the envy of the other kids." Very sighed again.

"Yes, and another little thing. Maybe, just maybe, there might be a position for her at Garces High School in the fall. Do you think she'd like that?" He sounded hesitant.

"But I thought that she was going to BHS, that she was keen on doing that as Maria went there?"

"But she has good grades and the family falls into the category of needing a scholarship. If she does well this summer at the new Catholic Boys and Girls Club, she would be in a good position to earn a complete scholarship."

"I suppose that she might be the envy of her friends. What would her family think? Scholarship students aren't always… Well, not always welcomed, shall we say?"

Father Sullivan laughed his big hearty laugh. "Half the kids who go there are on some sort of scholarship. We try not to make any distinctions. She's a good student, she'll be all right. But why don't we keep quiet about this possibility for the moment. Will you tell her about the summer internship, or shall I?"

"I'll call her, tell her the news. Thanks for all your help. Bye." Very hung up.

Gabby had a summer job, and the possibility of going to the private Catholic school on a scholarship. What was wrong with all of this? Why did Very's hackles rise at how handily Father Sullivan had solved all of the family's problems? He specialized in solving his parishioner's problems, everyone knew that. Why did this rankle so?

Very sat and thought for a long ten minutes before she found Gabby's phone number. She checked the time, she should be out of school by now. Retirement had made Very forgetful of other's timetables. Others worked or went to classes; not everyone was free to be called at any time of the day.

"Gabby, Very here."

"Yeah, I know, my phone says so. I don't answer just anybody's phone call. I'm aware of these things, scams and so forth. So, what can I do for you today?"

Very hesitated, taken aback by Gabby's assertive, grownup manner. "Today, you can thank Father Sullivan for helping to find a summer position for you. It's not paid, exactly, but it is a wonderful opportunity." Very outlined the job and the future opportunities that might come with it. She emphasized the work experience and possible free passes for family and friends. She tried hard to make it sound appealing and worthwhile. Very also hoped that no one had promised Gabby's two clever hands for the summer babysitting, cleaning someone's house or, worse, working in the fields. She knew that the family needed the money. At least Charlie's opportunity took him out of the house and someone else would feed him for the three months. But Gabby would still need her meals. "And on Saturday, there is a chance for you to go meet everyone there."

"Yeah, I know. There's a bunch of tours and free food and everything. We were planning on going."

"Well, you will be Father Sullivan's guest, so this is great. All set then?"

"Super. It sounds super. Thanks so much. See you around, huh?"

"See you around!"

Very sat back. One promise kept. She needed to remember to keep track of Gabby for this summer. Go to the club and check on her. Call her often. Very didn't know the people who were working at the new venture; didn't know what it was all about. Boys and girls clubs. Adults and children. Scout masters and young boys. Priests and ministers and young people. She wanted to check the Sex Offenders Index again, but what would that tell her? How could she keep Gabby safe? Or Charlie for that matter? How could she keep all those young children safe, from predators who lived next door, or predators who guided them in their youth activities?

Very vowed to be vigilant. TRUST NO ONE.

Chapter Nineteen: A Walk Outside

A walk, that's what was needed. Away from Five Points, not the usual walk around the clubhouse and down the cul-de-sacs. That had been very interesting the first five times she had done it, but now, Very wanted a different experience. Out of the gate and down the street. To the south of Five Points were neighborhoods, the middle-class neighborhoods of cookie-cutter houses and yards planted with the same tree, or more often, every fourth house planted with the same tree. The front yards were grass, a tree and a short row of bushes underneath the window. Small yards, small footprint, only a suggestion of the lawn that Very grew up with. But with recurring droughts, what was the point in a large lawn, thirsty bushes and flowers? Tradition?

Very took her keys, but decided that the rest of the usual hiking gear wasn't needed or wanted. Forget the phone, forget the water and the rest of the emergency gear. Just a stroll outside. She walked around the main part of the clubhouse and out the small gate to the north. In the distance, she saw undulating hills, soon to be yellowed with the dry grass, black if they caught fire and burned a swathe of the hillsides. Starting in a few weeks, she and all her neighbors would be on the lookout for tell-tale wisps of smoke. She scanned the hills all around, maybe she should have brought her phone. Well, there were no signs of fires and it was too late, she was here now.

A long cement brick fence surrounded the development. Gates on the north and south allowed egress, but the nature of the gates made Very think that they were of limited use. Anyone could tailgate a resident or someone with a code into the exclusive Five Points active retirement community. However, it did make her feel safer.

She walked west towards the city and looked at the new houses being built in this part of the heretofore undeveloped land. She looked at the dusty mounds and immediately thought of Valley Fever. Undisturbed soil was the hiding place of the fungal spores that caused the mysterious illness. It was not contagious like the flu, but mimicked it in the initial stages. Then, if a person was unlucky, the spores burrowed into the lungs, causing lung problems that lasted months or years. Rarely fatal, it was a nuisance that plagued agricultural workers and those who worked in the building trades. New soil, freshly disturbed, allowed the spores to fly into the air and windy days were the worst. Today was quiet, no victims were likely on this day.

Very passed the wide street that entered the new development. A billboard showed pictures of homes, small lawn, one tree and bushes with the note, "Single family homes starting from the low $200,000s." On the opposite side of the street, a smaller sign, perhaps meant to last longer than the initial offering read, "Welcome to Coyote Gulch." Very shook her head. Who would want to live in Coyote Gulch? It was a great name for the place, as just to the north, a small gulch swiftly fell to the river below with steep sides and brushy outcrops. A perfect habitat for the eponymous coyotes. Ah, this must be where they live, the ones she had heard at night. Hiding in their gulch during the day and roaming the neighborhoods at night, howling their presence.

Ahead of her was the new oil well. She had seen the derrick one evening as she drove from her mother's old house with goods to move to the new. It was tall and other-worldly, lit up all along its metal struts as it thrust into the sky. Very knew that Coyote Gulch was on its way, the fence was in construction and the roads and curbs defined. She had wondered why anyone would think of drilling for oil just a hundred yards away from houses, new houses? The derrick was now gone, but in its place was a large pumpjack, squatting on its cement platform. It wasn't currently pumping, but a pool of smelly black goo lay covering the cement. Very stood tall in front of it and shook her fist at the oil equipment, shouting a curse. Her mother maintained that oil was the origin of Bakersfield and that the black gold ran in the veins of all true Bakersfieldians, including her. Curse the stuff! Bring on electric vehicles and solar panels on all houses. As she turned away, Very made a note, find out if this was even legal. Poor residents of Coyote Gulch, they had to contend with both, oil and coyotes.

Very turned to walk back to her house. Suddenly, it was dark. She hadn't noticed the setting sun, it had been bright and daytime when she left. How far had she walked? Why hadn't she kept track of time? Where was her watch, or her phone? Never mind, she knew exactly where she was and home was just a few steps away.

But here, opposite the new development, there were no street lights and the oil field lay dark except for some buildings farther away. She could just stick by the side of the road. There was a bicycle path all along this stretch and at least any cyclists out at this time of night would have lights. She hoped they were better prepared than she.

She closed her eyes to help them adjust to the dark and then she heard it, a faint clack-clack accompanied by a low drone. It grew louder, came closer. Very looked up.

Bearing down on her, at high speed, was a cyclist with no light. Very jumped to the side, just as the cyclist swerved to the same side. Very could feel the heat from the cyclist's body and the waves in the air from his passing. "Ahhhh," she screamed.

An answering shout from the rider was snatched by the wind, but Very was positive she did not want to hear what it was. Walking in the neighborhood had never felt so dangerous. Treks in the Himalayas with rock falls, the tracks of snow leopards in the mud just inches from her tent, running out of water while watching a river hundreds of meters below down an impossibly steep scree slope. These were dangerous.

She shook herself and found the path again. At the second step she took, she felt her ankle twitch and then again on the third step. She stopped, bent over and rubbed it. Then she tried a warm up exercise, but that quickly caused the twitch again. She stood tall, calmed herself and walked slowly towards home.

In the distance, she heard growling. Dogs. She kept on her path towards home, ignoring the canine kerfuffle. The sound came closer, as if it was heading straight for her. Her breaths came closer together as she looked straight ahead on the bicycle path. Why was it so dark? It never got this dark in Bako. There was always ambient light from the downtown area that bounced off the clouds and the silvery fields. She reached up to rub her eyes and discovered she wore her sunglasses. She pulled them off and tried to stuff them in a pocket. She found no pocket big enough and folded them, hanging them off the front of her shirt. It was lighter now, but still darker than she had expected. The dog snuffling had not abated and she wondered if the canines were on a leash.

Then they stood in front of her, growling, snarling, snuffling, baring their teeth, preparing to go into full throttle barking. Two dogs that Very found were the embodiment of two hounds from Baskerville.

She ran, off the road towards the north and the steep hillside that eventually ended in the river. And that also contained the Coyote Gulch. She headed in that direction.

The dogs were still behind her, but for some reason did not seem to be following her. She turned to look and tripped. Her foot caught in a hole, a dip, a bush, on a rock, who knew? But it caused her to fall. She threw her hands out in front of her to arrest the fall. Whoosh, the wind went out of her lungs as she slammed into the ground.

She stopped and tried to get her breath back. She listened for the dogs, but heard only a vague noise off in the distance. And some human voices, male, or rather one male. Who lets their dogs off a leash out here? She lay quietly on the ground, hoping to evade whoever it was out there.

"Bang." A gunshot? Backfire? Firecracker? Very pressed her body against the earth, hugging the ground, trying to make herself smaller and flatter.

Again, two more shots. No closer, no farther away. Very slowed her breathing, trying to listen to the noises in the field. She heard a car start and drive away. She breathed in quietly.

As the night reverted to its own noises, Very heard some strange cat-like mews and whimpers. She held her breath and lifted her head. The darkness in front and all around her was deep. Was there a cat out here? Did someone decide that the Coyote Gulch was the new dumping ground for unwanted or feral cats? What about Hart Park, isn't that where one got rid of cats?

The whimpering was in front of her, so she lifted her head and peered into the darkness. She softly returned the sounds by mewing like a cat. The sounds stopped then and Very decided the cat had run off rather than face a human.

She began to rise from the ground, dusting herself off and talking to herself. The mewling began anew.

Kittens, small animal sounds. But where were the sounds coming from? Very inched forward and again came to the ground, kneeling in front of the sounds.

The ambient light revealed two large triangular ears, barely visible in the darkness.

Very inhaled quickly. This was no ordinary cat, a bobcat at least. What was she doing, going forward into the maw of this large wild cat?

She blinked and looked again. Yes, the ears were larger than a domestic cat, but they were very close together, not a big cat, something else. Very started to back away, when a car behind her swing its lights over the field in a wide turn. Very threw herself on the ground again, hoping the driver or passengers hadn't noticed the tall animal in the field.

She turned her face away from the light, but it disappeared as quickly as it had appeared. Very opened her eyes to stare almost directly into the face of the animal. Very had seen the face in the light and now knew who she faced. The poor kit fox was undoubtedly more scared than she. "Sorry, Mr. Kit Fox, didn't mean to disturb."

Very was answered with a whine, a high-pitched bark and scuffling. Two more sets of ears appeared, smaller ones, and Very could just make out the two babies. They snuffled and whimpered, and Very knew then that they were the ones who had made the cat-like mews. They cautiously hunkered down, out of sight in their den.

Very stayed where she lay for a few more minutes. Part of this caution was the cars, dogs and perhaps guns behind her, and the other part was so as not to disturb the kit fox family. They were on the endangered list or getting there quickly and Very knew that their habitat here was under threat. Just a few yards to the west were oil pumpjacks, with all the accompaniment of cars, trucks, and the oil. To the south were new homes being built. To the north was the river and to the east was the gulch, presumably aptly names as the home of coyotes. Those little pups would be a tasty meal for the larger canine. Should she try to save them? Gather them up and take them to the rehabilitation section at the zoo? But that was a place where animals brought in were designated to go back to the wild, back to their fate in the world. Short lives.

Leave them where they are.

Very stood and turned her back on the kit fox family and started walking towards the road. Or what she thought was the road because suddenly, she slipped.

She felt herself heading downhill in a steep dirt slide, on her back. Quickly, she flipped herself over so she was on her stomach. Still sliding downhill. Head first, but in a better position. Without thinking she reached out her right hand, grabbing a branch, a rock, the dirt, anything to stop or slow her slide and more importantly, to twist her body around so that she faced uphill. As soon as she found herself face down in the dirt, she reached her left hand out to dig into the dirt hillside, arresting her slide into the gulch. As she lay heaving and frightened, she heard sounds again. The high-pitched howls of coyotes.

Coyote Gulch. She had been closer than she thought and must have been turned around, not realizing how close she had come to the edge of the steep, deep canyon. She did not hesitate, with the wild sounds at her back and below her. She scrambled upwards with the energy of a much younger woman. Adrenalin-fueled fear pushed her upwards. Within twenty seconds she stood at the top of the gulch.

In front of her, she could easily see the road, lights from the small oil field and street lights from Five Points, only a few hundred yards down the road.

Heaving with fear, Very ran, or rather stumbled, towards the path and then towards the sidewalk on the other side of the road. She came to the well-lit entrance to the community and fumbled with the key fob to let herself in the pedestrian gate.

She stopped then and caught her breath. Her throat ached for water; her hands stung with cuts and bruises. She stopped herself from looking at her clothes which she knew were torn and filthy.

Like a thief, she sneaked through the community, sticking to the bushes, avoiding the street lights, longing to be respectably dressed and tucked up in her quiet home. With her domestic cat.

Chapter Twenty: The Pool is Open (and Heated)

Suit, yes. Cap, yes. Goggles, yes. Towel, yes. Which coverup? Warm or cooler? Warm, after all, it was only the middle of April. Very dressed for the pool then walked to the clubhouse. It was still early in the morning and no one was about. The few cuts and scrapes that seemed such a disaster yesterday were mostly healed and she was able to walk almost normally. She hoped the cuts wouldn't sting when she got into the water. Even then, the chlorine would probably do them good.

At the front desk, Very logged in and caught the eye of the girl, a different one, behind the counter. "The pool is heated, isn't it?"

"Yes, supposed to be." She smiled brightly.

Very made her way to the pool enclosure. She hadn't been inside the fence since the previous weekend, the day that she found the body. She marveled at the ordinariness of the place. Tables, chairs, lounges, umbrellas, everything as it should be.

The hot tub enclosure was still blocked off. Police tape encircled the whole place, but other things also blocked everyone's view. Fake plants had been brought in by the hot tub people to block everything from prying eyes. It all looked normal from the outside, but of course, everyone knew and could not forget what had happened just a week before.

Very went to a table with a red umbrella stuck in the center. Four chairs were placed around the table in a cozy conversational manner. Very plonked her bag on one and started removing the necessities. A whiff of wind picked up the bottom of her coverup and she shivered. She looked at the water. Supposed to be heated was a vague term, trying it out was the best course. She grabbed her goggles and cap and hurried to the shallow steps.

She slipped on her cap and then gingerly walked into the pool. Clear bluish water, warm as promised, greeted her. She eyed the grand pool. Twenty-five meters long and almost as wide, the deepest part was only five feet and the center part was only three, shallow enough to do aerobics or to walk across from one set of steps to the other. She had come early to beat the crowd of older women who did pool exercises every day at 9am. She put on her goggles and stepped in all the way. "Oooooo," she murmured.

She struck out for the end in a vigorous crawl. Before she hit the end of the pool, she heard a strange garbled noise. She stopped and lifted her head. Two ducks, one male with brilliant green feathers and one female, brown and drab, stood at the end of the pool. They balanced on the edge, as if they were preparing to dive in. Very yelled, "No."

Startled, they backed off a foot, but continued eyeing the clear water pool they had discovered. "No, not here, this isn't your pond, this is my swimming pool."

With dignity, they turned around and waddled away. Their walk was coordinated and dignified, as they strolled away from the edge. Waddle, waddle, bump, bump, like two teenagers getting to know each other. If they could have held wings, they would have. They wandered off about fifteen feet and sat down under a table, fluffing their feathers and settling in.

Very ignored them, and went on with her swim. She stretched her arms and legs in long strokes, reveling in the length of the pool. When she had done ten laps, she stopped for a breather. As she lifted her head, she saw the ducks, who had returned to gawp at the pool. "No, go away. This is my pool." She splashed water in their direction.

Startled, they turned and took off, missing Very's head by inches. Whap, whap, honk, honk, they took to the air, circling around the pool for one last look. Very knew they would be back. Wildlife here inside Five Points, as well as outside. Someone, maybe it was John, had mentioned the many Cooper's Hawks that nested in Five Points, as well as the cottontails that inhabited the many miniparks around the development. Very thought of these as dog parks mainly because each had a dog baggie dispenser at the entrance. But the hawks could prey on the bunnies as well as the many pigeons that nestled on every lamp post. And the coyotes? Did they prey on the cute little cottontail rabbits as well?

Very put her head in the water and hammered out two more laps. When she finished, she lifted her head to find herself staring straight at the hot tub enclosure, just a few feet from her. She shivered, but not with the cold. She turned to check out the pool. She was alone.

More laps, these were at a more leisurely pace, as she expected company at any moment. She began to feel lonely. Having the pool all to oneself is a good feeling, but not with the death machine at the end of every lap.

"Yoo-hoo," called out a female voice. "How's the water?"

Very lifted her head and looked around. "Great," she called back. "Nice and warm."

"Good, we're going in, aren't we?" she crowded around a table with two other women.

Very put her head down, vowing to herself to get in as many laps as she could before the aerobics class started. At every breath, she could hear the twitter of ladies who were there not so much to exercise, as to collect the latest gossip. Between twitters of greetings and asking after each other, Very heard their fears and concerns.

"Creepy being here," one said.

"Haven't been here since Saturday. Don't know if I want to be here now."

MaryAnne arrived and the twitters turned to her. Like a flock of birds, many of the women gathered around MaryAnne to kiss, hug and ask how she was.

Very stopped doing laps and tried her aerobics moves, washing machine twist side to side, stomach crunches, stretches, but had trouble keeping count. She found herself wanting to hear the conversations.

Gail came flying through the gate in a multicolored suit that she proclaimed was new this year. She came closer to where Very was stretching and accosted MaryAnne, "Are you okay to be here?"

MaryAnne's answer was to bat her eyelashes and grin.

"No bad thoughts, no regrets?" Gail pressed.

"I had nothing to do with what happened, and I know that neither did you. So, end of story. Words spoken can never be recalled. Loose lips sink ships. Gossip, gossip, gossip." MaryAnne took Gail's arm and they marched purposefully towards the table where Very had her things laid out. They began unloading their bags onto the table and all the chairs, putting their possessions directly on top of Very's.

Startled, Very decided her swim was over and got out. She approached the table and began gathering her stuff, "Sorry," Very said with an edge. "I didn't know I was putting my things on your table."

"Oh, sorry about that, we always use this table, every day. So, we thought this stuff belonged to one of our group. Judge not, lest you be judged. So sorry." MaryAnne and Gail gathered their things out of the way so that Very could move her swim items.

Very approached a nearby lounge chair and dumped her towel and things on the seat. So quick to move her things, so adamant that the table belonged to them every day. But also so quick to apologize, so quick to let her claim her items, so sorry that they had assumed. Forgive them?

Very sat on the lounge and dried herself and then her hair. She knew that she would go home and take a shower, but she wanted to hear more of the chit-chat at the pool.

Like at pickle ball, the point of the gathering was less the exercise than the camaraderie of the venue. Because this was the first day the pool had been heated, it had attracted some who may not have seen each other for the past week, since the ill-fated pool party. The whispers centered around the death.

"They did a nice job of covering it up. You can hardly see it."

"Can't see the tub at all! They've got all that fake greenery around it."

"You want to see the thing? Look into the watery depths? Good grief!"

"Does anyone know the plans, what's happening? Will they take it out? Renovate?"

"Would you ever get in again?"

"I heard that when this happens, and it happens more than you would think, that they completely redo it. Make it look totally different."

"I know that if one of my family members or close neighbors drowned in my pool, I would just fill it in. No way, would I 'renovate'. I'm not sure I'll ever go in again."

"Let's go ladies!" shouted the leader. She waded into the water with a satisfied splash.

Half the ladies had not dressed for swimming, not willing to brave the outside temperatures and not willing to believe the pool was up to their standards. Some took seats in lounge chairs and carried on the gossip. The brave half made their way into the blue water.

Very dried off, put on her wrap and made her way home. If she ever wanted to get the latest gossip, she needed to join the aerobics class.

At home, she showered, changed and sat to read the news on her computer. She had let the cat out when she went to the pool and now went in search of her new pet. The backyard was empty. It was small and held few places to hide. Cleopatra was not at home.

Very called. She shook the food box, making a rattling sound that carried as far as her voice. "Kitty, kitty, kitty!" Rattle, rattle.

She began to panic. What a bad mother she was to lose her baby so soon. She went outside and walked around the house. "Here kitty, kitty." She moved up and down the street, leaning over fences and calling. She began to knock on doors. She decided to start with her immediate neighbors, then go further.

The neighbor to the left was not at home. The neighbor on the other side did not answer. She walked around the block and counted houses, she was looking for the one immediately behind hers. When she knocked on the door, she heard a slow screech across the floor, then a pause, and another screech. She heard a person behind the door, breathing heavily and hesitating.

"Hi, I'm your new neighbor to the rear. And I've lost my cat, she's just new. Have you seen her?" Very called through the door.

"Umph." The door was opened, slowly. "Your cat? Is that the one that walks on the fence? Black and white? I saw her yesterday, but not today. Lost her?" The woman who appeared in the doorway was shrouded in dim light and Very could only make out the fact that she stood behind an old fashioned clunky walker, was gray-haired and wore something that resembled a bathrobe. Her voice was not strong, but she seemed certain about what she had seen, and not seen.

She shuffled with her walker to close the door.

"I'll get that," Very said, leaning forward to close the door.

Very frowned. The cat could be in her backyard and she not know it, but Very had called to Cleopatra over the fence, so believing the elderly neighbor was the only thing to do.

She went to the next house, but no one answered. She began to walk around the end of the block and thought she should call again. But then, she heard voices. On the other side of the cement brick fence.

She stopped. It was MaryAnne. Did she live here?

"Are you sure he didn't eat them? Fat, fat, can eat no lean. A moment on the lips is forever on the hips," MaryAnne's voice came loud and clear.

"My cookies? No, no, he said he'd keep them for later and I pushed them on him, but he was not going to touch them then."

"You know he was a diabetic. He'd never eat those sugary things. Whatever made you think he would?"

"The stuff is sugary, and I knew I could hide it in the sugar topping of the cookies."

"How much did you put in?"

"In for a penny, in for a pound."

"Just two tablets, not enough to kill him, just make him feel unwell. They are the stuff that you take for nausea, and they are sweet."

"Becky, that stuff is not really good for your heart, did you know that? Absence makes the heart grow fonder."

"You don't think it killed him, do you?"

"Maybe helped him along the way. The squeaky wheel gets the grease."

"But he didn't eat them, did he? You said he wouldn't. And what about your special sun cream? The stuff with bleach in it?"

"He hadn't used any. The jar was still on the table when he went into the pool. I picked it up, I didn't want anyone else using it. Obviously. In any case, it would only have made him itchy. Not kill him. A shower a day keeps the mosquitoes away."

"The cocktail?"

"I was just thinking of that. Gail's special cocktail. Where there's smoke, there's fire."

"What was in it? Milk of Magnesia was what she told me, made to look like a Grasshopper. Put that with the cookies and…"

"It spilled. I saw it all over the table top. I don't think he even tasted it. You can lead a horse to water, but you can't make him drink. You know the jump into the pool just happened so quickly. Boom, boom. A journey of a thousand miles starts with a single step. And then it was chaos."

"So, did he drink it or not?"

"Probably not. I don't think anything we did even contributed to what happened. You can't always get what you want."

Very held her breath waiting for more, but nothing more was said, or it was in whispers. Then a rustling on the other side of the fence alerted her to movement of the speakers. She needed to get out of there.

She scurried around the corner, back to her own street. As she passed the right door neighbor, she stopped again. Maybe the woman would answer this time. She hadn't met her properly, so now was the time.

She rang and then knocked. The door opened. "Hi! I'm your new neighbor, but I don't think we've met. I'm actually looking for my cat; she got out."

The woman looked at Very as she made these introductions and blinked, not saying anything.

Very looked down the long hallway as a small black and white cat sauntered along on her way to the open door, with her tail held high in a question mark.

"Kitty, Cleopatra?" Very held out her arms and the cat came closer, rubbing the legs of the neighbor as she passed. Very bent down and grabbed her, holding her tightly, all the while murmuring 'sweet kitties' in her ear.

"Oh, you mean that one?" said the neighbor.

"Where has she been?" Very asked.

"Eating at my house. You need to feed her properly and get her chipped. Not nice, letting a cat run wild."

"She is chipped and she has lots of food. She was just curious, weren't you? I think I need to keep her at home until she is fully acclimatized. Inside. But she loves to go outside."

The woman stared at Very. "Yeah, that's a good idea." She closed the door. Firmly.

Very turned and held Cleopatra tight. "Bad girl!" she scolded, as she turned and headed back home. As she neared the sidewalk, she skidded to a halt.

Davy was there, his large cat on a leash, smiling at her. He and the cat blocked the sidewalk. "What have we got here?" he asked with a smile.

Very hugged Cleopatra closer, keeping her from seeing the large fluffy cat at their feet. "She got out."

"Oh, gone walkabout, huh? Not a good thing to do around here."

"Walkabout, that's what she's done, but now I'm taking her home."

The big man smiled at Very, a lugubrious, smarmy smile.

Very shivered.

Chapter Twenty-one: Frankie Monroe Reappears

It was Friday at noon. She had had her swim for the day, her cat had been lost and found, and now it was time to think about going to the office. She sent a text to Darrell telling him she was coming in, probably in forty-five minutes or so. She knew that he would answer in the negative if he wasn't there or if it was inconvenient. She wasn't clear why she thought she needed to go, but it was a familiar place that needed to be checked into, at least every once in a while. What did that mean? Every week? She had been there on Monday, and there was nothing special to draw her back, just a vague feeling that it was time.

She got ready and went out to her car. She opened the garage door with a punch on the controls. Wow, an automatic door opener, and to her very own garage. This was a step up in the world. She knew it. She reveled in it. It was like the pool, why settle for a tiny puddle, when you could have a huge pool? Why settle for a car port when you could have an automatically controlled garage door opener and a large storage space? She smiled in satisfaction.

"Oh, there you are. I was looking for you."

Very turned at the voice and peered into the sunshine. Ruthie, Terry, Margie, Pammie, Joanie, Chrissie, Bonnie, Lynnie, Patty, Judy. "Judy, isn't it? Looking for me?"

"You missed the book club. And I'm Patty."

Very looked at Patty open-mouthed. What kind of accusation was this? Was she committed to doing something, bringing something, speaking about something, or heavens, reading something that she hadn't?

"I, uh, sorry, I didn't know when or where. And sorry, I forgot your name. Everything is new to me, I haven't really unpacked yet. And I didn't know I had committed."

"No, I understand, everyone takes their time. But in two weeks, on Thursday. It's in the library of course. We meet every two weeks. If you haven't read the book, it's okay, we always have someone give us a synopsis and some generic questions. But it's fun, it's community. You really need to join. I'll send you an email if you give me your address."

Very pulled out a small notepad and wrote down her email. "Here, send me an email and tell me what book we'll be discussing. I can always get it on my Kindle. I'm glad you caught me. Thanks for reminding me."

"You really need to join this group. It's a place for like-minded people. There aren't many here and we have to stick together. We can't let them take over everything here." Patty looked at Very's email address.

Which side was the right side? And which side was Very on? What did like-minded mean? Very's experience of Bakersfield was that few understood what made her tick and didn't care much either. Did that mean that Very wanted to join the exclusive club of the right-minded people? Had she been looking for exclusivity when she moved, or was it more mundane? Couldn't one wish for a gated entrance and nice facilities without belonging to one side or the other? Exclusive, right-minded people, to be found at the book club. Of course.

"Thanks again for reminding me, Patty. And don't forget to send me the name of the book." Very proceeded to get in her car and back out into the clean, well-kept street, lined with curbs and sidewalks.

Downtown, on 17ᵗʰ Street, Very found a parking place and proceeded to the office. As she climbed the stairs, she anticipated the gold lettering on the window pane in the door. Her name was now on it, but truth be told, she was beginning to tire of this. But still, her name on the door, in gold. As she neared and was about to open the door, she heard voices.

One was Darrell's, the other a woman's, a girl's voice. Very hesitated. If someone was here with Darrell, she couldn't barge in on him. What if it was a case, something important? Maybe she should knock? She listened again, then heard joint laughter. It sounded like they were having fun. It sounded…intimate?

She knocked and walked in. "Hi," she said to Darrell. "Did you get my message? That I was coming?"

Darrell looked at Very, a deer-in-the-headlights stupefied gaze. "Uh, oh, when did you send it?"

Very looked at her watch, "About an hour ago. No problem, you're here." She looked at the woman sitting in the chair in front of her computer. It was turned on, papers lay around the base and a coffee mug, not hers, sat to the side. At home, she was.

As she waited for Darrell to react, like introduce this newcomer at her computer and in her chair, she looked at the young woman. Very judged her to be about 25 to 30 years old, dressed appropriately for her age, in Bakersfield casual. Her curly hair was piled on top of her head revealing big hoop earrings dangling from her ear lobes. Her face was thin, almost gaunt, but what was the most startling feature were her eyes. They were huge, round and engaging. The moisture around them made the orbs and surrounds sparkle with life and enthusiasm. Very had never seen such eager eyes.

"Oh, this is Olivia," mumbled Darrell. "She, she is…"

"Sitting at my desk. Nice to meet you Olivia." Very smiled, a big smile, trying to show Olivia she meant her no harm.

"Hello, so nice to meet you. Darrell has talked a lot about you." She opened her mouth and showed her teeth in an enthusiastic smile. Snaggle-toothed was a polite euphemism for the state of her teeth. But it worked; Very liked her.

She smiled broader and made to get up out of the chair to give it to Very. Very demurred. She felt as if she should sit in the chair, but it was offered as a 'give up your seat to the old lady' and Very bristled at that.

"No, no, I'm not staying long, am I, Darrell? Anything to report, anything going on, or ongoing?"

Darrell looked at the two women, his tongue tied up in knots.

"So, are you working here?" Very turned to Olivia.

"Yeah," she began to answer.

Darrell leapt into the conversation. "You remember Very, I told you I needed some help. And you were so engrossed, so involved with your new life and new house and all. I just needed to get someone to do filing and accounts and stuff. And Olivia is an accountant. She has a degree from BC and all." He smiled towards Olivia, whose mouth curled into a return smile.

"That's great. It looks like it's working out well. But what if…" Very started to say.

"If you have need of a computer, I've got my laptop and remember, even that computer isn't the newest one I've ever owned. If we need to, we can manage to get another chair in here and I think the coffee making station can be moved a little."

Very laughed. "No, it's okay, I have my own computer and seeing as how I'm not really working on anything right now, Olivia can have the computer and the chair. We'll work it out."

Darrell looked alarmed. Olivia giggled and Very wished she hadn't arrived at this moment.

"Oh, but I do have something for you." Darrell began.

"Darrell, I don't need any work right now. I sorted out Gabby; Father Sullivan found her a volunteer place at the new Boys' and Girls' Club. I was just wondering if you had heard anything about the incident at Five Points last weekend?"

"I haven't, sorry. Maybe you can talk to your other source. You know Sergeant Sanchez and his sources are probably better than mine."

"Don't forget city versus county. We're city at Five Points. Sanchez and his sources are county."

"I wouldn't worry about it all if I were you. Really, it was an accident. Do you honestly think the cops are going to pursue any other avenue on this?" Darrell leaned forward. "Are you getting paranoid? I'm sure they don't suspect foul play from you. Have you been questioned again or anything?"

"No," admitted Very. "I thought they would try me again later, maybe after I had calmed down a bit and maybe I could remember more. But they never came back to me on that. In some ways, I feel disappointed. I mean, like, I'm the chief witness. I found the body."

"The murderer is the chief witness. He or she was presumably the last to see the man. Alive."

"Maybe. Poison is a sneaky way to kill someone. You don't have to be there. Alibis aren't the point."

"Are you telling me that the guy, what's his name, Peter Gunn, that old TV show name, was poisoned?"

"I have heard some gossip."

Darrell groaned and lowered his head, cutting off Very's view of his face.

"Gossip is important. It's what makes the world go around. How would we ever learn anything if it wasn't for gossip. I mean look at Facebook and the other social media things? Gossip, all gossip."

"But no one bothers to check the facts, and videos and photos can be altered. It's as though this kind of garbage information has taken over from the real thing." Darrell was a self-admitted Facebook hater.

Very stood her ground. "I'm calling this gossip, but it's more like information that the police have no knowledge of. I'm calling it gossip because it was overheard, and so maybe I didn't hear everything and besides, some of it was, I must admit, a bit dodgy.

"Okay, okay, let's have it." Darrell took out a notepad and pen. "Shoot."

Very laughed. "That's the one thing he wasn't, shot, that is. But here it is. Three women, all of whom disliked him, had been the targets of his amorous attempts, butt of his jokes and publicly humiliated by racist remarks, might have tried something. I overheard this, so it is truly gossip. But they maintain that their feeble attempts to poison him didn't work. You have to eat the poisoned apple before it is murder. And, according to this overheard gossip, he did not eat or drink the offending offerings."

"So, this means you are not going to say anything to the police." Darrell held his pen poised to write down anything important, which he determined he had not heard, so far.

"No, no. But I am going to keep my eyes open and my ears attuned."

"Where and how did you hear this gossip? Did someone tell you? Directly?"

"Over the fence," Very mumbled. "Hearsay, no more. Skip it."

Silence descended on the room as all fumbled for a new topic of conversation.

"Very, I found something. Here, Olivia, give Very your seat for a minute."

Olivia jumped up and offered her chair to Very. Very sat in the chair, the seat flattened and warmed by the last inhabitant. She swiveled around to look at Darrell.

"I know you've been busy, so I have done it by myself. You know it's been a long time, and we have looked just everywhere. But, when I have found a few minutes, I think of a new place. And with all the new programs and new computer innovations, it just keeps getting better. So I have kept going. And now…"

Very looked at Darrell, trying to decipher his rambling speech. "What?"

"In Sudbury, Ontario, Canada. I mean, we didn't really look too hard there, in Canada, did we? I thought it was worth a harder look. And being a little creative."

Very felt a shiver run up her back, and sit at the base of her skull. She gripped the table. "Frankie?"

"Not for sure. But I found a phone number, and a photo. Look here." Darrell held out a piece of paper with some numbers and a badly scanned black and white photo. "If you consider he's aged 35 or 40 years, gotten heavier, grayer, lines on the face. What do you think?"

Very gasped. It could be. The hairline was the same, the wide cheekbones, the lips, not thin, not too full. Then she looked at the other information on the page. "But this name?"

"Remember I told you that if someone was going to run, to hide, they would often change their name, but not too much."

"But Marvin Franks. Marvin. Marvin? The Franks part I see, but the first name. Who would choose Marvin?"

"I think that was the point, don't you?"

"Frankie was smart, but more of a street smart, not intellectual kind of smart. I don't think he'd say, 'Well, I'll change my name, but just a bit and choose a weird sort of first name, just to throw someone off my trail.' That doesn't sound like him."

"But maybe he was able to find some sort of document that had a Marvin name on it. Something he could steal."

"Did he steal this identity?" Very sat back in the chair and looked at the fuzzy picture. This was the only photo of a mature Frankie that she had ever seen. She had no idea what his life had been like since he left 39 years before. "I guess if the drug dealers that killed his friend and dumped his body in the orchard were after him, then changing his name was a no-brainer."

"That has been the idea all along. That he left, changed his name and started a new life elsewhere. And look at that birthdate."

"Wow, it's exactly two days, two months and two years different. That's either weird, or clever. This is what we've been looking for." Very lowered her head, not wanting Darrell to see the expression on her face. She had learned long ago that she had little or no control over her facial expressions and now, she wanted to be private.

"What do you think?"

"And there's a phone number," Very murmured.

"Sudbury, Ontario. Out of the way for a boy from Bakersfield."

Very's phone rang. She pulled it from her bag, saw it was Joey and answered automatically. "What's up?"

"Come for dinner tonight. Maybe there will be news," Joey said.

"Oh, yes, there will be news. Sure." Very hung up.

Darrell looked at Very with a question mark on his face. She ignored him, and stared again at the paper, at the photo of Frankie Monroe and the phone number.

She stood, folded the paper in half and shoved it deep into her bag.

"Maybe you're right, maybe Sergeant Sanchez has news. Bye."

She turned away as she saw Olivia and Darrell looking gooey-eyed at each other.

Chapter Twenty-two: The Video from the Hot Tub

Very worked on rearranging some of the boxes and made decisions about storing what and where. She spent some time playing with Cleopatra, but the cat only wanted to sleep. Exhausted, she lay down for a nap late in the afternoon. She tried to put the paper that lay in the bottom of her purse out of her mind. But the vision of the aged Frankie, and the only other memory she had of him as a young man, battled in her mind. She couldn't sleep, but when she got up, determined to do something about the paper, she found she needed to get ready for dinner at Joey's. She always brought something and felt inadequate if she didn't contribute. She found a can of whole black olives, Clara's favorite, and a bag of chips. She pointedly did not look at the expiration date, for fear she would be caught out delivering old food. She wouldn't eat any or not many, so she did not worry for herself. But what about the young ones? She glanced at the date. Months away, good to go.

It was the usual Friday night barbecue. The whole family was present, plus a few other friends. After Very had placed her offerings in the hands of Daughter-in-law #3 and greeted Joey, she wandered over to the barbecue station, manned by Sergeant Sanchez. The atmosphere was cheerful and Very couldn't help but be buoyed by the general company. But she looked in vain for the white Stetson.

"My favorite lawman." Very smiled at Bobby.

"Ah, Very. We need to find you your own lawman, I'm taken." Bobby said.

"That's okay. If I need one, I can find my own, thanks."

"How about your Private Investigator, Mr. Pitts?"

Very laughed. "I think he is taken too. He just hired himself a much younger woman as an assistant. A secretary, accountant, assistant."

"Ah, replacing you with a newer model? Feeling displaced?"

"No, I'm fine as I am. Life is exciting enough as it is." Very thought of the paper in her bag.

Bobby turned the meat on the grill, adjusted the flame and waited for Very.

"Ah, any news on our death in the hot tub? Should I be calling it Hot Tub Homicide? Or maybe Spa Suicide or just Accidental Death?"

Bobby looked at Very with a strange expression on his face. He looked up and away, as if he were checking with some higher authority, then back at Very. "Well…"

"I know, I know, you can't say anything. It's an ongoing investigation. But the expression on your face tells me a lot. In other words, it is not a simple drowning in the hot tub. Then why haven't I been questioned again? Did it ever occur to someone that I might know more than I was able to tell you that night? Really! I had had a little to drink and a big trauma. Why not revisit my statement?"

Bobby remained silent.

"It is not your investigation, obviously, but you know something."

"The real question is, do you know something? What is it that you have to tell?"

Very blew out her lips in a signal of dismissal. "Whuuut. What would I know? Gossip. You do know that Peter Gunn was a man who gathered dislike, or even hate.

Nobody liked him, not even his girlfriend. And he spent his time spreading around nastiness wherever he happened to be. The list of those who wanted to shut him up is long, very long. I wouldn't put my name on it exactly, but I was not a fan. And I have heard some gossip, that's all. Nothing definitive. I am assuming that the police are questioning those who have lived in Five Points longer than I, and those who knew him better." Very stopped and waited for Bobby to respond.

He turned again to the meat, using his tongs to poke, prod, push and punch the meat, forcing the beef to ooze red juice that ran into the flames. Very turned away from the sight of burning flesh.

"Hey there, Bobby, is that steak done yet?" came a shout from across the lawn.

"Yeah, coming right up." Bobby shouted back.

Lowering his voice, Bobby spoke to Very, "The case is not closed. The coroner may have something to say about it. And that's all I'm saying. Except to tell you that if you have information, you need to report it."

Very opened her mouth to answer back, but then closed it. She had nothing to say that she hadn't already said.

Dinner was announced and everyone got food and found a place to sit. Very chose a place with the 'girls', Joey, her daughters-in-law and the female guests. The men all gathered near the barbecue, many of them standing to eat.

"How do they eat steak standing up?" Very asked.

"Oh, their father cuts it up for them and then they just spear and gobble. Look," said daughter-in-law #1. "See how Dad has cut the beef?" She showed Very her plate with thin slices of bloody meat. Yeah, men and their spears and gobbling techniques.

The talk at the ladies table was babies and children. Joey caught Very's eye and shrugged with apology. The latest baby was passed around and lots of advice was given to the newest daughter-in-law who was hugely pregnant. Clara came and sat next to Very and listened carefully to the women's talk. Inculcate them young. Six years old and she was being taught the basics of being a woman, motherhood and all the jobs attending. All three younger women had college degrees and either currently worked, or had worked at interesting, meaningful jobs. In twenty years, maybe they, too, would be bored with breast-feeding stories and how to settle a fussy child.

"Clara," Very said to the inquisitive child beside her. "Did you know that I have a new pet, a cat. Her name is Cleopatra."

"Cleo what?"

"Cleopatra was a queen of Egypt, and my kitty is an Egyptian mau cat, so I think she is an Egyptian queen, or at least a princess. Look, here are some photos." For the next ten minutes, they discussed the beauties and the personality of felines, and the responsibilities and joys of being the caretaker of Cleopatra.

"Aunt Berry, if you ever need a babysitter, I'll do it. I know how. And I am sure she is a good kitty, so she will be easy to take care of. I can't wait."

"Well, the next time I go on vacation, I won't take her with me, so you can take care of her. But maybe you had better ask your mother first before you offer. Do you think?"

Avoiding this conundrum, Clara asked Very the moment's burning question, "Where are you going on your next vacation?"

Very reached down and touched her bag. "Maybe I'll go to Canada. I haven't explored it thoroughly yet."

"Not going back to Egypt, or Japan, or Mexico or, or?" Clara named the places that she knew Very had been to.

"No, not this time, but I'm working on another trip to South America."

"Ooh." This was not really brain-washing by Very, it was giving the child an education, a view of the world outside of Bakersfield and motherhood. A strike for a different kind of feminism.

Suddenly, Very felt tired, exhausted, bone-weary and wanted her bed. She said goodnight to Joey and the ladies. The men did not care if Very left now or later, so she simply headed out. As she approached her car parked two doors down, she saw another car approach the Sanchez family home. She got in and then looked in her rear-view mirror. She watched a man get out of the car and head towards the door. As he approached, he put on a white Stetson and strolled up to the side door, the family door. Very hesitated, then put her car in gear and headed home.

When she got home, she brushed her teeth and prepared for bed. But as she crawled in, she hesitated. It was still early and her tiredness had been muted on the ride home. She got her small laptop computer and took it into the bedroom with her. She checked her email, clicked on a news channel to see if any country had gone to war, a volcano or earthquake had happened, or a celebrity had gone rogue. Blah, blah, blah. She clicked over to check her Neighborhood Watch website. If nothing was happening in the big world, maybe something was happening in the neighborhood. Lost dogs, stolen packages, badly behaving teenagers, out of season fireworks, all were grist for the mill of the 'Neighborhood.'

Wow, something just put up. The message was headed, "Look who's getting into our mailboxes now." Very clicked onto the whole message. It was from someone, a name she didn't recognize, from Five Points. Oh no, was there a mail thief in the gated community? Or was it the usual following of mail deliverers and then raiding of front porches?

There was a short message, garbled and ranting, but then another link that read, 'Five Points Hot Tub Mystery.'

The sender signed him or herself as 'concerned neighbor.' "Watch this now!" Startled, Very clicked. It was a video.

Pulled into the web of messages and clicks, Very had lost the thread. Where did this come from? Was it safe to click? To view? Was she going to get some whacko video of hot tub trippers? Clothes optional? Pornography? But it did say specifically it was from Five Points. She clicked the 'play now' button.

The grainy surveillance video was hard to see. The point of view was downward towards the hot tub. The hot tub at Five Points, one that she recognized. She watched fascinated as Peter Gunn's figure stepped into the enclosure. She watched as he discarded his shirt, and flicked off his flip-flops. He stepped into the water. Opening his mouth, he uttered something that was not immediately intelligible. There was no sound, so unless Very was able to read lips, she would not know what he said. Maybe it was just the 'ah' of entering the hot water, which was the usual reaction to someone immersing themselves into hot water from the cool air. She had done it herself on more than one occasion getting into a hot tub. She continued to watch.

The shadowy shapes of three figures could be seen coming into the hot tub space. Very gasped as she watched, recognizing all three of the women. They had their party clothes on, the ones they had worn on the night of the pool party. Even though the film was in color, the colors were not clear, muted and washed out. Not surprising, given the time of day and the state of the lighting. Very watched as the three women spread out, facing the camera. A flash of an arm in the lower part of the picture showed where Peter Gunn was sitting in the pool. Words were exchanged. The arms and faces of the women moved. Mary Anne raised her arm and her mouth opened wide. Shouting? Becky stood at her tallest and sneered. Gail jerked her shoulders back and forth, but Very couldn't tell if she said anything or not.

Then they filed out of the enclosure. They had not come close to Fat Man Gunn, only stood and berated him. Very watched some more, but no other persons could be seen.

Then the camera went blank, dark, as if an unseen hand had covered the lens. The video continued, as Very could see that bits of light moved.

Suddenly, there was a break, as if the video had been interrupted, or patched together with earlier or later bits. Very knew this was certainly possible and easy to do, to manipulate the video to show someone who had been there earlier or later.

Then there was a change in the light. Now, among the shadows, she could see a dark patch in the pool. She gasped. It was the figure of the floating body of Peter Gunn. Then, the lights went out, but the film kept going.

It was not completely dark, however. The street lights gave ambient light and it was so dark, shapes were only the only things to be seen. Then she gasped again.

She saw herself. She saw a shadow approach and come into the hot tub enclosure. She remembered the night and knew that she was watching her own movements that Saturday, just six days ago. Like a hypnotized rabbit in the headlights, she could not stop herself from watching. She saw herself get into the pool, and then she saw the same shadow leap and throw her hands around. In her head, Very heard the screams.

The scene changed and became confused. People arrived from everywhere and the lights went on, casting harsh light on the dead body and the hysterical finder. Although she willed herself to click off and delete the video, Very watched with the horrified fascination of an onlooker to a crash scene. The big difference was that she was in the scene, at the same time as being an onlooker. The crowd that gathered now obscured her. The video ended.

A message appeared, "Watch again?"

Very felt her stomach flip over, and a nauseous bile rose in her mouth. Why would she want to watch that again? Relive the awfulness of that night?

Maybe she should, watch it again. Who sent this? Where did it come from? Who would post something like this? It had to have come from the office, from the staff in the office. What a breach of privacy laws! Was this private property? Certainly a private moment, not to be posted to the neighborhood everyone-can-see website.

Very looked back at her computer. She moved her mouse to the back button. The screen took her back to the Neighborhood page for her neighborhood. She saw a post that she had seen yesterday, but where was the one she had just seen? She scrolled up then down, then she went back to the main Neighborhood page. She found the Five Points page and clicked. Nothing. No recent message about mail boxes, and nothing about a hot tub. The whole message had been deleted.

Chapter Twenty-three: Call in the PI

Very knew that she needed to do two things, find the video, and let someone else watch it. But she had lost it somehow. For five minutes, she clicked and clicked, trying feverishly to recall the video. What if someone, the person who posted it, had taken it down? What was the purpose of putting it up, if only to take it down? Was it a mistake? Did they mean to post something about mailboxes, as the original teaser had said? Then why was the video posted, a rather gruesome one, that had to have come from a staff member or someone who had stolen the video?

She needed to get it back. How? Who would know how to do that? She looked at the clock. It was late, but Darrell had her back. She dialed his number.

"Hi Darrell, I know it's late. I hope not too late." Very waited a beat to see if Darrell would blow her off, or heaven forbid, say he was not at home.

"Uh, um, it is late. But what's up Very?"

"The most bizarre thing happened to me and I need your help." Very described the video, how it came to her and how it disappeared. "What do you think? Can you get it back?"

"Should I come over?"

"Only if you think it's strictly necessary. I didn't delete the video, so maybe it is still hanging around on my computer somewhere. Maybe?"

"I'll come over. Now? If you called me, you must be serious. Huh?"

"Is this like missing children? The sooner you start looking, the sooner they are found? And if you wait an hour, then something bad must have happened to them?"

"Very, I don't think that's a good analogy. I think I should bring someone with me, or maybe just consult. I'm on my way. If you find it again, try to save it."

Very went back to her computer, but gave up after fifteen minutes. She clicked on Facebook to find some animal videos to amuse herself while she waited.

Her phone rang. "Very, what's the gate code?"

Very had forgotten that any outsider needed a code to get in. She loved the idea that bad guys couldn't just drive in, but often forgot to give the code to her guests. She rattled off the number. Then she grabbed a jacket and went out to the front to wait for Darrell.

Soon, a car pulled up, not Darrell's, and two men emerged. Very went to the curb. "You had better park in the driveway, it's late and it's not allowed to park in the street," said Very to the driver.

"Wow, who polices this place?" He got back in the car and pulled into the driveway.

Very waited for him to get out of the car. "Private I think. We are super concerned about security here. Lots of elderly folks. When you get old, you'll understand."

"I guess," he mumbled. "Old f****."

Very stood, trying hard not be offended. Darrell waited and the three walked into the house.

"This is Jack," Darrell said. "He's my computer guy, the one I go to when I need some high-tech help." Jack was wearing black, just like Steve Jobs. He sported a kind of

Mohawk, with the center dyed white blonde, but his own hair showing black. Stubble showed on his chin, as if he hadn't decided to shave it or not. He was thin and slightly hunched, his body creating a question mark. He sported black-framed glasses that seemed too large for his face.

"Welcome to the old folks' home, Jack," Very said as they came in the door.

"Where's your office?" Darrell asked.

"No office, I didn't want a home office, but I've always wanted my own private library. I call it 'The Library.' Here it is." Very led them into a room that was lined with bookshelves with the exception of two glass-fronted cabinets, full of Very's souvenirs from years of travel around the world. Ostrich egg shells from Namibia, colorful pottery from Tunisia, Maasai necklaces from Kenya, raffia baskets from Botswana, dozens of skull caps from Central Asia, marionette puppets from Burma, miniature terra cotta warriors from China, a set of black stone cats from Egypt. On the floor lay a deep red carpet from Uzbekistan. A large oak desk sat next to the window with a computer and printer on top.

"Nice desk," Jack said, stroking the highly-polished wood of the heavy, solid behemoth.

"My grandfather's, so I guess you might call it an antique. For one of the old folks."

"A nice legacy," Darrell said, looking sideways at Jack. "Very, can you show us the website you found this video on?"

Very sat at the computer and put in her password. The website was still waiting on the sleeping computer. "Here," she indicated. "It was just put up, with the notation about people stealing mail from mailboxes. It wasn't a message for me, I think anyone who had signed up for this site could have accessed it."

Jack hovered over Very and reached over to click on something. Very excused herself and got up. "You sit here," she indicated to Jack.

Darrell assured Very, "We'll get onto it. In the meantime, Very, could you write down all you can think of about this website, this video, what it showed etc. If we can't find it again, the best evidence is collected as soon as possible. You are an eye-witness. And from what you said, this may be important."

As Jack and Darrell hovered over the computer, Very stepped aside. She found one of her PI small notebooks and opened it. She went into the dining room and pulled out a chair at the table. She wrote everything down that she could remember about the case. The overheard conversations, the innuendos, the video, all were grist for her notes. After 45 minutes, she wandered back into the library.

"Good, you've got it all down?" Darrell asked.

"Coffee?" Jack said, looked up from his concentration on the laptop.

"Sure, cream and sugar? Darrell?" Very turned to go make the coffee. "Does this mean you will be here a lot longer?"

"Oh, and your password, please, in case this logs off. And your WiFi password?"

Very gave them her passwords and went off to make a pot of coffee.

As the two men consulted, Jack pulled out his own computer and they began to work on two computers. Very listened in on snatches of conversation, moments of excitement, and some frustrated language. She brought back the coffee.

"Why two computers? Isn't mine good enough? I thought you were just going to try and retrieve that video?" she asked.

"We can't find the video on your computer, so we are going to try to go around, outside, do a squiggle and look for this video from another angle. We are looking for other venues of posting, including law enforcement."

"Is that legal?" Very asked, alarm creeping into her voice.

"Don't ask," Jack replied.

"I'll be out here," Very said as she drifted to the couch in the living room. She could still hear their muffled voices. She turned the lights low and closed her eyes. She felt Cleopatra's soft fur brushing against her hand. She pulled a crocheted afghan over her and puffed up a pillow.

"Meow," said a cat into her ear.

"Oh, kitty, what time is it?" Very sat up, light streaming into the room from the morning sun. She jumped up and ran to the Library. Empty. A note pad lay on the desk.

Very –

We got no satisfaction in finding the video, sorry. We also tried to find the origin and again, no satisfaction. But that particular website allows edits or retractions, so in case you change your mind within a minute or so of sending, you can take it back. This is probably what happened. Maybe the person who had the video decided to put it out there, but then changed his/her mind. Or it could have been the case of wanting to send that video to a particular person, but then the sender had a change of heart. Or perhaps putting it on the website was not the original intention, but the sender was a neophyte and put it up on the wrong website. Jack and I think the last is the real reason and that's why it was only up for a few minutes.

We also checked on your desktop, hard drive, all your other drives and again, no satisfaction with anything like finding a video labeled thieves and mailboxes or the Hot Tub

Homicide. It is all a mystery to us. By the way, Jack cleaned up your hard drive, emptied your trash and deleted all kinds of stupid duplicate folders and files. You need to thank him for that. (You should have heard what he said about old ladies and hoarding! Oh, actually, I think it was wise you didn't hear that.) If you want to retrieve anything, look in your trash folder, it won't go away for 30 days. Long enough for you to reconsider any junk you want to save.

Call if you need anything.

D

Very smiled at the thoughtfulness of Darrell to tell her what had happened in the wee hours of the morning while she slept. That she had actually slept all night, or what was left of it, was a surprise to Very. She had had a shock and she didn't often sleep well after bad experiences.

She made coffee for herself, fed the cat, and then let her out with express instructions not to leave the back yard. Perhaps Very was being hopeful that Cleopatra would stay close for the next weeks.

She wandered into the library and checked her computer. The desktop was almost empty, just six or seven neat files with clear labels. Beautiful job, Jack.

She drank one cup of coffee and then went out to swim. At this hour, she had the pool to herself. The air was still chilly and Very wished she had brought a heavier cover-up or a sweatshirt. But when she was in the heated water, everything seemed right. She floated on her back, gently doing backstrokes, but mostly listlessly staring at the clouds. She tried to see animals or scenes in them, but nothing appeared. Her mind wandered.

The paper in her purse, the one with Frankie's photo and his phone number. Early on a Saturday morning was a good time, wasn't it? It was time to deal with this problem, she shouldn't let it sit and fester longer. She tried to imagine what she would say, what he would reply, how the conversation would go. Could she ask right up front why he left? Or maybe it would be best to establish a relationship again, at least a mutual respect for one another, for decisions made…

Very stopped the scenario building and got to work, stretching her arms and legs, pushing hard to do her usual twenty laps. She wished, for just a heartbeat, that she could soak in the hot tub for a few minutes, letting the hot jets massage her stiff back and feet. But one glance at the direction of the small hot tub enclosure caused shivers and she turned away, quickly leaving the pool area.

At home, she had breakfast and then sat on the back patio, stroking her cat, soaking up the sun. The birds of spring were busy, as calls, tweets, and buzzes filled the air. She leaned back and relaxed.

The ringing of her phone in the distance penetrated the fog of her nap and she rushed inside to answer it. If she had been a millennial, her phone would have been by her side, sitting on the small table next to her cold coffee.

"Darrell. Oh wow, thanks for all you did last night. Sorry I wasn't awake to say goodbye. The clean desktop is brilliant."

"Very, you need to find those three women. You need to figure out why they were there."

"Oh, I saw them, near the enclosure, but they were just standing. I couldn't tell if they were coming or going. Everyone had on their suits, under their wraps or clothes, and now I can't tell you if they were wet or not, dressed in swimsuits or clothes. I don't remember, either from my view of them on Friday night, or from the video I saw, oh so briefly, last night."

"From what you've remembered, they were witnesses, or close witnesses or…"

"They were the ones to drown him? Don't forget Darrell, I was there too, and I am sure, positive, that I didn't drown him."

"He wasn't drowned."

"What? Not drowned? How do you know?"

"Inside information, and I didn't tell you that."

"Whew, that's news. So if he wasn't drowned, then what? He's still dead."

"Undecided, inconclusive. Maybe drugs in the system."

Very was silent. The overheard conversation of yesterday came wandering back to her. The anti-nausea medication, the milk of magnesia, were these enough? But then again, the speakers were sure that these things had NOT been ingested. But if Fat Man Gunn had been poisoned, it could have been in anything. Very thought of the long table, full of food, plates were filled and filled again. Easy to quietly slip something onto a plate. Or in a glass, or even into a beer can.

"But your informant wasn't sure what the conclusion was?"

"Not yet, need to wait. And remember Very, I didn't tell you any of this."

"Yes, yes, understood. Thanks again for the clean-up on the computer. I'm sure it will work better and faster. I appreciate it, really and truly. Tell Jack thanks for me. And if he needs anything…"

"And what about the information I gave you about…Frankie, a possible Frankie?"

"Not yet, no time to call. Or no energy to have a conversation. The paper is still here. I'll get to it soon. Bye."

Very reached for her big bag. She could see the paper, folded, in her bag. Leave it for now.

Chapter Twenty-four: The Cat Walker

The house was in need of a brush up and vacuuming. Very bent her back to the task for a vigorous thirty minutes, then sat down. She got a drink of water from the fridge door, but then cursed herself as the water ran down the outside of the fridge, creating puddles and a streak down the front. Stop using the cold water from the fridge, they never work properly. Just put a pitcher or water bottle in the fridge and drink from that. Who did Very know who had a functioning front door water and ice dispenser? The idea was nice, someone made money from it, but the reality was fraught with breakdowns and curses. She didn't need the aggravation at the moment.

A walk, that was it, a nice quiet stroll through the neighborhood. And she could use the excuse of checking her mailbox.

The smells of barbecue greeted her. This early in the day, it was not the smell of barbecue sauce or burning meat, that would come later, but now, it was the tell-tale smell of gas from the grill units. Now, the penny dropped and she realized why she never wanted to be first at Joey's house and the Friday night barbecues, because of this smell. Better the beef burning smell than the lung-searing artificial scent of gas.

She strolled out to the main street from her cul-de-sac and headed for the mailboxes. A breeze lifted her loose blouse and sent a cooling wind through her. She emptied her mailbox and tucked the letters into her pocket. Others were out this time of day, checking the mail, watering front porch plants, and the most important errand of all, walking their dogs.

A number of people had multiple dogs, usually two of the same kind. Small dogs were preferred, some even smaller than Very's cat. But there were all sizes and shapes, aggressively friendly and painfully shy, playfully pulling on leads and waddling sedately at their owner's feet.

Very greeted everyone, though not stopping to chat with anyone. She strolled, rather than walked, meandering down cul-de-sacs, checking out the pocket parks, nodding to the other walkers, joggers, bicyclists, even a motorized skateboard rider. The sun began to set and light up the western sky. Clouds were smeared across the west, promising a long, magnificent sunset of multicolors reflected in the various forms of the clouds. Very found a bench with a view of the sky.

She reveled in the safety of the community as she recalled her foray outside. Was it only two days ago? Just because there were gates and walls did not protect her from the wild animals outside, but at least they gave her a sense that they were on her turf, rather than she on theirs. This was her home, her neighborhood, her land, her place and she could say that they were not particularly wanted. The coyotes, kit foxes, raccoons and the human versions of those wild animals; not welcome here.

She spied a group of three neighbors talking with their dogs nestled around their feet. One was excited and pulled on the leash. Suddenly, the tiny dog was off and running. At first it appeared that the dog was just running out his long leash, but when the owner began to scream and chase, then

Very understood the dog had slipped out of his harness. She stood and caught the furball as he went by her feet. She carefully knelt with the wriggling animal until Mom arrived, trying to keep her fingers out of the way of the crying dog's mouth.

"Oh, naughty, naughty boy!" the owner cooed in a voice that was in total opposition to her words. "Here," she said to Very, "I'll take him." She bent to install the harness. Very could see that it was a little too loose, but knew that telling the owner would not garner any praise for doing so. The owner held the animal instead of confining him. Best. Very walked with the errant dog and owner back to the group of gossipers.

"Hard to keep them from being dogs, huh?" Very said. "The wide-open ranges here, and they want to go."

"Yeah, but if I keep him at home, I have the devil to pay. He cries all night and pees on the carpet."

"Oh, mine does that too."

Very tried to remember their names, but failed to conjure up even one. It wasn't worth the bother if this was only a short conversation.

"So," one woman continued the conversation, "he was poisoned?"

"Not officially, of course. My cousin can't say for sure, but that's the rumor from 'ye olde rumor mill.' This small town has leaks everywhere in officialdom. Could or could not be true."

"Oh, you're the one who found him, weren't you?" the woman with the escaping dog turned to Very.

"Yes, but that doesn't mean I know anything. He was just a big floating body when I saw him." Very replied in a subdued voice.

"Drowned or poisoned? Hummmm." The group fell silent.

"If he was poisoned, who could have done that?"

"Anybody at the party!"

"But would you do that, to anyone? Even if you didn't like him, would you kill someone?"

"Poisoning his beer is different from actually doing something, isn't it? Maybe someone just wanted to teach him a lesson."

"You would do something like that?"

"I am going to tell you something in confidence, I've done it. I slipped someone a little bit of LSD in a drink. Just a little bit. When I was young."

The small crowd moved closer including Very. "And..?"

"He didn't even notice. It was too small a dose, I guess. He never knew."

"How did you know he didn't feel anything?"

"He was my boyfriend and we spent the night together. He never said anything. I broke up with him after that. I guess if I was willing to drug him, then I didn't like him very much. It was a difficult time in my life."

"Could someone have done the same thing with Fat Man Gunn?"

"Like his girlfriend?" The question was met with silence.

"She wasn't the only one who had a grievance, you know. Lots of people had to put up with Peter Gunn and his snide comments about anything. He would call just about anyone 'fat', just like that, 'fat.' Who does that? I mean, even if he were thin, you can't call people fat, and he was one of the fattest. And remember what he called Stan? Said he was a cheat, and said that he sold him a lawnmower that was broken and then when he tried to give it back to Stan and get his money back, Stan refused. He was a terrible man and even if we aren't supposed to speak ill of the dead, I'm going to, because he doesn't deserve otherwise. I hope he rots in hell."

"What did he do to you? What was the terrible thing you can't forgive him for?"

"He kicked my dog, made her cry. He took his big fat foot and smashed it against her side. She cried. She was just trying to be friendly, you know her. And that man, that Satan, kicked her! You know what they say about animal abusers? People next. I wouldn't put it past him to have had something to do with those other men dying. Mr. Tom, dead before his time. And poor Bill."

"Really, he had something to do with their deaths?"

"And the trees he chopped down? Whose were they?"

"They made him move, didn't they? Oh, he might have been unhappy about that. What words went between those neighbors?"

"How about you?" the woman cradling her dog turned to Very.

"Oh, I'm new here. I didn't even know him, only saw him a couple of times, knew who he was, but that's all." Very tried to step back a bit, but the gossip fascinated her and she hung close until the small group started to move in the opposite direction to Very's house.

"Have a good evening," Very called out as she headed towards home.

As she started to walk to her house, she saw Davy with his cat on a leash. She walked on. As they neared one another Very said with a chirp, "Hi, nice evening, isn't it?"

"Umph, I guess you could say so." His mumble was not warm.

Very braved the brusque greeting. "How's your cat today?" Very bent to pet the huge animal.

It hissed and hair stood up on its back.

"Sorry, I thought Maine Coon cats were friendly, calm and very tame. But yours doesn't seem to be very welcoming today."

"Who told you that about Maine Coons? The internet? Did you just google Maine Coons and they told you it was perfectly alright to approach and touch my cat?"

"Sorry, no offense. But you have him on a leash, that must make him somewhat domesticated." Very grinned at Davy.

Davy laughed, a great belly-shaking guffaw. "Whoever said that cats were domesticated? No such thing. Cats are wild animals. They are only one meal away from reverting to their original wild state. Make no mistake about that, girlie."

"But my cat comes when I call and talks to me, telling me she is hungry or thirsty or wants to play."

"Ah, makes my point, doesn't it? Only when she feels like it. It's dangerous to assume they are anything but one generation away from fierce wild beasts. However, we rub along together, don't we?"

Very decided to act mollified, even though she was far from it. "I think it's sweet that you like cats. Cats reveal character."

"Whose? Mine or the cat's? Or yours that you choose to believe cats can be other than wild?"

Very gritted her teeth and continued, "My kitty's name is Cleopatra, she's an Egyptian mau. With an M on her forehead."

Smiling with his large yellow teeth showing, Davy bent closer to Very. "Some say that it is the sign of a scarab, renewal and rebirth. Auspicious, isn't it?"

"Rebirth, as what? Another cat? Don't scarabs protect the cats? Wouldn't they protect against wild animals, other cats, other beasts, like dogs and…coyotes?" Very replied without thinking too much about what she said.

"Don't tell me you believe all that hooey?"

"No, I'm just trying to figure out my cat, if she is special, like yours?" Very looked down at the Maine Coon who was now staring up at her and purring, loudly.

"Your cat is just a cat, like mine. One cat is just one cat. The same with people, a person is just that, a person, no different from other people. Some are good, some are bad, and most of us are somewhere in between."

"A sad thing, about Peter Gunn. Just another person, like others. I feel sorry for him," Very said.

"Not the best liked, so maybe we could say no loss. He said things about people. You remember Mr. Tom? He said nasty things about his son, or rather sons. Mr. Tom should have given him a god-almighty whack."

"Mr. Tom is dead. He couldn't have done that."

"Of course not, I'm just saying he should have. And he's not the only one. I, for one, am not sorry he's gone, Peter Gunn that is. I kind of liked Old Man Tom. Yeah, knew him for years and he was better than the rest."

"Yeah," Very agreed. "I met him, too, just days before he died. And I have one of his side tables. A nice souvenir."

Davy leaned forward, invading Very's space. "Did it have a magic drawer, a secret hiding place? I've heard stories about those. Treasure troves, I've heard."

Very hesitated a beat, "No, no secret drawers in mine, just a simple table."

"You were cheated, then."

"No, I don't think so, I'm happy with my purchase."

"Ah, that we should all be so happy with our lives and choices. Well, have a good one." He gave a chirrup to his cat and they strolled away.

Very stood on the sidewalk and looked as he walked away. She shook her head. What was he trying to say? What bits of wisdom did he leave with her? Cats are wild animals? Mr. Tom's sons cheated her on the table? Peter Gunn was a nasty man?

Chapter Twenty-five: A Late-Night Visit to the Pool

Back in her house, Very fidgeted, disturbed by the conversation she had had with Davy. She ate a quick dinner. She cuddled and brushed Cleopatra, but then let her out. "Do you want to become a coyote snack? Stay close."

She watched the very last of the sunset from her back window. The sky drew darker and darker. The street lights came on, but the shadows remained dim. She called Cleopatra who came into the house and headed for her food dish. She then gave herself a good wash and found a chair to settle in. Very couldn't stay still. The video came into her head, she closed her eyes and tried to remember as much as she could. She saw the three women come into the enclosure. Was Peter Gunn there? In the hot tub? Presumably. They talked, not long, but what did they say? They didn't approach the hot tub, only stood on the edge of the enclosure. Was the video complete, or had someone edited it? It must have been edited because everything happened so fast. Or perhaps it was one of those motion cameras that only recorded when someone, or some wildlife, moved within the camera range. Wild party goers like wild animals?

Very turned on the TV, flipped from one channel to the next and gave up after ten minutes. Restless, she mumbled to herself. The pool, she could go swimming. But she had already been in that day. Was that her mother's voice that whined in her ear? Why not twice? Why couldn't she go swimming more than once a day? Very stood up and found her suit and pulled it on. It was still a little wet and cooled her skin. She put on a pair of long shorts and a jacket. She checked on the cat, who seemed very happy to doze and groom without her company.

The warm spring air cheered her. She started walking towards the pool and wondered if she would run into anyone else. Also, would people be at the pool this time of night? Maybe. It was the adventure of it, the digging into her new home, starting a new phase of her life. She listened to the traffic noises just outside the community, but all appeared quiet and sleeping within. She walked slowly, savoring the solitude and somber scenery. Trees, with their new spring leaves, cast shadows and small bushes hid small wildlife.

She avoided the clubhouse, with only a few lights still on inside, and let herself into the recreational section of the grounds. The gate clanged shut behind her and she looked around. No one was splashing in the pool, the barbecue area had the lights doused for the night and the tennis and pickle ball courts lay in ghostly secretive quiet. There was no one there.

Very walked around to the back side of the pool enclosure, closest to the hot tub. She wanted to be the one to see someone, not have anyone see her. She cursed the loud click of the gate and slipped into the large pool enclosure, keeping to the shadows near the changing rooms. She stepped out into the light. The pool lights were on, as well as the small hidden lights that illuminated the cover plants. It looked romantic. Or was it sinister?

She walked quietly towards a group of lounge chairs to set her things down, or maybe to sit in the lounge chair and not go swimming after all. Just as she reached the chair, a huge figure arose like a leviathan out of the deep.

"G'day." Davy stood before her.

The hairs on the back of Very's neck curled and straightened. Her stomach did a lift and she found a large lump in her throat that caused her to suck for air. She looked up at him, realizing that he was even taller than she imagined, inches taller than she. And his arms were long, like great tentacles that could easily reach up and throw a towel over a CCTV camera that hid in the tree branches of the hot tub.

Where was Davy that night? It was just one week ago, about this time of night. Had she seen him? She tore back through her memory. Was he there?

"Are you asking if I was here that night?"

Very gasped. Had she said that out loud, or was he reading her mind?

"Are you talking to me? What is it you want to know?"

Very gasped weakly and looked him directly in the face, trying to judge him.

"Where was I? Well, right here with the rest of you, at the party."

"No, you weren't. You had left." Very looked up to the heavens to help her recapture her memories of the people and the place. There were a lot of people, a lot of movement, and Very hadn't been totally sober. But she hoped the blank black sky would cooperate and aid her recall. "You had a fight with Peter Gunn and you left. You weren't there when we were singing. We missed you and your voice. Someone asked, 'Where's Davy's voice? We need that big booming noise to help us keep on pitch and remember the words.' You had gone."

"Oh, I was there, but I was pushed out. That's what Pete did to me. Always pushing me out. Push, push. We don't want you, we don't need you, you don't belong here."

"But of course, you belong here, don't you live here? Own a house? That's not fair, everyone has a right to go to the parties and participate in everything. No one can prevent others from joining."

"But that's what he tried to do. He said things to me, things I'll never forget."

"He's passed on now, so maybe we can just let bygones be bygones?"

"I saw those three witches. I knew what they were up to. 'Here, Petey, have some cookies.' 'Here, Peter baby, have this drink that I made especially for you.' 'Oh you poor thing, here's some special cream for your sunburn.' And she tried to rub it on. But Petey was having none of it. He yelled at them. Nasty guy. Didn't you hear it? Didn't everyone hear it? Those three, up to no good, that was obvious. Evil little witches, all three."

Very hesitated. Did everyone in Five Points know about the cookies, the cream and the drink? Was this common knowledge, but no one would talk of it openly? Surely, not evil witches!

"But how do you know that? How could you see it if you weren't there?" Very shook her head with annoyance, or was it fear?

"You, all of you, think that because I am so big that I am always visible. I have my ways, I know all the nooks and crannies around here. And my ears, while large and misshapen, can still hear. It was a mistake that Peter Gunn made. A long time ago, years and years ago."

"You've known each other for years? I thought that…"

"That I came from Down Under last week? No, I met Petey years ago, when we were still kids. I was on a high school exchange trip, so we went to school together for a year. A long time for a kid to be bullied and spat upon and have anyone who tried to be friends pushed away. A lot of others took him up on his abuse. Including Mr. Tom."

"Mr. Tom was nice, a real nice guy. What does he have to do with Peter Gunn?"

"I told you, he was in on it."

Very sputtered. "No. I never heard anyone say anything about you, except the usual nice things."

"Mr. Tom was a friend of Gunn's and he didn't do anything, that's the problem. I might have said he was okay, but I was wrong. He didn't push back, he should have."

"But Mr. Tom died weeks ago." Very felt a frisson of anxiety. "We already had this conversation."

"Ah, so you think that just because someone died a few weeks ago that they had nothing to do with it? Oh, poor Mr. Tom has gone to his maker, and so he had nothing to do with it. You, lady, are naïve. Those three witches took you in, hook, line and sinker; their antics were part of it too."

"They were there," Very said softly.

"And you forgive them everything, because they are 'nice' ladies, part of the gang. They killed him. They killed my best friend."

Forgetting to be afraid, Very lashed out, "No they didn't. And your best friend? Since when? All that stuff may have made him feel bad, they even admitted that, but they didn't kill him. Whoever threw the towel over the camera, that's who killed him."

"What towel? What camera?" Davy said with increasing menace, leaning forward, coming within inches of Very, who stepped back.

"Don't make me out to be stupid. There was a towel there, all wet and mushy. I stepped on it. We all know, we all saw the video being covered up with a towel. It was Peter's towel, wasn't it? You covered up the camera and then you pushed him under. I saw the video. I know what happened." Very stood strong, but quaked inside.

"There was nothing on the video. Anyone who says there was is lying, making it up. Besides, why would I want to kill my best friend? Huh? Maybe as a little joke, we were always joking, Peter and I."

"So, you did push his head under?"

"Did I say that?"

"Was it a joke? But if you held him under, isn't that just the same as murdering him?"

"Drinking, maybe a little drugged, can that count too?" Davy swayed a little, as if he had been drinking and was now unsteady on his feet.

"So it was easy, was it? He was drowsy from the hot tub, from drinking, and you just thought a small push, a little foot on his head, just a wee shove, to teach him a lesson…" Very surprised herself with a boldness that had come from someone or somewhere else.

"He bullied me, always. Made fun of me, my big ears, my funny accent, the problems I had with understanding American slang. Whatever a sixteen-year-old could think of, he did. And it didn't stop when I came back here. He started all over again. He talked behind my back, told little lies, untruths, set people against me, made people hate me."

"No, people hated him! Don't you see, when a nasty person tells a story about someone, everyone believes the opposite. I've never heard any bad stories about you."

"Really? Everyone loves me? Naw. They despise me, and it was all his fault. He spread the lies, the rumors. He never stopped bullying."

"That's right, he never stopped and you were not the only one. No one here liked him. But pushing his head under water? Really, you did that?"

Davy was silent, but Very could hear his breathing, deep breaths, building, building, faster, faster. "You don't know what you're talking about. Blather, blather. That video, fake. No one can see anything."

"The towel," Very said. "It will have your DNA on it. They can tell. They can get evidence that way. It will be the last thing on that towel. You didn't wash it off, did you? It's there. They know."

Davy stood tall and took a short step closer to Very. "Speculation, all speculation."

The certainty of her speculations hit her. She remembered to be afraid. The prophetic words Davy had spoken on the first day she had met him came back to her. "Someday, someone should hold his head under water in his precious hot tub." She was alone here, with a killer. She inched backwards.

He grew large. He took a deep breath and his chest expanded, his arms lifted out to the sides, his legs spread apart. He reached out.

Very's immediate reactions were arrested. She always did this when faced with danger. Others had a fight or flight response, but Very was a deer in the headlights. She froze like a scared rabbit. Fighting was not an option with this colossus. One blow of his arm and she would go flying. One head butt and she would be totally winded. His grip would crush her arm. Flight was her only chance. Flight. Fly. Go.

She backed up and turned to run.

There was a click and then the lights went out. They faded slowly, but within seconds, the darkness was complete.

All around Very were tables, chairs, umbrellas, bushes and fences. All black, dark and all in her way. She saw a dark black space and moved swiftly towards it. Behind her, she heard the sound of scattering chairs, a loud 'ooooph' and footsteps.

Go, run.

Chapter Twenty-six: The Chase

But instead of running, she froze. She couldn't run any farther without being able to see. She let her eyes adjust and listened. A loud noise in the pool enclosure full of deck furniture let her know that he was still there and where he was. She saw a bush in front of her and to the side. She stealthily moved towards it and hunkered down. She turned to face the pool and realized that two small lights, attached to the clubhouse, were still on, giving some small amount of light to the scene. She turned away from them and tried to look at the blackest thing she could. Let her eyes adjust. She stilled her breathing and listened. She could hear muttered curses and the smack of a hand onto chairs and tables.

She looked up. The illumination from street lights, the small spots on the clubhouse and the glow from the sky gave her enough to see the outlines of the larger obstacles around her. But she was disoriented, and she wasn't familiar with the buildings, the bushes, the trees, the courts, the steps, the benches. And Davy was. He had said that he knew all the nooks and crannies. He knew the people, the conversations, the stories, the secrets. He was a collector, of all that went on in Five Points. He knew what had happened on that fateful night, he knew the comings and goings, and he thought he had been safe. Until Very showed up. Until she had goaded him. What had she said? What had made him essentially confess to her? It was not he who had sent the video out. Was it? Did he have the desire, as many criminals do, to brag about his deeds? Is that what coming here tonight was all about?

Stop, better not to go over irrelevant things at this point. He was a big man, he could harm her. Did he know that she had come alone? Had told no one where she was going? Who would wander around the pool at this time of night? The lights had gone out exactly the same way last week. Or had they? Had someone forced the lights to go out? Had Davy managed to get at the main switch and turn out the lights, thinking that everyone would assume the management had done it? They had said that, didn't they? The others had said the lights went out because someone cut them out, making them realize it was late and time to leave. But it wasn't the staff. Management wouldn't turn out the lights when so many people were standing around. It would have been dangerous and the staff knew that creating hazards like that was a big no-no. Insurance would be foremost on their minds. It was Davy. He turned off the lights, so that he could push Fat Man Gunn's head underwater.

Now was the time to get away, call the police. But he knew this place so much better than she. Could she outrun him? That she couldn't count on. She was capable of running, but to run faster than he?

Her phone. She had gotten into the habit of leaving her phone at home when she went out walking or to the pool. After the wild chase up the bluffs, she had made it a point to have her phone with her, charged, whenever she left the house. But here, with the quiet community, the locked gates, surrounded by people, she had felt safe. Shout? Could she shout and call someone to her rescue? Ah, making noise would only call attention to her own hiding place.

She shifted herself and tried to hunker down in the deeper shadows. She put her head down, trying to make her eyes adjust to the slightest light. When she opened them, she found two small round eyes, red in color, staring at her. Rabbit? No, rabbits' eyes were one on either side of its head. These were two small eyes directly looking at her. As her eyes adjusted, she could see a pale fur coat.

Then the animal opened its mouth, and hissed. Large, sharp teeth presented themselves and a rank animal odor came Very's way. She breathed in through her mouth and tried to put some distance between herself and the possum. "Tsst, go play possum," she whispered.

She listened. She heard small noises from the pool area. Was Davy still trying to look for her? Did he have any idea where she had gone? Was it better to stay where she was, or try to make a dash for it? He knew this place. Stay where she was.

She shifted her crouch, finding her legs and back starting to ache and then freeze up. The possum reacted to her movement and turned to scamper away. It made a noise in the undergrowth, scattering leaves and brushing against branches as it slowly exited.

"Oh, ho! I hear you!"

Very heard the heavy rumble of a large man making a path through the patio furniture. She jumped and began to run, hoping the path she chose was clear of the furniture and that the hot tub was where she thought it was. It was surrounded with heavy bushes. She made it to the enclosure, but the police tape wasn't just a decorative loop-de-loop, but a veritable forest of tightly twined tape. Not the place to hide. Go towards the pool, get to the other side.

She ran and then stopped when she thought she had come to the edge. She misjudged and slipped. "Splash!"

She went in feet first and so found her footing easily. But she heard the shout.

"Aha! Gotcha!" a big object splashed beside Very.

"Ahhhhhh," she put her feet onto the pool bottom and pushed off. Swim, she needed to get those arms moving.

She felt the light sweater she was wearing pull from her back. She reached to the front and jerked on the one button holding it together. Then she flung her arms out and let the sweater be tugged off.

"Yeahhhhh. You can't get away from me," Davy shouted as he pulled on the flimsy garment.

Very swam, put her arms out and thrashed for all she was worth. Not knowing where she was, Very knew that if she swam in a straight line, she would reach the other side. Disoriented, Very went on, finally leaving the shouting and thrashing behind her.

She turned and looked behind her. Her eyes were beginning to adjust to the low lights now and she could see the water in the pool, the edges, the deck, the tall palm trees that surrounded it. She took a few seconds to find the shallow steps that would take her directly out of the pool and away.

She leaned over and put her arms out, pushing off from the bottom. She felt the wave, the splashing behind her. Changing direction, she headed for the closest side of the pool. In three strokes, she touched the side. The stairs would have been easier, but this was faster. She hoped.

She reached for the edge with both hands, getting a purchase and then balancing her hands flat on the edge. She sank into the pool until her feet hit the bottom, then she sank some more until she knew she had room to push off and up to the edge.

Whoosh, her body leapt out of the water. Twist, twist, she told herself and landed butt first on the edge, feet still in the water.

She saw and felt at the same time, a hand grip her ankle. Kick, kick, push, push. First one foot and then both, together.

Bang! The noise reverberated across the water and was accompanied with a loud keening whine. "You bitch, you broke my nose!"

Very backed away from the edge and stood. She turned, leaving the hulk in the pool with what may have been a nasty injury. Breathing heavily, Very ran. She saw the gazebo's white lattice struts and headed for it, dodging the bushes and large boulders.

Before she reached it, she realized that she had lost a sandal. One waterproof sandal still clung to her foot, but the other had been torn off somewhere. She bent over and ran to the far side of the structure. Crouching down, she looked toward the pool. It was quiet. She saw nothing. She listened, trying to quiet her own breath. She heard the drip, drip, drip of water dribbling from her clothes. There was movement in the pool area, but she wasn't able to see anything.

She looked behind her. There was a wall all the way around the clubhouse grounds. A dirt path had been made there for walkers and the gardeners. It hugged the wall for most of the length, although Very couldn't tell where exactly she was. But it was here and if she went in this direction, she would come to the gate.

The gate, the gate to the outside. The street lights illuminated the sidewalks and the street. If there was a late-night traveler, she could stop them. It was easier outside than here, hemmed in by walls, hedges and places she was unfamiliar with in the dark.

In a burst of speed, Very struck out along the dirt path. She heard the squish of her sandaled foot and felt the rough, rock-strewn path with her unshod foot. Squish, ouch, squish, ouch. She pushed on. She also felt her wet, now clinging clothes. Her capris bunched in her crotch, her shirt grabbed at her arms and the cool night air raised goose bumps on her arms. She slowed.

Then she heard it, heavy breathing and plodding steps. She turned to look behind her. The sheltered path let no light in and the only thing that met her eyes was a deep inky blackness. She turned and went forward, more slowly now.

There, there was an opening and a way to get off the path and hide behind a bush. She slipped off the path and into the tight break. She dipped down and waited.

Whoosh. Whoosh. Slap, slap. Davy's heavy bulk lumbered along the path and passed Very in her hiding place.

When she heard him stop and rustle the bushes, Very decided on a risky plan. Run, run as fast as she could, in the opposite direction.

She leapt out, turned in the opposite direction and forced her legs to power up. Skip the irritation of the chafing, ignore the rough ground cutting into her bare foot, heat her body with adrenaline and run. As fast as she could. Ignore the lumbering elephant behind her.

Then she heard a thump, an oof and a ground-shaking whomp. Davy had fallen. Tripped on a rock, a branch or his own feet? No time to ascertain. He would be on his feet in no time and chasing her again.

She knew his secret, what he had done. He was hell-bent on silencing her. She needed to get out, go home. The fallen body was not her primary concern.

She ran along the wall until it opened up, just on the other side of the gazebo. She stepped out into the open area. She could see easily here, near the two small spotlights on the clubhouse and the streetlights. The gate. She saw it on the other side of the patio. But she also saw a clear path to it. She walked more slowly, trying to pick her way on the easier brick and cement patio.

Then she saw it, the gate. She lunged at the bar and felt it open under her push. She fell out of the gate and slammed it behind her. She stood and breathed for ten beats, then struck off for home.

It was only eight minutes, but Very attempted to make it in six. Her unclad foot hampered her stride. But the streetlamps looked as bright as day to her. The silence of the streets was eerie. It wasn't late. Wasn't there anyone coming home late? Wasn't anyone out on a late date? Gone to a movie, a concert, to visit a relative or friend? Very looked around, but saw no late-night travelers, no last chance dog walkers, not even any stray wildlife visitors from the outside.

At her door, Very struggled to find her keys, but they had been tucked deeply into her pants pocket and had survived the running and the pool dunking. Once inside, she locked the door behind her and rushed to grab for her phone.

"Darrell, I need you now. It's a long story, but I went to the clubhouse and found Davy there, Big Davy and he confessed, or rather I think he did. Anyway, he thought he had, so he chased me and I fell into the pool and he grabbed at me and I lost my shoe and now I'm home. But I need to go back. But I can't go alone."

"Don't worry, I'm coming. Give me your gate code again."

Very spat it out from memory and waited while he wrote it down. "Come quickly, please, please."

"I have your back, Very. You know that. I am your knight in shining armor."

Chapter Twenty-seven: Return to the Pool

Very quickly stripped off her clothes and took a short, hot shower. Cleopatra walked around the house mewing loudly. She knew that something bad had happened. It was not that she could do anything, but she wanted to add her voice to the chaos that streamed around her. The perfect pet, one who empathizes.

Very toweled her hair dry and put on warmer than needed clothes. She needed the heavy sweatshirt to cover her fear as well as her cold body. She listened for a car as she collected a flashlight and put it into a small backpack. It was the same backpack that had survived the journey up the side of the bluffs when she was being chased by the crazed drug dealer. The one with a gun. Now, she wished that she had a weapon, but had no intention of getting a gun. Maybe the flashlight would do, it was extremely heavy.

Very listened for Darrell's car and was at the curb before he could get out. "To the clubhouse," she demanded.

As they drove, Darrell asked Very to fill him in as much as she could.

"I went there this evening. I thought it would be quiet. I wanted to see the place in a quiet mood. But Davy, big Davy, was there. We talked. I told him I had seen the video tape. He didn't say he had done it, it was short of that, but he got very scared, or perhaps excited, when I said they could get DNA off the towel that was thrown over the camera. Maybe exaggerating there. Who knows if it was the towel or not. And if it was his or Peter Gunn's and if it was pulled over the camera or not. I was, perhaps, unwisely, throwing out ideas."

"Accusations, maybe?"

"Anyway, he started chasing me. I ran. But the lights were out. And I fell into the pool and then he chased me around to the back, where there's a small path. Then I heard him fall and that was all."

"So why are we going back there?" Darrell asked as they pulled into the empty parking lot.

"Park there," Very pointed to a parking space just next to the big service gate. Beside the big gate, normally locked with a padlock, was the small entry gate for people.

"The lights are back on, good. Maybe it will be easier this way."

As they neared the small 'person' gate, Very realized that, although there were lights scattered around everywhere now, they were a small fraction of the normal evening lighting pattern. Ambiance lights, Very would call them. They lit the undersides of bushes, outlined the trees, but they didn't quite make it easy to walk. Just enough to barely see.

Very took out her key fob and tried it on the gate. The monitor buzzed, but refused to let her in. She tried it again, and then again. "Damn, they must have locked the keypad at some point. Maybe when they locked up the lodge earlier. Or maybe it is on a timer."

"What do we do now? Is there another way in?" Darrell whined. "Maybe we should call the police."

"Not yet. You sound like you are glad we are locked out. But I know a place where we can probably get in. I don't know if there is security at that point, I would guess not, but let's try."

Very began to walk around the outside of the clubhouse enclosure. At one point, there were houses that abutted the grounds, but Very walked on. She muttered to herself about the lack of traffic.

"But these are old folks' houses. Aren't they all in bed by this time of night?" Darrell asked.

"Really Darrell! Are you going to just curl up and die when you hit sixty? Of course not, you are going to retire, take your savings and buy a place like this. You will play golf, or pickle ball, or pool, or cards, or whatever. You will go on vacations and out to dinner with your fellow retirees. You will be active. And that generally means that on a Saturday night, you might be out. Maybe not dancing and raving, but out." Very felt her energy flagging, but pushed on to round the corner.

"Here, we can find a place to get over here."

In front of them lay a long cement block wall surrounding the clubhouse grounds. They walked along it, while Very periodically reached up to look over. At one point, she turned back to Darrell with a hopeful look and went a few more feet. A tree hung over the fence, but the ground was marginally higher here in comparison to the wall.

"This is good, help me get up." Very indicated that he should cup his hands and help her get up and over the fence.

"Okay," he agreed tentatively, bending over and cupping his hands.

Very stepped gingerly into the stirrup and said, "Push." He gave a thrust and Very grabbed the top of the fence. Her shoes stuck to the concrete and she was up. She balanced on the top of the wall and grabbed a branch of the tree. With the other hand, she encouraged Darrell to grab her hand. "Use your shoes like climbing shoes. This is an easy rock wall, because of the concrete blocks, they're sticky."

Darrell huffed and puffed, but he, too made it up to the wall. The tree branches helped their descent and soon they were on the small dirt path. They looked out towards the pool area, which seemed well-lit compared to the depths of the mini forest near the wall.

"No security alarms. But that doesn't mean there aren't quiet alarms. Let's go, this way. But watch for Davy."

"What does he look like?" Darrell whispered.

"Big man, older, but light on his feet. Quiet."

Very started down the narrow dirt path in one direction and soon they came to an opening. She stopped, turned, looked, shook her head. "Do you see any footprints here?"

Darrell looked down and then asked for a flashlight. Very took off her small pack and stuck her hand inside, retrieving the long large three 'C' battery light. She pushed the button on the end of the handle and a bright round of light struck the ground at their feet.

Very gasped. An obviously bare foot print stared back at her. "Ooogh, just mine. At least we know I was here tonight." She shone the light around and identified a larger shoe print, also very fresh, and slightly wet. "We both went in the pool and then we left watery marks everywhere. But let's go this way, these shoe prints seem to be the ones on top, the latest."

They followed the imprints for a few yards, then stopped. Nothing. Dry, leaf covered path lay before them.

"We're going the wrong direction." Very swiveled and bumped into Darrell who followed too closely.

"How do you know?" Darrell asked. "You said this way, now it's that way. Which way were your feet pointing?"

Very looked out through the bushes. "The pool is there, the hot tub is just beyond that. There is the gazebo, there is the clubhouse. Let's head for the gazebo, and then I can get my bearings. Look for any signs of the big man having fallen. I never heard him get up. Frankly, I'm afraid that he is still here, injured. I'm afraid I left him here."

"Let's hope you left him here. Not following you home."

"But that is not good, to leave a man down. But you understand why I couldn't come alone?"

"Yes, I understand. And that's why I brought this." Darrell reached into the pocket of his pants and pulled out a gun.

"Good god, man, where did that come from?" Very shrank back into the branches.

"I have your back. Isn't that what you wanted?" Darrell's whine was small but unmistakable.

"Yes, I wanted you to have my back. But a gun?"

"It's not a very big one and at the moment, it's not loaded." Darrell reached again into the pocket and took out a box of ammunition. He opened the small box and shook out a few bullets.

Very watched him load the gun and put on the safety. He was right, it wasn't very big. But it looked like the lethal weapon that it was. Very armed herself with the flashlight.

"This way," she said, slipping through the bushes and walking softly towards the gazebo. Once there, they stopped and listened.

"I can't be totally lost, and I can't believe I have forgotten where I went and what I did. First I fell into the pool. When I got out, I wandered a bit, then I came here. Then I took to the small path and Davy followed me. I heard him fall. That's for sure. It was a great big ooffy fall. Like the wind got knocked out of him, or maybe he hit some soft body part or his head or back or something. Then I ran, but I never heard him get up and I never heard him following me again. Of course, I got the hell out. So, what happened to Davy?"

"We can look back along the path, which way did you go?" Darrell held himself tall, but with the gun in his hand.

Very closed her eyes, trying to recreate the panicked run. She ran it through her mind, then turned to Darrell. "This way." She set off along the path with Darrell following. "Careful with that little weapon of yours." She threw this comment over her shoulder as they made their way slowly along the darkened path.

"It's mostly for show, anyway," he replied. "It's because I'm a licensed PI. I get a concealed carry permit."

"Quiet," Very said. They walked carefully along the path, Very using the flashlight to sweep the ground from side to side, looking for something different.

She stopped. Darrell came up behind her. He stepped around her, gripping his gun. "What is it?"

"There," she pointed with the flashlight. She moved it gently from side to side and then into the bushes. "Broken branches. And divots."

"What?" Darrell asked, coming closer to get a better look.

"Holes in the ground, soft holes, like a big man falling, and using his elbows and knees to break his fall. And this rock and this branch. She reached down and touched the ground. "It's wet."

"Blood?" Darrell asked, fear invading his voice.

"Water," Very said, shining the light on her hand to show the absence of any red stuff. "This is where he must have landed. But he's not here now. He must have gotten up and gone. Where did he go?"

Very swept the area with the light, trying to find more clues about the chase, the fall and where Davy was now. She swung the light in an ever farther circle and then stopped. "My sandal. There's my sandal. How did it get here? I lost it by the pool, I think, I don't know." She reached for it and picked it up.

"No, leave it there," said Darrell.

"Why? It's mine. I recognize it. And I lost it here just an hour ago."

"Possible evidence. Well, now you have picked it up, handled it. Poof, the evidence is gone."

"Evidence of what? Losing my sandal? What? A murder weapon? The man chasing me? Oh, give me a break. There wasn't a crime here, except maybe last week. And it wasn't me 'losing' my sandal. Look, the Velcro has come loose, end of story."

"So, where is this man who you said confessed to the crime and then started chasing you? Where did he go?"

"Hiding," Very answered.

"We've been all around here. There is no one hiding here. He's a big guy. And we've made enough noise. The lights are obviously on 'nighttime' mode, just enough to see, but not burning too much energy. And this enclosure isn't that big. Let's go, one more circuit and then we say he's gone. Okay?"

"You're right. It was so much scarier when I was alone, it was dark and he was yelling things at me."

"Okay, let's go. Do we have to go over the fence again?" Darrell asked distastefully.

"Wait, wait," Very said, pulling out her phone. She took some photos of the slight indentations in the ground. "Just in case he comes back and tries to deny it."

They crept quietly across the pool deck, avoiding the chairs and tables that had been overturned. Very pointed to a spot that she identified as the place where she had heaved herself out of the pool. A small wet area was all that was left. Footsteps had dried up. As they came out into the open, not far from the gate, they stopped and Very looked back.

"What?" Darrell asked.

"Just checking. We looked, but he might still be here."

A high-pitched squeak was followed by the ghostly appearance of a set of white wings that silently flapped near Very's head. "Ahhhhh," she screamed.

Darrell ducked and stared as the wraith flew away. "What was that? Oh god, a ghost. The ghost of a dead man."

"An owl."

"That is a bad omen, if there ever was one," Darrell answered, quivering.

"No, it was just an owl, a barn owl. They live here too."

Chapter Twenty-eight: Another Death

Very and Darrell went out the gate easily. Very was sure they wouldn't lock the mechanism for getting out of the clubhouse grounds. Insurance considerations. They jumped into Darrell's car and within minutes were back in Very's house. When they got into the house, Very locked the door. She went around the house and checked all of the windows and doors, including the locking mechanism to the garage door. She doubled checked the sliding back door.

"Very, why are you locking everything? He wasn't there."

"Aha, that is why. Where is he? Where did he go? Did he go home? Did he come here? Will he come back here? No, Darrell, I'm scared. And I'm locking up everything. How could I sleep otherwise?" Very paced nervously up and down the long hallway.

"Do you know where he lives? Can we go check on him? Make sure he got back safely? I'll be with you. And I've got this," he patted his pocket.

"No. I mean, I don't know where he lives and I wouldn't want to go there even with you and your…weapon." Very sat on the couch. "Oh, I don't know what I want to do. I'm tired."

"Hot cocoa?" suggested Darrell. "Whiskey?"

"You know, the cocoa sounds good. Want some?" Very set about finding hot chocolate and milk, stirring and heating.

They sat at the dining room table. Very pulled the drapes and cut most of the lights. They looked on the back yard, now bathed in light from the street lights on the next street.

Cleopatra trotted across the lawn and headed for the back door.

"What the…" Very jumped up and opened the back door. "In, Kitty, in. How did you get out?"

Cleopatra ran in and meowed. Very checked her food dish and gave her some treats.

"Very," began Darrell tentatively. "We need to call the police."

"And tell them what? I mean, I know that Davy basically confessed to murder, but it wasn't exactly. So, I don't even have hearsay evidence to tell them. It's all 'he said, she said, I saw this, I know that' and nothing exact or specific. Maybe tomorrow, or Monday." Very sat on the couch and sighed deeply. "I'm worried about him, as a human being, because I think he hurt himself. But I am scared of him as well."

Silence hung over the room. Darrell got up and started wandering around the room, looking at the pictures and hangings on the wall, the cabinets full of strange objects, the souvenirs standing in corners and placed on top of the book cases. "Where'd this come from?" he asked, picking up an ebony carved mask.

Distractedly, Very looked at the black wooden object. "Borneo."

"And this?" Darrell held out a long walking stick with Chinese characters written on the sides. A bell was attached to the top by a string. "Japanese. The stick I took on the Eighty-Eight Temples Pilgrimage."

"A Pilgrimage? Like the Camino de Santiago? Walking?"

"Yeah, only longer. Well, if you do the whole thing, it's generally longer. It took me fifty-four days, about twelve hundred kilometers. I literally walked my butt off. Toned up the muscles."

"I had no idea you traveled so much, and such, interesting travel."

Very laughed. "The old maid school teacher? Never goes anywhere, never does anything? I had every summer off and during most of them I went places. I volunteered in orphanages, helped set up libraries, even helped in medical procedures for cleft palates. Not doing surgery, but support staff. I traveled, I visited places, I met people. I had a full life, including love affairs, dangerous mountain climbing, jumping from planes; you name it, it did it. I am not a shrinking violet. In the last few years, my mother needed me more and I stayed at home. Then I retired and I haven't quite decided what to do with my life. Moving here was a start."

"And looking for Frankie Monroe?" Darrell prompted.

"That was a fluke. Just something that happened. It was a thing that needed done. Maybe it gave some purpose to my life. The travel became a bit tedious. Travel for the sake of moving, checking off countries and World Heritage sites, one thousand places to see before I die? And collecting souvenirs."

"Nice carpet here," Darrell said, swiping his foot across the red camel's hair carpet in the living room.

"Bought in Bokhara, Uzbekistan, but made in Afghanistan."

"Okay, I'll stop asking. You surprise me."

"As I said, old maid librarian. Everybody thinks they know who I am."

Very collected the cups and put them in the sink. "It's late, stay here tonight. I need the protection, small gun though it is."

Darrell looked at Very with surprise and nervousness.

"You can stay in the front bedroom. Own bath, towels on the racks and the sheets are clean. I need the feeling of not being alone. I...I don't trust Davy." Very looked at Darrell. "Okay, is that okay? No complications?"

"Sure." Darrell said with a nervous twitch.

"I wouldn't impose, but you do understand, don't you? I just don't want to be here in this house, tonight, alone."

"Yes, I understand. It's okay. In fact, I don't know if I'd be safe driving home. I'm really tired and wound up."

"I hope you sleep well."

The clock said 6:45am. Very put some more kibble in the cat's dish and put her swimming suit on. It was light, the gardeners were already here, what was there to be afraid of?

When she arrived, she found two swimmers already in the pool. She joined them. They all swam their laps with no chatting. Very was sure she couldn't have done it otherwise.

It was cold when she got out, so she hurried on home. As she let herself into the house, she heard rustling from the kitchen. She flicked on the hall light and was met with Darrell standing at the end of the hall.

His small gun was pointed directly at her.

"Oh Darrell, who did you think it was?" Very slipped past him and into her bedroom, closing the door. She shouted through the door, "Coffee is in the pantry! I'll just do a quick shower."

As soon as she got out, she set to making a big breakfast, eggs, toast, hash browns, fresh pineapple. They sat on the patio eating. Cleopatra spent the entire meal rubbing against their legs, first Very's, then Darrell's and then back again. She purred as she did it and Very felt the soothing nature of her cat's purrs.

There was a knock on the door, a noise that was faint to Very, but it was repeated, louder. Very looked at Darrell.

"I'll get my gun and be right behind you."

"I'll look through the door peephole before I start opening doors," Very said as she scurried down the hallway. She stopped at the door and pressed her eye to the peephole.

She pulled the door open, even though she could feel the heat of Darrell's body as he stood behind her. "MaryAnne, Becky! So early."

Becky looked at her watch, "Well, not really. But we had to come."

MaryAnne jumped in, "Have you heard? Have you heard it through the grapevine? The gossip mill?"

"I guess not. Heard what?"

"Davy was found dead this morning!" Becky blurted.

Darrell looked out from behind Very and stood open-mouthed staring at the women.

MaryAnne's eyebrows raised into her bangs. A question, an accusation, wonderment?

Very, seeing MaryAnne and Becky's faces, said quickly, "Just a friend. Not to worry. Actually, he's a colleague. Nothing to see here." She turned to Darrell and urged furtively, "Hide that thing." She turned back to the door. "Coffee, ladies? Tell me everything." She stepped back and held the door open.

They trooped in and headed straight for the dining room. Very made a new pot of coffee and they waited until it had brewed and they were seated.

"Now, tell me all. Davy is dead and he was found this morning. Where?" Very tried to quell the feelings of fear, tried to keep her voice even and calm.

"At home. Just dead. Nothing seemed to have happened. Maybe a heart attack. That hits you quick, doesn't it? And you might not even know about your heart. Absence makes the heart grow fonder," MaryAnne babbled.

"His friend Don had a date to play pool. Get in early on a Sunday sort of thing," Becky resumed the tale. "Davy didn't show up, so Don went to his house. He banged on the door, everything. He called on his phone and by putting his ear against the door, he heard the phone ringing inside. He knew where the house key was hidden and let himself in. Lying on the floor of the kitchen. Dead, just dead."

"Didn't you hear the sirens? Where there's smoke, there's fire. Once burned, twice shy." MaryAnne said.

Very looked up and shook her head, "I didn't hear…"

Darrell intervened, "I did, but you can't think too much about it around here, can you? Must have lots of call for ambulances and such."

"When was this?" Very looked concerned. "Maybe it was while I was in the pool."

They all offered opinions on the time. Very disregarded this. Maybe she didn't want to hear any more sirens and so she didn't.

"We were wondering," began Becky, "if you had spoken to him lately, or seen him?"

"Why do you ask?" sputtered Very.

MaryAnne leaned forward, "The police are looking for you. They have a video, from last night. Honesty is the best policy. Hope for the best, prepare for the worst. No time like the present."

"And you're on it," interrupted Becky.

"How do you know this?" Very breathed evenly, trying to appear calm, even though her hands were shaking.

"The police are at the clubhouse. They asked the girl at the desk who the person was, but she didn't know. So she directed them to us. Asked us to look at it."

"And we recognized you. Knowledge is power. Keep your friends close and your enemies…" MaryAnne started to say.

Becky pushed herself forward again. "But we pretended we weren't sure what your name was. Only thing we said was that you were new here. Makes it more difficult to look you up. Anyway, we left."

"And came straight here. Heads up. The police are coming for you. I think they have questions. The squeaky wheel gets the grease. People who live in glass houses shouldn't throw stones."

"Why question me?" Very asked.

"Because Davy was on that tape as well. The last person standing? Two heads are better than one. Two wrongs don't make a right."

"What were you doing there?" Becky asked.

"I, I, went to see the place. Again. I have been having trouble sleeping and I've been thinking too much. So, I thought if I went back there, I could put the past behind me. I, I didn't think very clearly."

"Very," Darrell interrupted. "Where's your phone? I'm calling Sanchez."

MaryAnne looked at Darrell. "Who's that? The lawyer? The Go-To Man? The Fixer?"

"No, no just a friend." Very's voice fell to a squeak. "In law enforcement." She heard Darrell speaking to Joey and the words, 'come immediately.'

MaryAnne fussed in the kitchen. "The police will be here soon, I'm sure and they need a fresh pot of coffee, so come on, Becky, let's get to making it. Busy hands make short work. There's no place like home, and a fresh cup of coffee. If you want something done right, do it yourself."

Very saw Cleopatra through the glass on the back door. She looked scared. A new person last night, two new people now. What would she think of police and Joey and Bobby Sanchez, all at once.

The doorbell rang, Cleo took off, under the bushes in the back. Very moved slowly towards the door. "Joey, Bobby!"

"We were on our way to Mass. Darrell said immediately, so here we are. This had better be important." Joey pushed her way in. Bobby followed, dressed in a sports jacket and freshly laundered and ironed shirt. Both, wearing their Sunday best.

MaryAnne and Becky scurried out the door, saying over their shoulders, "Coffee." And "Freshly made, and done right."

"What is it this time?" Bobby said quietly.

"Davy died and I think he may have confessed to murder. Before he died. To me. Well, maybe he confessed."

"Rewind, Very. Start from the beginning." Joey sat on the couch, in the seat vacated by MaryAnne. Bobby stood, feet apart, hands behind his back. At attention.

Very sat, took a deep breath and narrated the last night's events. Calmly. Methodically. She left out some bits. One was the 'confession', if indeed it was. Very grew more and more confused the more she told the tale. She couldn't remember exactly what he said, so she paraphrased. When she got to the part where Darrell accompanied her, she gave the tale over to him.

Darrell was methodical as well, and he also left out pieces of the story. The gun, for one thing, was conveniently forgotten.

Very jumped up. "I never touched him. Never. He grabbed for me, look, here are the bruises from his grip on my leg. But I never did anything to him. Well, a few pushes with my feet. But I had nothing to do with his death. God, I don't even know where he lives. I didn't go there. And when Darrell and I went back, no one was there. No one!"

"Very, the police will ask. Just tell the story, don't make up things, and don't leave anything out. It sounds like he died a natural death. Just the facts, ma'm." Bobby was cool, level-headed and bent forward when he talked to Very, softening his stance.

The doorbell rang, Darrell answered. The police, two officers in uniform, came in and walked the long hallway to the great room.

The interview was swift and, considering the subject matter, calm. Very told the story again, this time more coherently, if not more truthfully.

At one point Joey pointed to her wrist and tapped it. "We are going to catch the next mass. See you tonight, for dinner. You too, Darrell." She and Sargent Sanchez left.

Within minutes, the police also took their leave, cautioning Very that they might have more questions. Darrell showed them out.

They stood in the hallway. Darrell looked tired, he was unshaven and with wrinkled clothes.

"Thanks Darrell. For everything."

"You know Very, if you lie down with dogs, you get up with fleas." He shook his head sorrowfully.

"But…" Very stared at her feet, silent. She felt the barbed rebuke. But could she have avoided the dog, or dogs? Aren't they everywhere? Don't we all have a little dog in us, accompanied with fleas? "Will you come to the Sanchez's for dinner this evening?"

Darrell hung his head. "No, I don't think so. I have something else on."

"Oh, a date?" Very said brightly.

Darrell looked at Very with wide open eyes as his face began to turn a deep red, starting at his neck and seeping upwards.

"It's okay. Don't worry. It was just a polite thing. You won't be missed, much. I guess I can hold my own. You're busy. Nice." Very fumbled to a halt.

Darrell stood at the door and mumbled incoherently.

"And I want to thank you again. What an ending. If it is an ending. And all your discretion, that was much appreciated." Very said with a weariness to her voice.

"Well, at least one thing has been solved. He won't come after you again. Davy won't be bothering you."

"That's convenient. Too convenient. But what did he die of? Did I have anything to do with it, I wonder. Did I do something?"

"No, Very, it wasn't you. He probably died of a guilty conscience."

Chapter Twenty-Nine: The Promise of the Village

Very woke on Monday morning very early. She had come home a little earlier than usual from the Sanchez dinner, but yesterday was a tiring day and she craved her bed. There were no crazed hot tub goers to threaten her, but getting to sleep wasn't easy either. She dreamed of water, of dark gardens; she dreamed of the gazebo as a haunted place; she dreamed of Five Points as an asylum for misfits. She woke up many times, but she was tired and went back to sleep immediately, only to dream again.

Groggy, she made coffee and found the newspaper deposited in the exact center of her driveway. She went to the back porch, and invited the cat to sit on her lap, but Cleopatra declined. She took the paper and her coffee and delighted in the cool morning air. Summer was coming soon and even this early it was going to be too hot to sit like this. She knew to enjoy it while she could. The obituaries were duplicates of Sunday's, the funnies weren't funny and the Sudoku took less than five minutes to do. She leaned her head back and closed her eyes.

Thinking about the last two days was too painful, so she determined to question herself on whether she was glad she had moved to Five Points. Sometimes people, Very included, made decisions that were not the best thought out, but were spur of the moment. Sometimes they were brilliant choices, other times they ended disastrously. Very had thought she contemplated this move to Five Points carefully. She had visited active retirement communities and liked the idea of the communal facilities, the giving up of care for the lawns and bushes and trees. The clubs were a nice way to make friends, get some exercise, get out and socialize. It wasn't as though she needed to drop her other friends, but the proximity of neighbors with the same concerns as she gave her a sense of security, and purpose. The friends she left in the old neighborhood had been her mother's friends, her mother's generation, her mother's choice of companions.

But she knew she had needed to break away, but not too far. She had thought about it, a lot, and was sure this was going to be good for her. It was her choice, her house, her activities. She leaned down and petted Cleopatra, who purred her appreciation. Her own patio, with her plants scattered about.

But, the reality of Five Points was not what she had imagined. Now, there had been four deaths in as many weeks. True, all had been up in years and perhaps not unexpected, but four. It was the one in the hot tub, the one she had found, that gave her nightmares. It seemed as if there were more nightmares this week than last. Getting worse? Like PTSD from the war? At first, it was the horror of it all, and those around could understand. But then, time went on, no one else shared, so the sufferer was alone. Then, the nights brought terror that only daylight could chase away. And then…

Maybe she should see a therapist. Actually, the body was dead, never threatened her. The chase by the big man Davy, now that would be a problem. But that issue was gone as well. Dead? How did he die? Not her, she had nothing to do with it. But still, another dead body. All men, all well past their use-by date.

Did she make a horrible mistake coming here? Was this the right move? Maybe she should have chosen a different place. That big place just up the road, closer to the mouth of the canyon, Luna. Maybe she should have looked a little harder there. Their pool, although much smaller, was rumored to be heated all year. She wanted community. Did it matter which community? She was never going to play pickle ball, but the fact that she could, there was a group, they would teach her how, that was the point.

But all the bickering, the bad vibes, the ill-will, the fighting over the temperature at the pool, the shrubs in front of the clubhouse, who said what to whom and when. This wasn't what she came here for. The three women walking at the pool as Fat Man Gunn sang that ditty about the dusky maid. That kind of stuff was everywhere here. The not-so-subtle racism, the classism, the snubbing of those 'not our sort.' Should she just ignore this and carry on?

On the other hand, would leaving here stop this bad behavior? Would her tepid protest make any difference to the lives of those being swept under the rug? She had heard a man say that this place was so white. No multi-cultural life here. But Very had heard a myriad of languages being spoken as she walked around the cul-de-sacs. Arabic, Korean, Chinese, Spanish and a couple she couldn't recognize, Hindi or Gujarati perhaps. Maybe those people felt that they weren't welcome in the clubs and at the gathering places. But they had as much right to join as anyone here. Was she supposed to be a one-woman campaign against bad manners?

But they kept dying. Would staying here bring her closer to the Marble Forest? What was there about this place that made death so close? Or was it just that all of us are getting older and our day is coming? Sooner rather than later. This wasn't a retirement home or nursing home, or an assisted living place. Assisted dying place was more like it.

No, this was living in the later years. All of us get older, we have aches and pains, we get nasty diseases like cancer and need heart pacemakers and artificial hips. The art of forgetting was coming for all of us like a freight train with its lights off. Fast, furious, full-tilt. All of it, the saggy bosom, the need to take a nap every day at two in the afternoon, the creaky knee joints, the malaise of losing our childhood friends. This was aging, and this was a place to do it with as much dignity and fellowship as was possible.

It was a village. This place was like those old-fashioned small towns. Everyone knew everyone else, and their business. And knowing the neighbor's business was part of it. It was bad in that there was too much gossip, but it also had an upside. Davy's body was found by his neighbor. He knew where the key was hidden, and knew that going inside, looking for his pool playing partner, was what was expected of him. Many here didn't have a child, or sibling, living around the corner. Instead they relied on their neighbors, those artificial members of the family, their village. They waved at you as you walked down the street. They didn't ask your political affiliation before they did it. They gave rides to the doctor, they asked after you, they took care of your pets when you were on vacation. They were your village and they were responsible. That was the promise.

Very cleaned up her kitchen. Where did all these coffee cups come from? They must have used every single cup in the cupboard yesterday. She cleaned the cat's dish, the litter box, gave Cleo some pets, even as she slept on the couch. Her mother would have objected to an animal on her couch, but Cleopatra didn't know that; she knew that it was a grand place to take a nap.

Very put on her suit and wandered down to the pool. She enthusiastically waved at four people who went by in their cars. She had no idea who they might be, but she knew that they were her neighbors and it was neighborly to wave.

At the pool, she saw MaryAnne and went over to sit at a table near her. "Good morning, how are you today?"

"Great, I hope things with the police are okay? I mean, we've had enough of that hubbub. Let bygones be bygones. Life is too short to sweat the small stuff. Life is long if you know how to use it. Go forward. You never know when the Grim Reaper comes. Have a seat. I have some news!"

Very sat and placed her bag on the table and took out her water bottle. Life may be short, but it could be shorter if she didn't rehydrate properly. "What news?"

"Fat Man Gunn's wife is moving in. To his house. It's hers now, so she thought, why not? I met her and she is lovely!! So sweet, so nice. Her name is Annie, by the way. It's a wonder she got caught up with that man. I don't know why she did."

"But I thought you and he… Pardon me, it's not my business, but I heard some things." Very sputtered in panic.

"Water under the bridge. Forgive and forget. Get over it. Put it behind you and charge ahead."

"What a great philosophy." Very smiled. A village. It took all types and sizes, shapes and philosophies.

"She's already moved in. Most, at least three-quarters of the furniture, is hers in any case. She just had her clothes and some personal items to move. Should be receiving in two or three days. She asked for my help in deciding on where to hang some pictures and to decorate. Wow, I'm excited. You know, they never divorced, so things are going to be very easy about the house, not like being a divorced widow, just a plain old widow. Lots of those around here. Did you ever marry?"

Very smiled, "No, but I got close once. And then, I never found the right man."

"It's not too late. Keep your eyes open. Hope springs eternal. Better late than never."

"Thanks for the advice," Vera said quickly. Was this supposed to comfort her? "Yeah, I will. Keep looking." Very thought of the white Stetson and the craggy face beneath it. And she remembered the paper in her bag, the one with the phone number and the bad photo. She sat for fifteen minutes and then, unable to pretend anymore, she excused herself.

She walked home, measured steps, trying to maintain calm even though her heart raced. She remembered to wave at the crazy lady across the street. No, misguided perhaps, but not with a black heart.

Once inside, she retrieved the paper from her bag. It had been folded and stuck inside, so it was wrinkled and torn on one corner. She smoothed it out. Cleopatra came to investigate, reaching up and sinking her teeth into the corner. "Oh no, bad kitty. That's mine." Very found another paper to crumple up for the cat to chase.

She got her phone out and looked at it. She looked at the phone number and the information that it was in Ontario. What time zone was that? She googled it. Ahead by three hours. Daytime, but would anyone answer? At work? No, Frankie Monroe would have retired by now. At home, fussing with a hobby? Helping his wife cook dinner?

Could she leave it? Two years ago, she would have said that she had put it all behind her. It was only after the finding the body in the orchard, Frankie's friend Danny Boy Harger, that it came up again. She thought she had buried it all, but that one discovery had created a cascade of developments that had thrown her backwards. Now, she couldn't ignore, couldn't leave it. She needed to know.

But was this really Frankie? And if it was, what should she say to him? How could she explain the intrusion into his life? Obviously, he had attempted a disguise, a way to escape many years ago. Who was she to disrupt the new life? Was it best to call, to possibly startle, in a stealthy manner, this man who had not wanted to be found?

But he had never acknowledged the flight. He had never given any explanation for his abandonment. Did he not care about their child? It seemed that he did not care about her, but what about his family, his child? And what of his mother and sister, however tenuous that biological relationship was? Did he know about Cassandra? He must have known that the child that Danny Boy Harger's wife carried may have been his. A decision taken when young can seem for the best. But did he still believe that now? Maybe he wanted to know as well.

It was a phone call. Nothing more.

She punched in the number. She heard the ring, ring, ring, ring.

It was answered. Very inhaled.

"Hello," a deep throaty voice said.

Very hesitated. But she had called, she had started this, and now, she needed to answer. Now was not the time for fake cowardice.

"Hi. I'm looking for someone. Is this Marvin?"

There was hesitation on the other end. But finally, he answered, "Yes, that's my name."

"Frank, Frankie, is that you?" Very whispered.

There was silence, a short one, but definite hesitation.

"Very?"

"Yes."

The phone went dead.

Chapter Thirty: Epilogue, The Reopening of the Hot Tub

Very looked at her open suitcase. It was already warm here in Bakersfield, they predicted high eighties for the next week, although it had been cooler since Monday. Late May was usually warmer and she was sure it would be HOT before she got back. Her return ticket was for a week, and she had no idea what was going to happen. What was the weather in Canada? Cooler for sure, and it would feel much cooler to a girl who had acclimatized to the heat over a lifetime.

She had tried calling Frankie back. After an hour, the phone had been disconnected. She had asked Darrell and they had come up with an address. Very dragged her feet, not wanting to pursue the man who obviously did not want to be found. She had checked the internet map website and got a view of a house. Simple wooden house. On a middle-class street in a suburb. She had decided to go there. No more phone calls. Just confront him. If it was him. Of course, it was. But why should he avoid her? A wife? Secrets?

But she had one more thing to do before she could go to Sudbury, Ontario tomorrow. She had been invited to be the first into the newly renovated hot tub. At first, she had demurred, saying that it should be the head of the board of directors, but MaryAnne had convinced her she should be the one. After all, she was the last one in, and it was a 'karma' thing. If she could go in, be happy about it, then everyone else would also feel happier about taking the plunge. What could Very do but agree. She was glad that the hot tub would once more be seen as a happy place, and the stigma of death erased.

But first, she had to call Gabby. Darrell had indicated that she had called and wanted to talk with her. Gabby had called the office as it was an 'official' thing. Maybe the girl wanted to hire her again? Very was preoccupied with her upcoming trip, but knew she needed to make this one call.

"Gabby, how nice to hear your voice! What did you want to talk about?" Very tried not to be too short with Gabby. She didn't want to give the impression that Gabby's concerns were unimportant to her, but today was not the day for idle gossip.

"Just checking in. I'm official. I start work tomorrow. For pay!! It's not much, because I'm underage. But they asked for my Social Security number and all. Wow." Gabby babbled on about her duties checking in and out equipment. Keeping it clean and neat. She would answer the phone if no one else was around and greatest of all, she would count the change every day and log it in. Very didn't say anything, but doubted that Gabby would be allowed to do that alone and unsupervised. Never mind, she described a wonderful opportunity. "It's a grown-up job."

"That is wonderful," Very answered.

"And there's more. I'm going to Garces next year. The uniform is all sorted. And I got a scholarship. This is just a fabulous dream."

"And what about your brother Carlos?"

"He's going to Bakersfield High. He's going to be a Driller. He has friends going there and that what he wants. We are twins, but we are not identical and he's a boy, so maybe it's time to just go our own ways. We need this separation. We need to have our own friends, our own interests, our own lives. We are very different, you know. He's much more into sports and well, boy things. And I like exploring the various parts of the intellectual life. But we will always be close, that's for sure. We are from the same family."

"That's great about Garces. Are you prepared for the private school stuff? Maybe you will be surprised at how, well, uh, different they are."

"Oh, you mean the snooty girls who go to a private school and think they are better than the rest of us? Yeah, I'm ready for them. I mean, we are all just from Bakersfield. People don't come from San Francisco or Montecito to go to school in Bakersfield, do they? They are nothing special. None of us are special. We just want the best we can get. Bring 'em on!"

"Good attitude. I'm sure you'll be fine. Just make the most of what you can get. And may I ask, to whom do you owe for this? Father Sullivan?"

"How did you know?" Gabby went quiet.

"He's helped you so much, what is one more favor you owe him?" Very felt happy for Gabby, but there was unease as well. Even though Gabby said she could handle the pressure, Very knew that high school girls could be cruel. And what about Father Sullivan? Was this a good omen? She felt unease there as well. Too much indebtedness was always cause for apprehension. She remembered Joey's words, she and her family supported Father Sullivan against his enemies, those who would malign him. Trust was something Very lacked and she needed to restock the supply.

"Great Gabby, I'm so happy for you. I'll be gone for a week or so, but when I get back, I'll be back in touch, okay?"

Very thought of the $43. Why not give it to Gabby, help her out with expenses? "One more thing, do you have a bank account? I've got some 'seed' money for it. Maybe you need to pay off old debts, or buy something new. And of course, you'll put your pay in a bank account. How about it?"

"Wow. Seed money, huh? I need to look that one up."

"Well talk later." Very hung up.

Very counted out underwear and checked her toiletry bag for supplies. Only a few minutes to go before the hot tub ceremony. She had a new swimsuit to model. Hot pink. And a good tan.

She was just on time. The hot tub area had been closed off for so many weeks. A large canvas had gone up, surrounding the workmen as they changed everything. The crowd gathered closer to the tape that held the onlookers back.

MaryAnne sidled up to Very. "You know the latest on Davy's death?"

Very stood still, her mind racing for what to say. Nothing, MaryAnne was capable of getting on with it without a response from Very.

"It was ruled an accidental death. You know he had a fall. You, of all people, know that. Anyway, he got up and went home. He probably thought that because he could walk and get home, that he was okay. He had had a concussion. He should have called a doctor or gone to the hospital, but he didn't. And because he lived alone, no one noticed that he wasn't doing well. Apparently, this is unusual, but not completely unheard of. He died of brain damage. Alone. Anyway, nothing to do with you!"

"For that I am grateful. So, is the matter closed? Do you know?" Very said this quietly, not wanting the rest of the crowd to listen in.

"Let's hope so. It has been unpleasant and as far as we are concerned, the wheel has turned. Right has triumphed. The comeback is always stronger than the setback. Onward.

Okay, here we go!" MaryAnne started the applause as the staff from the clubhouse brought out bottles of bubbly poured into plastic glasses on big trays. "It's just apple cider," whispered MaryAnne. "No alcohol in the pool area!"

The manager smiled and made a little speech and then had Very cut the ribbon.

Very entered the new enclosure and gasped. "It's not the same, not the same at all. Look everybody, it's completely different. You come in from this direction and then there are these little seats, and it's octagonal. Oh yeah, new hot tub." She threw off her sheer wrap and entered. "Oooooh, good! Come on, everyone!"

Soon, the manager had to cajole some to get out so they wouldn't exceed the new limit of twenty-four. Water sloshed out, making the deck slippery, and despite the bubbly being non-alcoholic, someone has sneaked in some of the real thing. The grand opening was getting out of hand. Very retreated.

Very took the opportunity for one last swim on Saturday morning. When she got back, she noticed a text from Darrell. "Come in at nine for a short meeting on a new case? Coffee and breakfast provided."

She showered and then called. "Short meeting, Darrell? I'm leaving at noon."

"Sure, I understand. You go to Canada and then come back. It's a big case, it won't be solved overnight."

"Yeah, the last big case was when you landed me into the middle of a gang war."

"But you solved the case."

"And people died."

Darrell was silent and let Very think a minute, quiet down.

"It's a cold case. Nothing immediate. How long will you be gone?"

"My ticket is for a week."

"What if there is a reunion? Or a rekindle?"

"I live here, I have a cat. I will come back." Very sighed. She had not asked herself this question. But a week was enough. Actually, one hour would be enough. But what if?

"Nine, and I will get my own breakfast. Coffee will be appreciated."

At nine, Very climbed the steps to the second floor office. She heard voices as she walked down the hall. Darrell's door was open and it appeared there was already a crowd in the tiny office.

Very stood in the doorway. "Good morning everyone."

Darrell sat in his chair, his new secretary Olivia had wedged herself into the corner behind the second desk. A young man, thin to the point of anorexia, leaned against the wall, his arms crossed over his chest, and a nervous tic attacked his upper body. Her chair, or rather the only other chair in the room, was occupied by the white Stetson, minus the hat. He turned to her and nodded his head in recognition. His craggy face was solemn.

Darrell made introductions. "I've asked Very to join us because of a special knowledge she has. This case happened almost fifty years ago. But it's still a cold case. And Very lived there, in Cuyama."

"I was a kid." Very said in protest.

"That's not the only reason why I asked you to be in on this case. You are very good, you know how to research, you can help us. We need your skills. And we're willing to wait until you get back. There's a lot of work to do in the meantime. Cold cases are not easy. And this Cuyama cold case promises to be a difficult one. So, Very?"

About the Author

Phyllis Wachob grew up in the Central Valley of California, loving to read and use her imagination. After college at UC Santa Cruz, she began a career of travel and adventure, studying for an MA in England, traveling by bicycle through France and Italy, and then busing through Greece and Turkey. While trying to settle to life in California, working at a desk in an office, she stretched even further during vacations to Asia and beyond. She then became a full-time traveler and writer, spending a year in India, followed by a year traveling in Africa. She has continued to travel throughout her life and has to date, traveled to 76 countries.

English teaching as a profession was embraced during a spell in China, where she fell in love with the wild scenery and peoples of Chinese Turkestan. She subsequently lived in Japan, Taiwan, Australia (where she earned a Doctorate of Education in Teaching English to Speakers of Other Languages), China, Singapore, Egypt and Turkey, teaching and traveling. These extensive experiences are reflected in her mystery novels in the Teachers Abroad Mystery series. She took her knowledge of the people, places, food and customs and wove fictional stories of mystery and murder.

She has been influenced by the great mystery writers, (although she started with the Nancy Drew mysteries), enjoying Sherlock Holmes and Agatha Christie's books among others. She believes that characters and their vicissitudes form the crux of mysteries and the motivation to solve the whodunit is the driver of the story. The colorful, exotic, and unfamiliar should draw the reader into the core of the mystery, while the mundane and conventional hold the keys to the solution.

Currently she resides in Bakersfield, California where she was born. Her newest series, the Kern Kapers Mysteries, is set in Bakersfield and environs and features the characters who live there. She is a member of Writers of Kern and benefits from the connections of this professional writing community.

More information and blog posts can be found on the webpage: phylliswachob.com.

Questions for Reading Groups

1. Very meets a lot of new people at once. She also has trouble remembering names. Have you ever experienced this? For example, the first day in a new school, a new job, a conference? What did you so?

2. Within a short period of time, there are two deaths at Five Points. Very contemplates the fact that if you chose to live with old(er) people, you have to expect this. True or not?

3. Every now and then, and especially at the pool party, Very is surprised at the gossip, much of it petty and cruel. Perhaps teenagers might act like this, but Very thinks the adults should be kinder. Why do we gossip or pass on information? Is there a function to this? Do we grow out of it?

4. Very 'buys' a cat at the Pet Store. It is a rescue cat and they immediately take to each other. How important are pets? To single people especially? What do you think about rescue dogs and cats compared to bred animals?

5. Very wants to join activities at Five Points, after all, that's why she moved there. She finds the Crafters Club full of gossip, the pickle ball people are aggressive and only want to win, and the Pool Party ends in disaster. If you were Very, what would you do?

6. In Chapter Twenty-nine, Very thinks about why she moved to Five Points. She thinks she will have community, friendship and activities, but she has also found discord and

death. She thinks about what the last years of her life are supposed to be like. What do you expect of retirement?

7. Thirty-nine years ago, Very was left at the altar, pregnant, by her fiancé. He disappeared and Very has heard nothing about him since. Now, there is a strong possibility that he is alive in Canada and Very has made plans to go and search for him. Is this a good idea? Will finding Frankie make her happy?